SEIZE

St. Martin Family Saga
Emergency Responders Series

GINA
WATSON

Interior format by The Killion Group
http://thekilliongroupinc.com

CHAPTER 1

Augustine Charles Roy had been tailing Eve's sister, Mia, for a few hours. She'd fueled up her car, picked up a bicycle from the shop, gone to the post office, and done her grocery shopping. Now she seemed to be heading back home. That worked out well for him because he'd be able to introduce himself to her and then they could drive to Toronto where he would deal with Nicolas Renaud, her sister's abusive husband.

He followed her out of town. From the file Augie'd compiled, he knew she lived with her mother outside the tiny Ontario town of Elora, a town so small one artery was all it took to lead a driver in and out.

It wouldn't do to be spotted, so to put space between them, he stopped at a convenience store to pick up a pack of smokes. Walking out to his car, he felt the wind pick up. He lit a match and cupped it to light the fresh cigarette between his lips.

He'd memorized the directions to her country home. He made the turn and felt the earth shift beneath the car. The ground wasn't completely dry, and the soft terrain made the steering loose. Her car was parked in front of a modest log cabin. First thing Augie noticed were two sets of tire tracks, the second set leading off to the side and possibly around the back of the house.

He parked his car in a bank of trees and stealthily approached the log home. He was alone, with no backup and no one to call. Recon was a necessity, and the extra time now might save both of their asses later. He skirted the side of the home, stopping at the back edge. He peeked around his corner and was able to confirm an additional vehicle on the scene. And not just any vehicle, but a buffed and shined Chevrolet

Tahoe with illegal-grade tint and wireless amplifiers with cellphone signal boosters sprouting from the roof. Plates were Illinois.

Before he'd left Baton Rouge, Augie had compiled a file on Nicolas Renaud. He was into some heavy and illegal shit and had been connected to members deep within the National Crime Syndicate, an organized crime organization with connections all across the globe. Several of Nicolas's connections operated out of Chicago. The man was crooked through and through. So crooked, his picture was on America's top one hundred most wanted criminals list.

Augie inched his way to a high window and peered in. Immediately his skin pricked and his mouth went dry. One man leaned against the kitchen counter, casually cleaning under his nails with a wicked-looking knife. A second man had Mia's arms locked behind her in a tight grip. One meaty hand was around her throat.

Shit, he'd have to act quickly to get her out of there alive.

"Stop it you idiot. Renaud wants her alive." The man against the counter said.

He heard Mia wheeze and gasp for breath.

With his back hugging the house, he organized his thoughts. If he took out the guy at the counter first, the fat guy could hurt her, kill her even. He'd have to go for the one with his hands on her. The element of surprise would have Thug Two moving slowly. Augie had no weapons but himself, so surprise would need to work.

Without further thought, he used his foot to bust through the door. Pudgy hands groped at her breasts and between her legs. She'd scratched her attacker's hands bloody, but that had provoked him to squeeze tighter. His hands were on her neck again. Her eyes met Augie's, and she sputtered something inarticulate before passing out. Her attacker dropped her to the floor. The guy behind Augie began to move, so he lunged at the large man in front of him, knocking him to his back. He pelted his face with blow after blow, intending to take care of Thug Two first. He felt the give of the man's jaw and watched blood spatter on the floor. The pain pounding at his knuckles suddenly connected with an excruciating snap radiating from his skull; slivers of wood rained down around him. He fell to the side but kept moving, and rolled until he was on his feet. The guy on the floor choked and coughed up blood, but the other guy was in better shape and had a knife.

Blood trickled into Augie's eyes, blurring his vision. Thug One lunged at him, but Augie ducked and, using his own weight, he bent the knife-wielding arm at the elbow, dislocating it. An agonized scream arced through the air, and the attacker backed away. The fat man was up, swaying.

In the back of Augie's mind a phrase kept repeating: *the girl isn't moving.*

He picked up the knife as well as a butcher knife he grabbed out of the block on the counter. He faced off with the assailants, but they ran out the back door and into the SUV. He chased after them, but his head was talking to him again: *Go help the girl.*

In the kitchen, he rolled her to her back and positioned his hands on her chest. He pumped thirty times and then administered a breath. He resumed pumping, and she gasped violently, throwing herself into a sitting position and pushing at him. Her hands went to her throat and she coughed, spit flying from her mouth. She wheezed in a deep breath and her eyes watered. Augie sat on his knees next to her. Her gaze darted frantically around the room.

"They're gone," Augie said.

She started backing away in a crab walk. When she was halfway across the kitchen she jumped up, turned, and began to run. He followed after her, pulling her arm to stop her. She screamed, but her voice was raspy and ineffective. She whacked him in the head.

"Fuck!" He released her to cradle his aching skull.

She ran out the front door and toward her car. He hated to use force after what she'd been through, but she left him no choice. She was in shock and nothing he could say would have her trusting him. He held her wrists with one hand and with his other hand at the small of her back, he guided her from the car, but not before he plucked her purse from the front seat; she'd need ID to cross the border.

He put her in the back seat of his vehicle and activated the child locks so she couldn't jump out. About halfway down the driveway, she bashed him in the head again.

"Goddammit! Will you please stop doing that. Can't you see the blood trickling down the side of my head? That fucking hurts. Next time you do it I'll have to restrain you."

"Let me out of the car." She furiously jiggled the handle.

"I'm not going to hurt you. Your sister sent me to help you."

Her head shot up and her eyes met his in the rearview mirror—tormented and worried eyes.

"Eve is safe and so are you now. You can stop hitting me."

Without answering, she lay on the back seat and kicked the glass on the rear door repeatedly. Augie pulled the car over, and she sat up immediately. His backpack was on the floor, and he reached down, feeling around until he found the rope inside the pack. Then he climbed over the seat and into the back. Her eyes went wide and then glassy, and her breathing sped up. She was frantic and he felt shitty for what he had to do, but he couldn't risk her fleeing or hurting herself trying to run away. He buckled her tightly into the seat and then tied her wrists together in front of her body. When he had her secured, he tilted her head up and looked into her furious eyes.

"Mia, I promise I won't hurt you. I'm sorry for restraining you, but it's only to keep you safe. Eve *did* send me to help you." She didn't respond.

As he put the miles behind them, his mind kept recalling the color of her eyes. They weren't gray. Were they purple? No, lavender? A cross between gray and lavender. The color was mesmerizing. Her eyes were definitely her greatest asset. In comparison, the rest of her was plain and thin, what was referred to as the girl next door. Nothing special. Her hair was a mousy light brown. Her skin was beautiful, like her sister's, but Eve had won the gene-pool lottery in that family with her abundant curves. Instead, Mia was a little slip of a thing. She was bony and spindly. He'd felt her thinness when he'd manhandled her to the car. He frowned at the memory.

He drove for two and a half hours before they entered Toronto. She stirred in the back seat.

She coughed. "I need to use the restroom." Her voice was still raspy from the fucker's rough treatment.

"We'll stop and get a room for the night in Toronto. You can tend to your needs at that time."

She looked out the window and mumbled, "Are you going to escort me *hogtied* through the hotel lobby?"

He couldn't stop the laugh that broke free. Her head shot up and her eyes simmered at him.

"There's nothing at all funny about any of this. First chance I get, I'm going to have you arrested."

"That wouldn't be wise. As I said before, I'm here to help you."

"I don't need your help."

"Really? Because it does seem that you were passed out from strangulation when I found you. When I *rescued* you." He grinned into the rearview mirror. "When I sent two armed assailants running."

Her knotted hands instinctively went to her throat before she frowned at the rope and knot and lowered them.

He exited the highway and then drove to a fast food seafood restaurant. He drew a hat from his pack and jammed it on his head. Then he turned and untied her wrists. She rubbed them, and he offered an apology.

"Fish and chips any good here?" He pulled the car into the ordering line. In the rearview mirror, he saw that her neck showed bruising and irritation. Damn, he'd already failed her. A chill spread through him when he considered what would have happened if he'd delayed another second.

"My name's Augie. As I said before, Eve sent me to get you. It seems Renaud has finally exhausted his options, and so any hopes he has of finding her rest with you. He knew that going after you would lead to Eve."

"Why do you keep calling her that?"

"When she left she changed her name to Eve." He moved up in the drive-thru line. "So is it any good?"

She turned her head from where she gazed out the window. "Is what any good?"

"The food."

"I've never eaten here."

"Maybe we should go somewhere else. What's good?"

"I don't know."

"What do you like?"

"I don't often eat restaurant food."

At the window, he paid for their meals. As he drove he thought about what she'd said. She was a strange one. "So you don't have a favorite restaurant?"

"Be hard to say. The last time I ate at one would be family vacation as a child. Seems like we went to a diner; I really liked the waffles."

"What about McDonald's?" He rolled down his window and pressed a button to retrieve a receipt allowing him to enter a parking structure.

She shook her head. "Never been." They walked from the garage to a motel around the corner.

"That's so weird." She was definitely the most peculiar woman he'd ever met.

And he'd met more than his share of peculiar folks.

Could Mia trust this man who said he knew her sister? She recalled the thick hands that had been on her throat and not being able to breathe, and she placed her own hands at her neck and gasped.

Augie's hand landed on her arm as he regarded her with wide eyes. "Are you okay? You need some water?" He dug around in his backpack and offered her a bottle. She took it, and then he lightly traced the tender skin at her neck. "I'm sorry."

After what had happened in her kitchen she didn't know who to trust. He seemed honest, and in her gut she felt he was truthful, but she didn't understand what was going on.

He was a nice-looking man, even with the blood dried in his hair and scalp. Tall and muscular. His clothes fit pretty snug and with him standing before her, she could see just how tight his body was. His jeans were faded and he wore cowboy boots. He even had one of those belts with the big buckles. His snug and threadbare light blue T-shirt completed the contemporary cowboy look. His hair was a dusty blond, dark at the scalp and sun lightened on the ends. He wore it messy, a look she liked.

His hands were full, and he handed her an envelope. "Get the door, will you?"

"I'll need the key." And the lock. She didn't see one.

"It's a keycard." *Keycard?* She saw the slot in the door and put the pieces together. She dug around in the envelope and removed what seemed to be a credit card. She swiped it in the slot, heard a click, and opened the door.

"Shall we eat?"

"I'm not hungry, I want to shower, and I need . . ."

"Right." He tugged her to the bathroom.

"Unlucky for you, there's a window so I'll have to monitor your bath." He pointed at the tub. "Draw a bath."

"But I take showers."

"If you want to get clean tonight, it'll be a bath. Fill the tub first. Once the water is off, you can get into the tub. One more rule: I'll need you to strip down out here. And no towels. When you're done, I'll greet you with a towel."

Her blood simmered. "I don't think so."

"No? Okay, how about an option? You're very scrappy and I've yet to thoroughly search you, so you can strip down in front of me to demonstrate that you aren't hiding anything that could cause me or yourself harm or"—he raised his palms in the air and wiggled his fingers—"I can thoroughly search you. Mind you, this requires my hands on you."

So he wasn't dumb. She'd actually snagged a fork from the lobby and thought of bending the prongs back into a makeshift knife. She turned away from his knowing gaze, plugged the tub, and turned on the water. On second thought, a bath would be calming.

She started undressing.

And took a very long, very deep breath.

She'd never undressed before a man. But he wasn't really looking, at least not obviously ogling, so she removed her shoes and socks, followed by her jeans. Her shirt was long enough that she was still covered. He took the clothes from her. When he discovered the fork, he held it in up and cocked a brow at her.

"Going to fashion this into some kind of prison weapon?"

"I thought I might stab you in the throat while you slept."

He started laughing. Loud. Great, she was overwhelmingly nonthreatening. His full smile stretched his face, startling a tingle from her belly.

Wow, the man was a hottie; who would have guessed?

Yet tingling girl parts aside, he still wanted her to strip down in front of him. Was he a pervert?

"Hey!"

His attention was diverted from the faux knife as he angled toward her, brow raised.

"How can I be sure you aren't going to try something with me once I'm naked?"

He placed an open palm on his chest. "I'm flattered you think so highly of me, but you don't have to worry, because I really am a nice guy. Besides, you're so not my type, you're forever safe."

His cocky smile infuriated her.

"Do you know how badly I want to hit you in the face right now?"

He wagged a finger at her. "Extremely hostile, Miss Brown."

Of course she wasn't his type. She wasn't anybody's type. She should have been a boy. She was built like a board with barely a curve, so his comment didn't faze her. She pulled her shirt over her head, unclasped her bra, and dangled it slowly to the floor. Finally she hooked her thumbs in her panties and slid them down. She picked everything up and piled the clothes in his arms. As she waited for him to make the next move, she saw his forehead crease ever so slightly and his jaw clench tight. Hmm, so he really hated her body. She shrugged and turned toward the tub.

"Earrings too."

She froze and turned back to him. "What?"

"Take off the earrings."

"They're studs."

"The back is sharp, and I understand you have a fondness for pronged items."

She huffed and walked toward him at the sink. He held his palm out, and she placed the earrings in the center. "Happy now?"

"Immensely."

She moved to close the door, but his hand stopped it. "Door stays open."

"Oh, for God's sake. Are you a perv or what? You gonna stand there and watch me go?"

He swallowed and ran his free hand through his hair. "Er, no, I'll just eat my dinner."

"Good. You do that."

She hoped he'd choke on his drive-thru fish. Serve him right, the cocky bastard.

CHAPTER 2

Augie moved the furniture around, putting the table and chairs in line with the front door so he'd hear if she tried to escape. The window in the bathroom was an issue, but with the water off he'd for sure hear if she slid it open. And now he wished he hadn't thought of that damned bathroom window because it had him thinking of her wet and sudsy in the tub. No, she didn't have huge round tits or thick graspable hips, but she'd been confident as she stood naked before him. And her body suited her. Really well. Too well. He'd never seen a woman built like her. Or maybe he had, but he'd definitely never noticed them. There was no excess. That meant there was nothing left over for pleasure or fun, but that didn't mean she couldn't use that body to accomplish those things as well.

What was he thinking? He rubbed his jaw, the rough skin reminding him he needed to clean up and maybe shave. But how would he manage that with her wanting to escape him?

He tried to eat, but with every chew his head pounded. He would love to stand under a hot shower.

He heard the water swish before Mia said, "I need a towel."

He held a towel out for her as she backed into it, her skin pink and silky, wet and smooth. *Fuck!* He needed to keep his head in the game. He shook off thoughts stirred by her before his head exploded.

"I need to take a shower."

She eyed him curiously. "So what's stopping you?"

"Quite frankly, you are." He studied her a moment and then went to his pack and retrieved two pieces of rope. "I need you to sit on the toilet seat." He collected her clothes and shoved them into his backpack, placing it on the rack above the toilet.

Then he removed her towel.

"I wasn't done with that."

"Yes, you were." He grabbed the other towels and placed them all on the rack in the shower, high above his head.

"I hate you so very much."

He smiled and pointed. "Sit on the toilet."

"Why?"

"Please just do it. My head is pounding, and I'd like to have a shower."

Her face softened. "Fine."

She sat on the toilet lid, and he tied her wrists.

"So while I was passed out, they attacked you?"

"Yeah, I guess they did."

"As far as white knights go, I'd rather hoped to get a more official-looking one."

He tried to keep his eyes focused on her wrists, but other parts were in his peripheral vision. "Are you questioning my skills?"

Mocking him further, her nipples hardened before his eyes. He started binding her ankles.

"I'm not questioning them, I'm stating they're not very good and this isn't necessary. I'm not going to leave without my clothes."

"Well, if I'm showering, you could easily retrieve your clothes from the rack. Plus I'm not entirely convinced you wouldn't flee completely naked. You seem like a fighter."

"What if I give you my word that I won't?"

"Do you trust me?"

"I don't even know you."

"My thoughts exactly. Your word is of no value to me." He stood and pulled his shirt over his head. Then he started the water for a shower.

"Am I supposed to sit here while you do that?" She gestured with her tied hands toward the tub.

"I won't take long. And for the record, you can trust me. I'm in law enforcement back home. Sheriff of East Baton Rouge Parish."

"That's very comforting."

As he waited for the water to warm, he removed his boots and jeans. Mia watched him. Closely. Trying to hide her body from him—her parts might not be too curvy, but the ones she had worked just fine—she held her knotted hands to her chest. Unfortunately his cock was hard, so he turned his back to her before removing his shorts and cupped himself. He didn't typically show any modesty, but he'd sensed an air of innocence in her and didn't want to make her nervous.

He stepped into the tub and sudsed up. As he washed, he heard Mia clear her throat several times. Heard also one long sigh from the other side of the shower curtain. He stuck his head through the curtain. "You still here?"

"Hey, watch it! You're getting me all wet."

Back under the pulsing shower head, he made short work of rinsing. He chuckled under his breath as he thought of her sitting on the toilet seat, simmering mad, while she waited for him to untie her. He shut off the water and opened the curtain. He reached for a towel and she turned, her eyes at the level of his crotch. Luckily he wasn't still hard. She shot up and teeter-tottered before he caught her.

"Easy does it."

"Will you just untie me please!"

He wrapped the towel around his waist and undid the knots that held her wrists together. Then he worked on the ankle rope until she was free. He unzipped his bag and tossed her clothes at her. She grabbed them and stormed out in a huff and he got a great shot of her ass as she walked away.

When he came out of the bathroom, she was on the bed, flipping through TV channels and wearing her underwear and shirt. "When can I see my sister?"

"I have to take care of something before we can leave."

"Then I want to call her."

"No phones."

"Why not?"

"It's too risky. Too easy to trace."

She clicked off the television and groaned. Leaning on one side, she punched a pillow three times and then squished it in her hands. She laid her head on the fluffed mound and closed her eyes.

She was asleep in no time, and Augie wondered what that felt like. It took him hours to fall asleep, if he even could. He sat in the chair next to the door and rested his head back against the hard edge.

He heard when she got up and used the bathroom. He heard her pad back to the bedroom, and then he listened harder when she stopped. Pretending to be asleep, he didn't rise from the chair, but squinted one eye open. She was standing in the center of the room, looking around. She pulled her jeans on, followed by her socks and shoes. Grabbing her purse, she went to the bathroom and shut and locked the door.

Damn, she was going out the window. He jumped up and into his shoes. He opened the door and jogged around the perimeter to the window that lined up with their room. Not a moment too soon, he thought, as a long denim-clad leg dangled from the window. She continued out until her body straddled the sill, her back to him. Placing her hands between her legs, she managed a pretty decent dismount into his waiting arms.

She hit with a thud.

"Howdy." He smiled down at her.

She squinted at him and squirmed.

"I'm not putting you down, so you can stop that."

"Let me go!"

"I can't."

"Why not?"

He walked and said, "I made a promise to Eve and Clay."

"Who's Clay?"

"Clay is the man who loves Eve."

Her eyes widened. "Does she love him?"

"That I wouldn't know. She's a woman."

"What's that supposed to mean?"

"I try to stay out of your heads. Crazy things go on in there."

"*You're* crazy."

He shrugged. "Been called worse."

"Will you put me down?"

"Can't—you tried to escape. And after giving your word."

"You said my word was of no value to you."

He cocked his head. "Is that what I said?"

"I have an excellent memory. It's exactly what you said."

"Huh. Well, that seems to be pretty clear."

She scratched at his arms, but he still didn't let go. He carried her in silence the rest of the way and when he got to the room, he dumped her on the bed.

She stood on her knees and waved her finger in the air.

"I'll have you know I am an upstanding, truthful, and respectful individual. You have no right to judge me or decide what kind of person I am. Had you accepted my word, I would have abided by it."

She was really cute as she tried to convince him of her character. Too cute. He wanted to use his charms to soothe her. He imagined how her slim, feminine body would feel in his arms—silky and taut, warm and writhing. He wanted to see if she'd respond as most women did when he dialed up his game.

His fingers were laced together, his hands on top of his head as he leaned back in the chair, balancing against the door. He just sat and stared into nothing.

"What are you doing?" Mia demanded.

"Thinking."

"Thinking about what?"

He smirked. And he looked great doing even that.

"The plan."

When he didn't divulge more, she turned his smirk back on him. He laughed. And still told her nothing else.

She gritted her teeth and politely asked, "What plan is that, Augie?"

"I've got a friend coming with a car, and she's going to see you reunited with your sister."

"I'm not getting into a car with some girl I don't know."

"You got into a car with me." His fingers scratched across his bare chest. His very bare, very chiseled chest.

"You forced me."

"A repeat can be arranged."

"I may not look like much, but I can fight a woman. I won't go with her."

"She was special ops—marines—so I think you might just go with her."

He infuriated her. She wanted to slap that smug attitude out of him. Pulling her knees to her chest, she wrapped her arms around her legs. "Where is she?"

"Who?"

"Evie."

"Your sister? She's in Louisiana."

"And you say she met someone."

"Yeah, my buddy Clay."

"Do you know why those thugs wanted to know where she is?"

"Those thugs can be traced back to her husband."

"To Nicolas?"

He nodded and resumed his staring.

"Will you tell me what's going on?"

His brow furrowed as he regarded her. "Eve—*Evie*—left her husband."

"Yeah, I got that part. What does that have to do with me?"

"He wants her back. I'm not sure if he thinks you know where she is, but he does know he can use you in a negative way to pull Eve out of hiding."

"Why is she hiding from him?"

"You don't know?"

She shook her head. "We're not that close. I know they've had problems in the past. She came back to Elora once before, but he came and took her back with him to Toronto. After that I didn't hear from her very often."

"He hurt her. Badly. Repeatedly. She had to leave everything behind to get away from him. She had no idea he'd come after you."

Her hands cupped her mouth as she thought about how someone could hurt her beautiful, sweet baby sister. "He hurt her?"

"Yes." His voice was a whispered rasp.

"How?"

"I'm afraid he abused her. Physically, emotionally, sexually."

Mia slid down in the bed and with her head on the crisp, cool pillow, she thought of Evie. Tears leaked from her eyes as she thought of how she could have, should have, helped her. Had she only known, she would have fought with her life to save her sister.

Augie climbed on the bed and took her hands.

"Hey, she's safe now. And in love. She'll have a wonderful life with Clay. She's going to be fine."

He wiped the tears from her face with the pads of his thumbs.

"Thank you."

"She made me memorize something to tell you." He scratched his head with his thumb. "Uh, let's see if I can remember . . .

"Take the old dog out back, let him run round with the yak—hippity dippity hoppity doppity. Wash your hands and feet, after you eat brush your hair and teeth—jippity pippity joppity poppity.

"Go to school, make good marks, come home we'll go for some butter tarts. Yippity nippity yoppity noppity."

She stood to her knees and dug her nails into his forearm. "Why didn't you tell me this earlier?"

He shrugged. "You were in shock; you wouldn't have listened."

"I would have. It's proof that you were sent by Evie. That was a song our mom made up."

"I'm glad that's settled. Does this mean you'll trust me now?"

"Yeah, I trust you." She looked down at her hands. "I didn't get a chance to thank you for saving my life. I guess I *was* a little in shock, but thank you. I owe you everything. Truce?"

She held her hand out, and his warm, masculine hand molded to hers. A tingling started at her fingertips and ran up her arm, down her back, and toward the top of her head. It had her gasping. His eyes narrowed, and he jerked his palm out of hers.

"What is that song about anyway?"

She sighed. "My mom sang it to us when we were very young." Before the family was split apart by divorce. She frowned at the memory of it all. Then she realized he watched her intently.

"What's wrong?" he asked.

She sat back on the bed and he followed. They bunched the pillows behind them.

"My mom had some mental problems. She went undiagnosed for a while, but her mood swings were hard on the family. My parents split, and Evie went with my father; I stayed with my mother."

"Did they go far?"

"No, actually they lived in the same small town."

"I don't mean to pry, but I did investigate your background. One report listed your mother as an inpatient in a behavioral hospital."

Mia's lips tightened. She didn't want to talk about this with him. Then, looking down at her hands, she realized he was an answer to one of her prayers. She'd wished for someone to talk to, to confide in, to bounce ideas off of. Someone who wouldn't judge. So, correction, she *did* want to talk to him about this. He had a trustworthy face, and she hoped that trust was reflected deep down to his bones.

"She's okay, but she was diagnosed with schizophrenia. It's horrible. She thinks the entire world is out to get her. As far back as I can remember, she suffered from isolation and loneliness, but the last five years have been especially hard. That's why my dad left with Evie—he couldn't take it. I wanted to help her. I enrolled in an online university. Took some core courses and then majored in psychology. I never finished because it's quite expensive and we sort of ran out of extra money after dad died and the hospital isn't so cheap. I did learn a lot, though, and I tried to counsel her." She shrugged.

She expected to see pity in his face, his eyes, but instead she saw something else. Understanding? His eyes simmered, and his mouth was stretched into a slight smile. His gaze was confident on her. Unblinking.

"You're very strong. Children shouldn't have to take care of their parents, yet you did. And successfully, apparently."

"I don't know." She inhaled through an open mouth. "She's in that hospital."

"She's getting what she needs. Meanwhile, you sacrificed so much, put your life on hold to see her through the darkness. That's very selfless of you, Miss Brown."

She didn't know what to say. The need was strong in her to break their gaze because he was reading her soul with those penetrating brown eyes. But she couldn't break away, the connection was too strong. She'd never had anyone recognize her sacrifices before. Her lips did a slow turn upward, and she couldn't have done anything to stop them.

"What?" His eyebrows lifted.

She shook her head. "I've just never spoken about this before. It's nice to have someone to talk to."

"Well, it's also nice to have an actual conversation with you. I prefer it to *I hate you so much* and *I want to slap you in the face so hard.*" They laughed.

"I volunteer at the grief counseling center. I'll need to make a call to let them know I'm going to miss my shift."

He shook his head. "No phones."

"Can I use email?"

"Do you have a computer?"

"I meant on the phone."

"What part of *no phones* don't you get?"

At her grimace, his eyes pleaded. "These precautions are for your protection and the protection of your sister."

"I know. It's just that if someone in dire straits calls my phone and I'm not there . . ."

He steepled his fingers over his chest. "We can go to a public library. You can use a computer to access your email so you can make provisions for the grief center."

"Thank you." She smiled. He really was kind, and she felt at ease around him now. Truth told, she had before. She wouldn't have undressed in front of him if she hadn't. But now she had confirmation with the silly nursery rhyme that he'd taken the time to memorize. She giggled.

"What?"

"I can't believe you memorized that song for me."

"I can't believe I remembered it."

Their arms met in the middle of the bed, ever so slightly touching, his warmth seeping from him and into her. It wasn't the most comfortable way to sleep since she preferred to be on her side, but she was content to remain in that position so she could stay connected to him.

Mia woke to the sounds of a crunching in her ear.

"I hope you like doughnuts and"—Augie leaned over and produced a steaming paper cup of coffee—"mocha latte. Girls like that, right?"

"Absolutely." She sat up and smiled, and then she laughed.

"What's so funny?"

"You have powdered sugar on your nose." She swiped her finger across the corner of his mouth. "And is that cherry?" She put the finger in her mouth, confirming her suspicions.

"Yeah, kind of messy to eat."

He was blushing as he wiped his face with a napkin.

"Mmm, I love strudel." She took a large bite and the warm apple cinnamon filling oozed into her mouth.

"I was wondering something."

She lifted her chin at his serious manner.

"Evie didn't mention her mother was in the hospital."

"I didn't tell her."

"I gathered. Why?"

"Evie knows what she knows from my father. Honestly, Dad didn't believe in mental illness. He thought Mom was being selfish and was lashing out against him because she'd grown to hate him." She gauged the feedback his body was giving her. He frowned slightly, but she thought it was from curiosity. Or maybe confusion. At least he wasn't a stone wall like her father with his crossed arms and implacable expressions. Augie seemed open to what she was telling him.

"The illness is biological; there's a chemical imbalance in the brain that causes the hallucinations and episodes of psychosis. Medication can level it out."

He nodded. "I get it. My mother suffers from anxiety, takes medication for it. We call them her happy pills because she's so nice after she's taken one. It's the only time I ever see her let go of all that she worries about."

"Exactly. With schizophrenia, patients are put in a hospital to determine a course of treatment. Certain medications can make the delusions worse, and others can make them go away altogether; it depends on the chemical that needs adjusting. Only way to find out is to try the medications and monitor the patient."

"So is your mom in the hospital for that?"

"No, she already found a drug that helps her." She inhaled and sighed. "She's in there because she started drinking, and alcohol doesn't mix well with Thorazine."

"Oh." His brows rose. "My mom's medication doesn't do well with her amaretto sours either." He shrugged. "Doesn't stop her from swallowing down her pills with it."

She enjoyed talking with him. It was easy, and he seemed to enjoy the give and take as much as she did. "What happens when she does that?"

"She passes out." He shook his head. "We had to take her to the emergency room twice. Combination of the pills with the alcohol slowed her heart rate. But even after all that, she still combines the two."

"That's hard."

"Yeah." He scratched his head with the car key. "Shall we go to the library? And we need to ditch the car."

"Oh." Her eyebrows rose. "Why?"

"A precaution. It may have been identified by the thugs. Doesn't seem likely they'd give up on their mission. I wouldn't."

His words made Mia uneasy, and she was doubly thankful he was with her.

CHAPTER 3

They went to the library so Mia could send her email. While there, she purchased a couple of used books, excited about her finds. Augie enjoyed how something so simple delighted her.

As they exited the library, he pointed to a super-center store. "Would you like to get a few things: toothbrush, hair brush? Anything?"

"That'd be great."

"Come on."

When they left the store with their purchases, they watched a man attempt to tie a cast-iron mixer to a motorized scooter using one bungee cord. Mia's hand landed on Augie's forearm.

"Augie, look. He's going to lose that load." She clicked her tongue. "Oh, and there's a white bow on top of the box. It's probably for his girlfriend or wife. Let's help him."

"What kind of idiot drives a scooter to do his birthday shopping?"

"Maybe that's all he has."

Before he could answer, she took off.

She tried to reason with the man, but he was agitated.

"Sir, please let us help you. We can follow in the car with the mixer."

His hand held stiffly between them indicated she should keep her distance.

"Just go away. I don't need your help."

"But the mixer is too heavy for this small fender. It's going to hit the ground."

"I said go away."

Augie looped his arm in hers. "Come on, Mia, he said he's got it."

"That's right, go on," he yelled over his shoulder.

He sat on the scooter and started the engine. They stopped behind him. As soon as he put the scooter in drive, the mixer wobbled and Augie was there to catch it as it fell.

The man slammed the scooter onto the kickstand and jumped off, ready to strike, but Mia tried talking to soothe his agitation.

"Sir, your mixer was about to fall to the ground. It would have broken if not for this man. Please, can we offer you some help?"

The man was speaking gibberish under his breath and was clearly flustered about something.

Augie set the mixer on the ground. "Mia, forget it. Let's get out of here."

Mia's eyes pleaded with him as she held up her index finger to ask him to wait. "Sir, it's okay, where do you need to go?"

"For my mother." The man rocked on his feet, but wouldn't make eye contact with her.

"Okay. Is she close by?"

"Oakridge."

"I know where that is. Shall we follow you with the mixer in our car?"

"No!"

"Mia, I don't think this—"

"Augie, please. He needs our help."

They ended up driving beside him so he could see Mia, in the passenger side of the car, holding the mixer. At every intersection she waved and smiled to the crazy bastard. When they arrived at his mother's apartment in an assisted living facility, Mia suggested he wrap the gift, but he didn't have any paper. Augie watched as she helped him wrap it in old comics from the stack of papers in the apartment.

"She's going to love it!"

Mia smiled and so did the man. When they were leaving, he lunged at Mia, and Augie almost pounced on him, but the man only hugged and then released her.

"Thank you for letting us help you, Russell. Your mom is going to be thrilled with the mixer." He said something under his breath and then waved goodbye like a small boy.

As they drove, Augie marveled at her patience with the aggressive man. "You're really good with people."

"Not all people. I work well with the afflicted."

"Why do you say that?"

"I've just never been good at making friends. Normal people don't typically gravitate to me; most think I'm strange."

Still, he assumed that her being from a small town meant she'd have some long-lasting friendships.

"Don't you have friends from high school?"

"There were roughly four hundred students at my high school. If anything, the small number just made me stand out more. I wasn't very popular."

He nodded as he pictured her during her awkward years. "Were you in sports or anything?"

"No, I had to get home to Mom."

"Prom? Homecoming?"

She shook her head. "No."

"You really mean no friends."

"I know it seems weird, but the school really was small, and I worked hard to keep our private family business from being spread all over town." She shrugged and looked at him. "I bet you were popular."

"I did all right."

"Did you play sports?"

"I did."

"Which?"

"All of them, I think."

"That doesn't surprise me."

"I wasn't very good at any of them, so that's why I played them all."

"Is that how they do it in Louisiana?"

"Yeah, everything's backwards there."

She laughed, and Augie was rewarded with a beautiful pearly white angelic smile. It was breathtaking. He needed to make her laugh more often. He was going to make it his new mission.

He drove the car to a junkyard. "Ready?" He grabbed the sack of toiletries from the back seat.

"What are we doing here?"

"I'm having the car destroyed."

"Isn't that excessive?"

"Not at all."

"Couldn't we give the car to someone in need? Like Russell."

"Car has to be destroyed. We must erase all traces of me ever being here."

She frowned.

"Please trust me."

When she looked into his pleading brown eyes, she saw warmth and honesty.

"Okay."

She opened her door and followed after him. A man stepped out from a metal building and shared a funny-looking handshake with Augie. He was American, tall and wide, with a deep scar across his left cheek. After a few exchanges, she learned they'd fought together in Afghanistan. Augie and Scott discussed the car. He said he'd drain the tank and then the car would be destroyed within the hour.

"Let me give you a lift."

"That'd be great. To the train station."

Train station?

Mia wondered if she should introduce herself—since Augie hadn't—but once they started driving, she just sat back and listened.

"How are the nightmares?" Augie asked.

"Every night. Sleeping pills they give me make 'em worse. It's always the same thing—what would have happened if you hadn't come when you did." He shook his head vigorously. "And then I see their faces."

Augie squeezed Scott's forearm. "Hey, I was there and that wasn't our fault; we were sent for the civilians, and we got to all of them."

"We did, but their faces—those sweet faces—haunt my dreams."

His voice was shrill and so highly pitched, it sounded painful. Was he referring to children? What had he and Augie been involved with?

"Do you keep up with Gloria?" Scott asked.

Who's Gloria?

"Not really."

"You guys were great together."

And when were they together?

"Not great enough."

Looking out the window, Mia realized they'd reached their extremely odd destination.

"Good seeing you, Scott."

They did their handshake again and Scott backed the car out. Augie watched as the car drove off.

"Augie? Everything okay?"

Their eyes met and his pained, saddened eyes blinked at her. She squeezed his arm. "You okay?"

He nodded. "Let's go."

"What are we doing at the train station?"

"No trails."

"Trails?"

"The less Scott knows the better so I had him drop us here. It's close enough that we can walk back to a hotel, and if anybody comes sniffing around it won't put him in a compromising position."

"Are we switching hotels too?"

"Yes."

"Was Scott referring to children?"

He froze.

"He said *sweet faces*. I was wondering if he meant children."

He walked slowly, hands locked behind his back. "Yes, children."

"Did some die?"

"Yes."

"He . . . he was trying to save them?"

Augie stopped walking and pointed. "Do you want a soft pretzel?" They each got one and took a seat on a nearby bench. She sensed the moment was over and though she wanted information, she didn't want to pry. The overwhelming compassion she felt for him and his friend at what she imagined they'd endured twisted in her gut. If he didn't discuss it with her, she hoped he'd find someone he could confide in. She understood how the negative festered, bringing sickness and weakness to all parts of the body and mind.

Augie was a good man. She didn't want him weighed down with unchecked and heavy emotional burdens.

They ate in silence and luckily Mia didn't press him anymore about Scott's admissions in the car. He didn't want to talk about that mission or those days.

When they finished they walked, fingers laced, to their motel two blocks away. He couldn't explain it, but he didn't want to break their connection, so he kept hold of her hand. She didn't seem to think anything of it, but her touch meant everything to him—she was a mountain guide in a blinding blizzard. A Sherpa. Seeing Scott again had Augie back where he never wanted to be—forever lost in an arid desert. But her warm hand in his anchored him to the present.

She pulled him through the station. He still hadn't said anything, but she was undemanding. She stopped at a candy shop and only dropped his hand to fill a bag with . . . *Runts*. No wonder she smelled fruity and sweet; she still ate this candy he'd given up as an adult. A cool refreshing, like an internal breeze, rushed through him, linking the good memories from his past to the very real present. And there *had* been good memories. Lots of them before the war and before death and loss. Hell, he even had good memories of his buddies from the combat zone.

He shook his head, but couldn't hold back a smile. This slight girl and her sugar craving had saved him from floundering into an abyss after the meet with Scott. He scratched his head. Clay had saved him when he'd returned from the Middle East, but that had been a different, rougher, kind of therapy. He'd needed that demanding presence of a buddy kicking his butt then, but now he needed her sincere compassion. Or maybe he just wanted it. Or shit, maybe because he'd been denying himself the gentle concern of a woman for far too long he now craved it. She was gentle yet concerned and seemed to know his innate needs, needs he wasn't aware he had, such as talking about the darkness and devouring sugary, enamel-damaging junk.

She popped a handful of fruit shapes into her mouth and laced her fingers through his.

"Sherpa," he whispered as he smiled down at their linked hands.

She blinked her eyes at him. "Did you just call me a Sherpa?"

"You led me away from the darkness."

She smiled and squeezed his fingers.

"It's true—the damning thoughts didn't overtake me. It's gotta be the first time I've ever thought about what happened and didn't vomit and feel the walls closing in on me, cutting off my oxygen."

Her jaw dropped and her intake of air was sharp. She held the bag of candy up in the space between them.

"Runts?"

People swirled around them, and he laughed. Cleansing, all-consuming laughter until tears dripped from his eyes. She did the same, and he scooped up a handful of the fruity candy.

As they walked to the hotel he thought about the effect she had on him: she kept his demons at bay. There was a lot of downtime in the desert and he'd filled it by memorizing poems and literary passages. She reminded him of one particular Will Fitzgerald haiku:

I needed her
not because
her kiss
lit up my days
but because
the scent of
her skin
guided me through
the dark

At the motel he stood in line to register for a room. Pointing to a beverage stand, she whispered in his ear, "I'm going to grab a hot tea. You want one?"

"I'll take a coffee. Lots of cream, no sugar."

He waited in line for several minutes while the elderly couple ahead of him tried to hurry, but failed miserably. The woman had misplaced her wallet. They searched the luggage and her purse, twice. She smiled at him.

"It's hell to get old and senile. I apologize for the delay."

When she turned, he saw a strip of red leather poking out from her jacket pocket. "I think what you're looking for may be in your pocket."

He gestured and she pulled it out with a giggle while her husband rolled his eyes.

Finally he paid for their room and then searched the lobby for Mia. He observed her as she watched a couple with a child swipe crackers and condiments from a shelf outside the hotel restaurant. A man in an apron approached, gesturing wildly and pointing to a stack of menus. The father shook his head. Mia stepped in and had an exchange with the efficient employee, and not a very nice one by the look of it. The couple put the items back, and Augie watched as Mia pointed to the restaurant and placed cash in the woman's hand. Mia shook her head, holding her hands in the air, obviously refusing to take back the money, and then placed a hand on the mother's back and prodded her into the restaurant.

Augie crossed the lobby and took his coffee from her.

"Thanks, Mia." Still smiling at her sweetly bossy ways, he took a sip.

And he naturally wondered how she'd react to being bossed around.

Hot images of her responding to a dominant man, to *him*, heated him more than his coffee.

CHAPTER 4

They occupied the same bed.

Last night he'd slept in a chair, but she'd said there was plenty of room in the king bed.

She'd started out under the covers and that had been a good thing since they had nothing to sleep in. But Mia wasn't a quiet sleeper, and she'd shifted excessively the last few hours. Augie glanced *again* at the woman currently taking up two-thirds of the mattress, the woman who wore only her underwear. He'd taken off his shirt, but knew better than to remove his jeans. A slender arm landed across his chest. He exhaled loudly, hoping to disturb her enough so she'd reposition herself. She rolled and her thigh slid onto his, but she was still asleep. He'd be changing his name to *Saint* Augustine as soon as he got back to Baton Rouge. His hand went to her hip in an effort to move her, but that was a mistake.

She was warm and smooth and her hips were displayed in a provocative manner that had him going full-on hard. He clicked on the television and the shopping network came blaring to life. She stirred and raised her head from his chest. She eyed him with one eye open and one squinted shut, looking disoriented.

"Were you deliberately trying to wake me up?"

"I don't know—were you *deliberately* trying to give me a hard-on?"

She pushed herself up, attempting to push away from him, but the bed was shit—soft in the middle and hard on the edge, creating a bowl effect.

"God, do you have to answer using vulgar language and descriptions?" She ran her hand through her hair. "And for the record, I wasn't aware I was disturbing you. I apologize."

"Human-body pillow aside, can you at least get under the covers so I'm not in pain?"

From the glow of the television he could see that she turned as red as an apple when she eyed his erection. She quickly pulled back the covers and slid under them.

He turned off the television and rested his eyes. Her warmth seeped through the comforter, but she was safely covered, so at last he could get some sleep. His muscles slowly relaxed.

A blood-curdling scream pierced the room and hit his brain like a two by four. She jumped up and he followed. Eyes wide, they gawked at each other across the bed.

"What the hell?" he demanded.

She was shuddering as she rubbed one leg and pointed with an unsteady hand to the bed.

"Something bit me on the leg. Something huge. Oh God, it was on me."

Her voice was so high, she squeaked. She shrieked again, and his head pounded.

"Goddamn, woman." He took a deep breath. Patience wasn't his strongest character trait. He pulled back the sheets and identified the culprit. A huge beetle. He approached from the back and was closing in on it when Mia screamed again, causing his pulse to hammer in his ear.

"Oh my God, is that what bit me?" She cupped her hands to her mouth.

"*Stop* screaming. Let me get rid of it, and then I'll look at your leg. Sit in the desk chair."

She was shaking her head and hugging herself.

"Mia, sit in the desk chair."

She stopped rubbing and made eye contact with him.

"Sit."

She slowly lowered herself into the plastic chair.

He scooped up the bug and flushed it. Walking back into the room, he was attacked by warm, soft, sugary woman. She clamped her legs around his waist and her arms around his neck.

"Thank you. I can't believe it bit me." She shivered. "Do you think it's poisonous?"

He set her on the bed. "Let me look at it."

"Oh no!" She clutched her leg. "You do, don't you?"

"No."

"But you would have just said no. You hesitated."

"Well, dammit, some beetles are. Now sit still and let me look at you."

Shit, the damn thing had left a welt on her smooth skin. He grabbed a towel and some ice from the bucket. The welt was large, about an inch and a half in diameter. When he set the ice pack on her leg, she winced.

"I don't think that's necessary." She pushed the pack away.

"Do you want to scar?"

She looked at the bite, then back to him with pleading eyes. "No." Her voice was a deflated whisper.

She was so sadly pathetic. He couldn't take it, so he climbed onto the bed behind her and pulled her to his lap. He delicately set the compress on her leg. She needed a distraction, at least until the ice melted.

"When I was in the marines, we had to do these drills. We'd go out in the field and stay for two to four weeks, learn to survive off the land and stuff. One of the gigs was in western Texas, dry and hot. One morning this guy we called *Nuts*—he had a pair of the hugest balls any of us had ever seen—well, the crazy fucker took out an Iraqi FROG in Fallujah all by himself. Later that morning he used one of the field toilets, basically a Port-O-Pot. Now would you think a two-hundred-twenty-pound, six-foot-four marine named Nuts could scream like a girl getting sand thrown in her eyes on a playground?"

She was laughing so hard tears leaked from her eyes. He thought it was the cutest sound he'd ever heard.

"Your scream, Miss Brown, was manlier than his. Seriously, his screech woke up the entire company and had us scrambling. We thought a woman was being murdered. It sounded like a cross between a seal and a hyena captured in a jaw-tooth trap. When we got to him he was rolling in the dirt in front of the toilets, his pants around his knees. Sand was stuck in the tear tracks on his face. The enormous marine had been brought down by a teeny spider bite to the ass.

"To be fair, it wasn't your average house spider. It was a goddamn tarantula. Poor bastard had to let his ass air out for two weeks. He carried a donut around to sit on."

Mia's laughter eventually evened out and, given her proximity, they shared a way-too-intimate look. Her shy sweetness was playing tricks on his libido. He lifted the bag from her leg and lightly traced the swelling tissue. She turned in his lap and straddled him, leaning her head against his shoulder like she was going to drift off.

"Did you check the bed for any more beetles?" Her soft voice in his ear made his cock twitch. Her head lifted, and sincere lavender eyes met his.

"I did. We're safe."

"You're a real-life hero." Her lips feathered a kiss to his cheek and then to the busted skin at his temple and jaw. "My hero." She pulled away slowly, her eyes hooded. She held up two fingers, "That's twice you've rescued me now."

She was so close, her breath heated his skin. Wanting to taste her rosy lips, he closed the gap between them. And he tasted. Her warm, soft mouth vibrated with sounds of pleasure.

He pulled away to keep from getting carried away. He caught her gaze before she stared down in a shy gesture—gray laced with lavender. Spectacular. She snuggled into him and sighed.

Great, a moral dilemma. The warm female on top of him was as sweet as Louisiana iced tea, and her soft groans had him as hard as oak. He'd rescued her from two life-threatening situations—though the beetle hardly counted. Still, he wasn't one to quibble over details. He wondered if he was taking advantage of this bashful but passionate, honeyed woman.

Thank God he still had his jeans on, because with the way she was straddling him, he surely would have come like a teenage boy without them. With her in just her white cotton panties and a bra with tiny black polka dots, Augie could see the perkiness of her small breasts and the way the hard peaks poked against the thin fabric. She was fresh, too fresh, and innocent to boot—he felt it in his gut. She seemed much younger than twenty-five, with the kind of innocence that came from inexperience. He wanted to take her youthful inexperience and incinerate it. Wanted her to be a woman who knew the score so they could share some hot sex without him having to even *think* about worrying about it. Without worrying about her.

From what he'd read in the file he had on her, she'd been caring for her mother for years. She'd lived at the same address, in that small town, her entire life. She didn't have the moves to impress, so she was simply herself—pure and honest. When was the last time he'd had a woman like that? He couldn't remember. He thought he liked sophisticated and aggressive—the kind of woman he didn't have to teach for her to know what he liked. But the thought of teaching Mia had him so close to coming that he squeezed his eyes shut and thought about Afghanistan.

Then his thoughts shifted to Nicolas Claude Renaud. The bastard he'd hired had had his hands around Mia's neck when he'd intervened. Yet despite her situation—being attacked by Renaud's goons and then being pulled away from her home by *him*—she remained upbeat and constantly put others before herself. What would it be like to have a woman like that? Augie still couldn't believe they'd spent an hour getting Russell situated with his mixer. An *hour*. And then she'd helped that family in the lobby, expecting nothing in return. She did it just for the joy of giving to someone in need. Most of the women he knew were egocentric, thinking only of their hair, their lipstick, their nails, but she didn't seem to care about any of those things.

She bent and kissed him innocently on the mouth before lightly running her fingertips down his neck.

He wanted her. And couldn't believe he'd thought her plain at first glance. She was anything but. Granted, she was a far cry from the forced perfection he was used to in the South, but he loved her dewy freshness. Her hair was a natural light brown with sun-kissed blond threads running through it. She didn't flatten it into an unimaginable slickness, nor was it artificially curled. It was just her hair and it suited her. He didn't think she wore any make-up, but she didn't need to—her skin was as smooth as porcelain.

But something had changed.

Her eyes were darker now, the color more intense, hazy and sleepy. He wanted to know what had caused them to change.

Could it be their bodies pressed so close together?

Her hand landed on his jaw as her lips nuzzled near his ear. She rubbed her body against him, and it took all his discipline to not roll her beneath him and pump away into her tight heat.

There was that smell again from his childhood, fruity and sweet. *Runts.* Her scent. It had him off balance.

Shit, he had to put a stop to this. He'd never been out of control when it came to women, but she held his mind in a fogbank.

But maybe just a minute more . . .

She squeezed his cock through his jeans and licked her top lip. Groaning, he palmed her core, and the moisture he felt on her panties made him lose his tight control. He frantically unhooked her bra, her small tits hardening as he slid the material down her arms. She unbuttoned his jeans as he hooked his thumbs in her underwear and removed them. He lifted his ass from the mattress and she pulled his jeans down with his boxers and then they were skin on skin. Their heated bodies gave off so much heat that they were covered in a light sheen of sweat, silk and satin rubbing against one another, and it felt so right. God, it felt good.

Rolling her beneath him, he ran his cock through her wetness. Shit! Condom. Hovering over her, he grabbed his wallet from the nightstand. She raked her hands up and down his chest as he fiddled with the package, then rolled the latex over his erection. He fisted himself and aligned with her, but there was no easy passage. She was small, so he positioned her better to take him by putting a pillow beneath her ass. He tried to push in again, but thought he might hurt her if he forced himself. Yet he needed to be inside of her. Now.

"Fuck, how long has it been for you?"

She inhaled sharply, panting against his skin.

"Um, I haven't ever actually had sex."

She writhed beneath him, her hands squeezing his ass.

No. She didn't just say . . .

"Are you fucking kidding me?" He rose to his knees, threading both hands through his hair. He jumped off the bed, so wound up he couldn't hold still. Hell, he needed *some* kind of release. The water bottle from the nightstand took the brunt of his wrath as he hurled it against the wall. It splintered and water rained down.

Mia sat up on the bed, her hands behind her for support.

"So you're some twenty-five-year-old virgin? How's that even possible?"

"Not because I was saving myself. I just haven't met anyone in the small corner of the globe where I live. But I want to have sex with you."

Their eyes met for the shortest of seconds, and then she bit at her lip.

"I can't take your innocence."

"My innocence? I've never had sex, but I'm not innocent. I know what's involved."

"Your virginity. I can't take your virginity."

"But I don't want to be a virgin, and I'd like to have sex with you right now. Can we please try again?"

He looked at her offering herself to him in the sweetest, most primal way as she leaned back naked and exposed. Her taut breasts and stomach, down to her bare cleft, were calling to him and he wanted to devour her. His dick was so hard he'd explode if she were to reach out and touch him.

"I want you so badly I'm in pain, but I can't give you all the expectations that *should* accompany your first time." Shit. He didn't know how to talk to her about the loss of her virginity. He'd never met a virgin before. Far from it. All the women he'd been with came highly experienced and skilled, and he liked it that way. Or he had until now. He still wanted her. He was dying to taste her, and he was curious about the noises she made when she was aroused. Curious about what she looked like when she came.

He sat on the edge of the mattress. She pressed her palms to his chest, pushing him down to his back on the bed.

"What expectations?" she asked.

He didn't fucking know what expectations. She slid her knee between his legs, and he instinctively rolled beneath her. The way her heat was riding him had him unable to put together a coherent thought. Her long narrow torso and toned legs called to him like a beacon to a ship. He was about to take it too far, and she didn't get it. This moment would be something she could never get back. She'd remember it forever. Hell, he wasn't prepared to be her first.

He placed his hands on her firm but pliant hips and lifted her from him. He sat up, threw his legs over the bed, and scrubbed his face with his hands. This was wrong. He should have insisted on sleeping in the chair, but she'd been irresistible when she'd told him they could share the bed. She hadn't thought anything of it, but he knew where it would lead.

"Mia." He stood and they gazed at each other from opposite sides of the bed. Opposing camps. "I think you can see it's clear I want you." He grabbed his erection.

Her jaw dropped as her eyes focused on his hand stroking his cock. He dropped his hand when she made a sound between a moan and a sigh.

"You should wait. You'll meet some guy, and he'll give you everything you want."

Their eyes locked. "What do I want?"

He exhaled loudly and rubbed the back of his head. "Fuck if I know. All the things women want. Marriage, house, babies, my balls around your neck."

She stood directly across from him now. Her height imposing; she had to be at least five feet eight. Her lips pressed together, and her forehead crinkled. "I don't want any of those things I just want a night with you." She shook her head. "I've not had a chance to meet anyone, not anyone I've been attracted to. I've been taking care of my mom since I was a kid. This is my first time away from home. I have the time and, with you here, I actually have the circumstance. If you don't want to have sex with a virgin because you're nervous you won't measure up, that's fine. At least be honest. But don't stand there and tell me what it is I expect."

What the fuck was he going to say to that? He'd apprehended criminals less intimidating than Mia Brown.

She snapped her bra into place and pulled the straps up her arms.

"I'm sorry I've upset you," he said, the words sounding lame.

"I'm not upset."

She bent over in front of him to pick up her clothes from the floor. He didn't know if she was deliberately trying to be provocative but, given the way she was standing, he could see all of her. The sight made his body tense, and his balls had grown two sizes. He was going to have a serious case of blue balls if he didn't get release soon.

"I'm frustrated, humiliated, and embarrassed, but I should be thanking you."

"Thanking me?"

"Yes, you've saved me from making it with a coward."

He was a coward? Shit, he thought he deserved the Congressional Medal of fucking Honor.

She was dressing. "I don't know how it is where you're from, but in Canada, women are taught that they can have their own thoughts and express their opinions. Canadian men aren't afraid of strong-minded women, they embrace them. I guess this energy between me and you just wasn't meant to be."

"Where are you going?"

"To get my own room."

He stood, aiming for her. She held one hand up.

"Leave me alone, Augie. I don't want to be in here with you."

She grabbed her purse and was gone just that fast, leaving him reeling. He immediately missed her. It was like someone had turned off the lights. And what she'd said had stung. Damn, he'd wanted her fresh lips around his cock and he hadn't gotten to taste her sweetness.

He fell across the bed and dialed up some porn, but was turned off at the fake, grotesque proportions of the women's tits and their subpar, overindulgent acting. He switched off the television, closed his eyes, and thought of Mia: her slim figure, small breasts, fresh face, and her humor. To his surprise, his erection grew until the demand for release simmered through him. He grabbed his cock and thought of the lean curves that were already burned into his memory. She'd been willing to give herself to him, and he'd let her go. He'd meant to say she deserved someone better than him. He certainly didn't deserve someone like her.

He'd done bad things. Then he'd done worse things. And then he just existed. There was nothing remotely redeeming about him. Yeah, he was doing her a favor, but he wanted her there in the bed with him—to keep the demons at bay. He didn't want to dream tonight. He didn't want her where he couldn't see her. Just as the poem said, he needed her scent to guide him from the darkness.

He thought of her sweet, gentle exploration of his body when she'd been on top of him and immediately came in his hand.

What the fuck? There was no denying it—he was into her.

Mia slowly walked along the sidewalk that led to the front of the motel. A chill in the air had her wrapping her arms around herself. She kicked a rock and picked at the disastrous series of comical events: she'd thrown herself at Augie, begged him to have sex with her; he pushed her away; she called him a coward; he called her a ball-busting man trapper. Not in so many words, but that was what he meant. She exhaled harshly and squeezed her eyes closed, thinking she could erase his body from her memory. No luck. His taut chest and six-pack abs were there to stay—a great image to entertain her mind, but one that didn't do anything to relieve her yearning body.

At the front desk, she paid for the room using her credit card and asked for extra pillows.

The room smelled musty, so Mia left the door open while she flipped through channels on the television. She landed on an adult-only channel. Her father had subscribed to something similar and when she was a teen; she used to sneak into his room to quench her curiosity. And while knowledge and experience were two different things, she definitely hadn't been innocent since she was a seven-year-old staring down at her mother on the kitchen floor, her face bobbing in a pool of vomit made up of alcohol and pills.

She sighed and closed the door. With the television on late-night comedy, she settled into the bed, unable to focus on anything but piercing brown eyes and that muscular stomach. His crazy sexy smirk and bright smile had her blood pumping—in the wrong direction if she intended to sleep.

Geez, the man was hot.

She rolled to her stomach and groaned. Every time she closed her eyes, she saw his dark eyes fixed on her. It was unnerving, so she opened her eyes wide. Which didn't help much—she couldn't stop picturing his body. His bulging muscles. His intense eyes. And yeah, his cock. She wanted him inside her. She wanted to taste him and rub up against him and feel an orgasm roar through her while her legs were wrapped around him.

She wanted to enjoy sex with a man, all the messy, hot and wonderful glory of it.

Augie would be the perfect guy for her first time.

He seemed carved from marble with his bulky tightness. His ass in those worn jeans had caught and held her eye. It should be illegal for him to wear those jeans with that belt buckle. And then he'd caught her checking him out and let loose that cocky smile—the smile that was currently making her grin even though she didn't want to because she was mad at the asshole. When she'd finally gotten her hands on him, she'd attacked. And maybe that had turned him off.

She wanted to touch every peak and valley of his chest, run her hands over muscle and skin. She'd never touched a male body before tonight, and now her body wanted more.

It wanted a lot more.

Her fingers played over her own skin, even though she tried not to stroke herself. But she hadn't gotten near enough from Augie.

Yes, her body definitely wanted more.

CHAPTER 5

Not having slept in three days, Augie was exhausted and dog tired, but the repetitive knocking against the wall and the sighs of a woman's satisfaction kept him from sleeping. That and his huge erection. He'd banged one out before he went to bed, but he was again hard as stone.

"It's three in the morning. *Fucking* Canadians."

He sat up and put on his jeans and T-shirt. He needed a cigarette, but Mia had thrown his last pack out the car window. He pulled on his boots and left the room. Outside he'd seen one of those old-fashioned cigarette machines from the good ol' days, where you dropped in your money and pulled the lever for a pack of smokes. He walked to where he thought he'd seen the machine. The lights in the eaves were out in that wing of the building, but he could make out the machine. He put in his money and pulled. Before he even opened the pack he smelled menthol.

"Damn." Still he lit up and inhaled, not liking the aftertaste.

He was worried about Mia, knowing he shouldn't have let her go. But he knew she wouldn't leave. Something had changed in her when she realized the dire situation her sister had been in. Nicolas could have killed Eve; the fucker still wanted to. And he'd been willing to sacrifice Mia to get to her.

He walked along the dark outdoor corridor that led to the lobby.

Inside, he approached the counter. The attendant was a woman. Game on.

"Hey there," he said, adding just the right amount of southern drawl. She smiled widely, and her eyes made their way down his chest.

"Howdy, cowboy. Need a room?"

"I've got a room. What I need is to see if you'd be sweet enough to give me some information." He smiled. Women could never resist his smile. He held her gaze and could see the increase in her respiration at the pulse point between her breasts. He was in.

She wet her lips. "Sure. What do you want to know?"

"A woman by the name of Mia Brown would have come in here around eleven thirty and paid for a room. I need that room number."

She clicked a few buttons on the computer, its plastic shell yellow tinged from age and smoke. "No Mia Brown. I've got a Michael Brown."

"That's her."

"Room one fourteen. It's the fourteenth room to the left when you walk out the front door."

"You've been very helpful. Thank you."

"You need anything else, you give me a call."

He winked at her as he strolled away.

At one fourteen he knocked and scratched on the window. A light glowed to life, and then a shadow passed in front of him.

"Mia, it's me. Open up."

"Augie?"

"Yeah."

The door cracked and she was there, standing in only her tank top, her hands folded across her chest. Again she seemed confused. He'd remember that, that sleep fuzzed her brain.

"What's wrong?"

"Nothing. I just got worried about you."

Her hands rubbed her arms and she moved away from the door and hopped under the covers. "I'm fine."

He hated when a woman said *I'm fine* because it meant anything but. "Are you *fine* because you want me to leave you alone or are you *fine* because you want to go back to sleep?"

"Both."

He stretched out next to her. "Look, I'm sorry about what happened. I didn't intend to embarrass and humiliate you."

"You forgot frustrate."

"Right. I didn't intend to frustrate you either. I'm not at all good with women."

"Forget it."

"That's more girl speak for *I will never forget.*"

"I don't know what kind of girls you've been around, but I never say anything I don't mean. I want to put this behind us and to do that, you need to let it go. I have. I'm focused on helping Evie."

She was surprisingly and refreshingly easy to be around; he'd never found women to be that way before. Even his mother fussed so much, he could only tolerate her in small doses, like at Sunday brunch.

The room was warm and quiet and his eyes grew heavy. He closed them, thinking about the color lavender and slim curves and long limbs.

"Augie."

No way out. He carried two women, one over his shoulder, one in his arms. Too much weight and he fell to his knees. No way out. Smoke clouded his vision. They will all die.

"Get up!" he screamed.

"Augie."

A silver whisper guided him through the mines. Through the smoke.

"Augie."

There it was again. The voice took on light and became visible. He was going to survive.

Warm, moist, soft skin skimmed his neck.

"Hi, Augie."

His hands seized her upper arms and pulled her to his chest. He held her too tight, but he couldn't let go. She possessed virtue and kindness, and he wanted some of it. He needed to feel her warmth, her breath, her life. "Mia."

"You were having a nightmare. You screamed and were sweating and kept shouting *get up* and *we're going to die.*"

Her eyes weren't lavender, but an intense deep amethyst as she stared intently into his face.

"Where were you?"

He gasped and pulled her close again. "I just need to hold you for a while. It might be weird, I hardly know you, but I need . . . I've never had . . . I can't explain it, but I hope you don't mind."

"I don't mind." She settled against his chest. "I never had this either. I like having a friend. I need a friend."

She sighed, and he felt her lips form a contented smile against his neck. They could be friends. She really had meant what she'd said—she'd moved on from their spat. Forgiven. Fresh. New. The words bombarded his brain.

So this was friendly touching? Then why was he getting an erection? Soon it would be reaching for her . . . "Shit. Sorry."

She giggled, but there was another sound mixed in with that laughter—the sound of creaking metal. She heard it the second time. He put his finger to his lips to keep her quiet and mouthed, *Get dressed*.

They'd been located, and instantly he knew how—she'd used her goddamn credit card to pay for the room. Traveling with a woman was never a good thing.

He scooped up her purse and motioned her into the bathroom. The door handle jiggled, and he heard mumbling. At least they were dumb thugs.

He pressed close to Mia's ear and whispered, "We're going out the window."

She nodded, and he opened the window. He crawled through behind her, closing the window behind him. He pulled her by the hand and started a light jog. They crossed the main thoroughfare and then he led them down a back road.

"Where are we going?" She was short of breath.

"Don't worry about it. I need you to keep quiet so I can stay focused."

At the train station he purchased two tickets in a sleeper car, anxious to board and hide.

"I need to use the restroom," Mia said.

"Hold it until we board the train."

This was going to royally fuck up his plans. Gloria had been set to meet them at the hotel. Now he would have to figure out a way to get a message to her. He didn't even know where they'd end up. He dragged Mia to an attendant; she had to skip to keep up with him.

"We'd like to board." He held out his tickets.

"Sorry, sir, we are only boarding—"

Augie held his identification and badge out. "It's imperative that we be allowed to board now."

"Certainly, sir. Right this way."

Their compartment was small. Even smaller with Mia standing in the middle of it with her arms crossed over her chest. "Restroom's in here."

While she tended to her needs, he assessed the window. He hated feeling trapped, but that's exactly what they were—goldfish in a glass bowl. Beneath a red handle, a plaque read: *In case of fire pull latch and push.* He scanned the seam where the wall would break away. At least that was something.

When Mia came out, she resumed standing in his way. He pointed to the couch. "Sit." At least she did as she was told. He inspected the door and lock. It was shit. He would have no peace unless he watched each passenger board the train, but that would expose him and leave her where? His only option was to stay put.

A knock on the door had him on full alert.

"Attendant."

He opened the door a fraction of an inch and saw the man from the deck.

"May I take down your bed?"

Augie stepped aside and let him by. Mia stood, and the man inserted a key into the cabinet that housed the bed and it unfolded from the wall.

"I'll be around at eight o'clock to pin it back into position. If that's too early, please display your Do Not Disturb sign. Goodnight."

Augie dropped to the couch below the bed. His fingers tapped his thigh as he waited for the whistle and the rhythmic movement indicating they were on the move. He hated being a sitting duck.

"Augie." She stood before him.

"What?"

"Is everything okay?"

"No, it's pretty far from fucking okay."

Her lips tightened. Her hands rubbed her arms. It was cold in the cabin and she wore only a tank top. She had to be cold; her nipples said she was. He stood and dug in the bed cabinet for a blanket. He found a lightweight blue fleece throw and passed it to her.

"Thank you." She wrapped the blanket around her shoulders. "Is there anything I can do to help?"

"Well, I don't know, Mia. Are you in possession of a time machine?"

Her brows inched together.

"Because that's the only way you can help me with this goat fuck."

She took a deep breath and sat beside him. "What's wrong, Augie? Who were those people? Why did we run?"

"The plans I had to fix things for Eve and to protect you and your sister have been destroyed."

"What happened?" Her eyes widened.

He sighed. "You happened."

"What?"

"How'd you pay for the hotel room?"

"I used my credit card."

"*And . . .*? Do you understand the problem?"

"No."

"Are you seriously that fucking stupid?"

For lack of something to throw, his fingers rubbed vigorously against his scalp. "If you use a credit card to pay for something, it can be traced via satellite."

Understanding settled across her face.

"One or both of us could die tonight. So you see, Mia, you totally fucked me in the ass."

Her hands cupped her ears and tears fell from her eyes. "Can you please stop talking like that?"

She was a quiet crier. She didn't snort and sniff and carry on like his mother or any of the women he'd been with. She turned her body away from him.

"I'm sorry." Her voice was soft, barely audible. "I would never knowingly do anything to jeopardize your safety."

"Will you please just get in bed so I can stay focused on this detour and try to keep us one step ahead of the men who are trying to kill me and hurt you and your sister." She immediately climbed up into the bed.

He'd made a promise to Clay, and he intended to see it through. During college he'd moved in with Clay; he was the reason Augie had gone into the marines and straightened out his life. He'd do anything for Clay. When he'd seen that gleam in Clay's eye when Eve was around, Augie knew his buddy needed her like he needed air to breathe. Hell, he'd said as much. When Clay thought she was leaving him to go after Mia, he went to a dark place and Augie vowed he'd bring Mia back safely.

It seemed like an eternity as he paced and held his breath whenever footsteps stopped outside their door. Finally the train jerked and rolled to life, the whistle sounded, and they were catapulted forward as the train picked up speed. He sighed, plopped to the couch, and closed his eyes. A feather's touch whispered across his arms and hands. He opened his eyes to a head hanging above him, with hair cascading like a waterfall.

"Are you still mad at me, friend?"

He couldn't help but smile at her. Was she mad at him? He'd said some nasty, hurtful things to her.

"No. And I'm sorry I lost my cool."

She completed an impressive dismount from the top bunk and scooched next to him on the couch.

"It's okay. I totally screwed up. I'm really sorry—I honestly didn't know. I should have, and I guess most people probably would have, but you got stuck with me." She bumped her shoulder into his. "Are we still going to be besties?"

"Besties?"

"Best friends. I guess that's weird, huh? Just friends then?"

She offered her hand, and he took it.

"You're my first and only one, so I'd rather like to keep you. Even once we get to our destination if that works out."

He felt his forehead crease as he frowned. He'd never met anyone who worked so hard to preserve friendship with him. Maybe Clay, but they had their ups and downs. Augie knew he was an ass, and people struggled to keep him around. That was fine with him; he didn't mind being alone. Plus he had his brothers. But he did like this girl. She was easy to get along with, like a guy. More so than any woman he'd ever met.

"Yeah, we can be besties." He smiled. Couldn't help it.

She rewarded him with a fresh laugh that could light the darkest, most demented hole.

"Really? So I'm forgiven?"

"You're forgiven, just don't use any technology."

"Done. Do you think we're in the clear?"

"I do. They'd rather have apprehended us before the train took off."

"That's a relief."

"So what's in East Bay?"

"East Bay?"

"That's where we're headed."

"Oh. Well, not a lot. It's good for fishing."

"Fishing?"

"Yeah, walleye. Why are we going there?"

He cocked a brow a her, was she being deliberately obtuse? "We had to flee because we were being pursued by men who want to kill me and kidnap you."

"Great, thank you for that. What I meant was, wasn't there another destination available?"

"I just took the first thing I saw."

She scratched under her chin. "We can make it work."

"Glad to hear it." He laced his fingers together and rested them on his head.

"So what's the plan?"

"You mean the immediate plan or the overall plan?"

"I guess the overall plan."

She leaned forward and rested her elbow on her leg, her head in her hand—the twenty-first-century version of The Thinker. He bit back a grin.

"I have to get Nicolas to sign for an uncontested divorce and then convince him to leave Evie and her family alone."

"Hmm." She stood and turned off the overhead light, leaving the glow from the floorboard lights and the occasional flash from outside the window. "Seems like the only thing within our control is a good night's sleep. Come."

She held out her hand, and they climbed into the bed.

"I think these are actually meant for one," he said. He landed on top of her, his weight smothering her. She giggled and tickled his side until he rolled over. She positioned herself on her side against the wall, offering him more room. They lay on their sides face to face.

"I wanted to ask you a question." She spoke softly, and he couldn't guess what she was going to ask. He hoped it was something simple; he needed simple after the last couple of days.

"Go ahead—what are you waiting for?"

"I'd like to call my mother today. I didn't see her yesterday, and I obviously won't be able to see her today or maybe not even tomorrow, so I really need to call her."

He held her hand in his. "I know you're worried about your mother, but I'm afraid it's impossible to contact her without revealing your location, so that's out for a while."

She was so close, he could feel the heat from her words on his skin. She nodded and worried her bottom lip between her teeth before it popped free, pink and wet and luscious. He wanted to suck on that lip; it drew him like pollen draws a bee. His finger beneath her chin lifted her face to align with his, and he covered her mouth with his own.

A low moan escaped her throat. She tasted fruity and when she opened her mouth to wet her lips, he deepened their kiss. His tongue reached hers, and he felt the tentative wave of her tongue as she explored his mouth. He liked that she didn't come with a bag full of overly dramatic tricks or put on a provocative display for his benefit. He'd grown bored lately. It was always the same thing: the woman would try to entice him with her skills and he'd play along, seemingly engaged, when he really wanted to bypass all the bullshit and just have sex. But with Mia nothing was fake; her innocence was the real deal. She was different and the difference made the act of kissing and touching quite refreshing.

By the time they broke apart, she'd developed a lovely blush across her cheeks and chest. She wore an embarrassed smile and looked down, shielding her eyes from him.

"Hey."

Her head jerked up, and her amethyst eyes found his.

"You really are quite beautiful, Mia."

More blushing. It was rather becoming, and he wondered how long she could do it.

"Are you embarrassed?"

"I don't know. You're just so close."

He leaned down and took her earlobe between his teeth. "You invited me up here," he whispered.

"I don't want you to go, it's just extremely intimate."

"It is that." He nuzzled behind her ear, his nose in her hair, inhaling. "I'm sorry I upset you before, about your virginity. I want you; take a look for yourself."

Her eyes traveled down his torso and stopped at his growing erection. "How 'bout we take things much slower?"

He knew that playing around would be safe. Plus the ability to move around much was inhibited by the small space they occupied. To cool himself down he focused on her face and rubbed his nose against hers, taking in her scent and the feel of her silky skin.

"Your skin is beautiful, like satin." He nipped at her shoulder. "Your eyes change colors with your emotions, and I'm fascinated by them."

"Can I touch you?"

There was that blush again, but she held her gaze steady, and it devoured him.

"Yeah, baby, touch me."

She slid her hand down his torso to his cock and timidly palmed him, rubbing back and forth. Her cautious exploration lit a slow burn within him.

"I want you," she said. Her eyes were hooded and her blush had dipped down to her chest.

"I want you too. Roll over and put your back to me."

When she complied, he snaked his hands around her small waist, sliding over her hips. He popped the button on her jeans and slid the zipper down. That was enough. He was thankful they were both fully clothed; otherwise, his willpower wouldn't last. His fingers found their way between her legs and then between her folds. She was wet but he didn't tell her that because he thought she'd be embarrassed. But wet was good.

He liked wet. He found her clit, hard and exposed. He imagined what it would look like and he wished he could see it.

She responded to his touch, arching her back into his chest and moaning his name on a whisper. His finger slid into her and she was hot and so tight . . . Her muscles squeezed around him, and he pulsed in time with the contractions.

His other hand came up and cupped her breast, and his fingers pinched her nipple. She moved in an erotic rocking motion that had her ass riding his cock.

"Let me make you come," he said.

"Yes," she whispered.

He massaged her clit until she was panting and writhing, but she wouldn't let it happen. His lips nibbled at her ear.

"You have to let go."

"How . . . How do I do that?" Her voice was breathy.

"You've never come before?"

"I don't know how," she whispered.

He spoke low into her ear. "Clear your mind. Imagine you're jumping off of a cliff and free falling for miles into a crystal-blue sea."

He didn't know where the poetic came from, but he guessed it was her influence. She was his muse. His touch became more intense as he lathered her toward the place she longed to be.

"Jump off now."

Her body bowed and her head pressed back, into his shoulder. His lips found the pulsing vein in her neck, and he traced the line with his teeth as she came apart in his arms.

His massage continued.

"Keep falling, let it come."

When she shuddered a final time and went still, her heart was racing and she was short of breath. The marks on her neck where she had been choked were still visible, and he bent his head to gently kiss the skin there.

"Does it hurt?"

"Not any more."

He liked touching her, so he didn't move his hand from between her legs. He wrapped around her like a boa constrictor, not wanting to let go. He hoped she wouldn't make him.

CHAPTER 6

He was asleep. His breathing had changed from light to heavy, and he exhaled against Mia's neck. His hand was still between her legs, and she winced as she thought of the intimacy it represented. He was draped around her so tight she felt every muscle twitch, heard every sigh, smelled his earthiness—a combination of grass and leather. She could still recall his taste, a combination of mint and citrus and a faint taste of tobacco, a habit she wished he'd forgo for the sake of his health.

She felt more connected to Augie than to anyone she'd ever known. He seemed to sense it too, given the way he held her. He'd said she guided him away from his demons as a Sherpa guides mountaineers from danger. Maybe they had both been lost at sea, but together could survive the storm.

Yeah, and wasn't that a fanciful thought? How many years had she longed for a companion? At least since she turned sixteen. She closed her eyes and basked in the hold he had on her. Aware of the ridiculous smile on her face, she focused on the sway of the train and the rhythm of his body.

A shrill, high-pitched scream came from behind her, from Augie. She tried to twist in his arms, but couldn't move because of his tight hold. The back of her shirt was wet from his perspiration. "Augie." She slid her fingers over his arm and rubbed.

"No. Please, no." Another scream. "I can't do it."

"Augie." She pulled at the hair on his arm and immediately felt the change in his respiration as his body tensed. He moved, disengaging from her. First his hand slid from her pants. Then his arm pulled from beneath her. With his warmth no longer pressed against her, she felt cold. She turned to rest on her other side and to watch him. He had his knee bent, and his right hand rested under his head as his left scrubbed at his face.

He was different now, not the way he'd been a few hours ago when he'd talked her through her climax with his soft and sultry breath in her ear.

"You were having another nightmare. Was it about the children? Were you at the rescue?"

He scrubbed his face again, but this time his hand moved to his hair and rubbed vigorously. "I was."

She started to trace the length of his arm with her fingers, but stopped when he flinched. His demeanor had turned a complete one eighty, and she hoped she could help him get back to that carefree, happy place.

"Something bad happened with the rescue."

His head turned; his eyes were slits. "It was the fucking Afghan war. So yeah, bad shit happened."

Lots of people she'd helped at the crisis center screamed and yelled and shouted expletives when they were coming to terms with their past. Not surprised, she pressed on. "What happened to the children?"

"It's been nine years. I haven't spoken to anyone about what happened, and I'm not going to start now, so spare me your psychoanalysis."

"I'm not psychoanalyzing you, Augie. I'm offering an ear, if you need to talk, as a friend."

"Just because you were isolated and alone with no friends doesn't mean I was. If I'd needed to talk to someone, I would have found someone *nine years ago*. I don't need you to save me."

He sat up, hitting his head against the ceiling. "Fuck!" He rubbed at the spot with his hand. "What are you playing at anyway? You're coming on very strong, wanting to be best friends and trying to get me to take your virginity. It's like you want to trap me." He turned to look at her. "And besides, I've got enough friends back home. People I've known much longer than I've known you . . . and women too for that matter, older than you and more experienced. I don't need anyone else in my life, especially not a girl from the Canadian countryside."

He climbed down and started pacing.

Mia rolled to the wall. Tears rolled down across her nose and onto the sheets. She willed herself not to make a sound. They were stuck on this train until they reached their destination and while she might be crying right now, she'd never let him see her.

It was stupid of her to ask him to be her friend, but she was so desperate for a lasting connection with someone other than her mother. She was introverted and had a hard time making friends. If he didn't want to be friends, he could have just said so. But they'd gotten along well and fairly quickly She felt she could trust him already.

So he thought she was trying to ensnare him. How exactly? Hadn't she told him she didn't expect anything from him in exchange for sex? The things he did to her body were from another world. She'd never experienced so much pleasure, but she would never use their intimacy against him.

She wished she wasn't attracted to him, but she was, and not just in a sexual way. She was impressed with all of him: the soldier, protector, lover, and friend. She loved his playful side, when he was sparring with her.

Part of her knew he was reacting to his deep-seated pain, but his words still hurt. Her nose was now stopped up and she opened her mouth, taking a deep breath. She unwittingly sighed, the kind of sigh that was broken due to a hard cry. Damn it. She hadn't wanted to make a sound. Why couldn't she just act natural, normal? Normal—what did that look like?

She bet he dated a big-haired blonde with huge breasts—she'd seen the reality shows. The women in the South all had blond hair and huge boobs, hips, and lips. She wondered if that were the definition of a normal twenty-something woman.

She was miserable, but at least the tears had stopped. She closed her eyes, but the only thing she could focus on was how her body had responded to his touch.

What he'd done was wrong. He knew immediately after he'd said the words that he'd hurt her. She was getting too close, and he needed to push her away. No, it wasn't really that, because he liked being next to her. He simply didn't want to talk to her about his time in Afghanistan, tarnish her with his past. He wanted her kept free from those demons because if he told her, he'd no longer want to be around her. Just like he felt about his fellow soldiers. Seeing them brought back memories he'd buried and wanted kept buried. And now she'd heard the intimate, desperate things he screamed in his sleep. During his nightmares he knew he screamed like a small child, not like a marine. He didn't want her to know him like that, vulnerable and helpless.

Would she forgive him for the hurtful words he'd spoken, especially after what she'd told him about making friends? He'd told her they could be *besties,* and she'd beamed that glorious smile that told him she'd been truly happy.

But at his words, the fire left her eyes and was replaced by something else. Sadness. Dejection. Her shoulders slumped and she seemed to deflate altogether on her last exhale. Her throat worked as she swallowed thickly and turned from him. Then he'd barely heard her sigh. It was so soft, but he'd heard it, and he knew she was crying because of him.

"Mia," he whispered. She sniffled and his gut seized. "Mia." His hand gently rested on her back.

"Just leave me be, please." Her voice was low and lacked inflection.

"I'm sorry I said those things. You can come to me for anything, and I'll always try to help."

She turned to him. Her face was red and her eyes puffy, but she was no longer crying. He grasped her shoulders, but she wouldn't look him in the eye, just down at the bed.

"Did you hear me? I'm sorry. You can come to me whenever you have a problem."

She nodded. Her fire was definitely gone. He squeezed her shoulder tight as he looked at her in the bunk.

"Look, I've never had anyone constantly pressing me for information. The only girlfriend I've ever had was from my company in the marines, so I don't know how to be around you."

"I'm sorry too. I didn't intend to pressure you. It's just you have night terrors, and I wanted to help you. I won't do it again."

"Don't give up on me." He shook her shoulder. Her entire body moved, and her large bright eyes grew even more rounded. He let go and turned from her, taking a seat on the opposite side of the compartment. He was so fucked in the head. He rested his elbows on his knees and his head in his hands. Escape, he needed it right now. This was the beginning of a panic attack. That doctor had given him those pills, but he refused to take them. Shit. The walls were closing in; he was unable to get away. He couldn't get out. The moving train swished around him, back and forth, side to side. "Ah." He couldn't keep his head from spinning. Sickness was hitting him strong—he'd throw up soon. He shut his eyes tight as he tried to hold on.

"Augie."

Opening his eyes, he saw her squatting between his knees, her eyes bright. Her hands went to his cheeks.

"Augie, I'm here."

When he sat up she straddled him on the bench, and he reached his arms around her, squeezing tight. "Mia." He gasped, almost sobbed into her neck. "Why are you here? I've hurt you again and again."

"People say things they don't mean when they're in pain. You're guarded, you raise walls when people get too close."

"But you were crying. I hurt you."

"I know. Letting go and letting people in—it's painful for everyone involved. But the ones who love you will always be there. No matter how great the pain."

Her sincerity cut him to the bone. She was squeezing his upper arms, and that motion tethered him to the present. Just her spirit could save him. She didn't even have to say a word. He needed her. She should know that, but he was afraid to tell her. Afraid to have anyone know. Afraid that something he needed might be used against him.

"I'm sorry. Can you forgive me?"

"Augie, I'm okay. But I could have really used our friendship, don't use my weaknesses against me.

He grimaced. That was exactly what he'd done. He rested his forehead on her shoulder. "I'm sorry Mia."

She understood he was only protecting his heart and his secrets, but his words were some of the meanest she'd endured, and she'd endured a lot from her clients at the crisis center.

He was remorseful and that meant a lot, but she wanted an open-ended friendship and sensed he wasn't offering that sort of companionship. She translated what he'd said about coming to him for anything. He'd said she could come to him, *whenever she had a problem*. But what about other times, times she didn't have a problem but just wanted and needed a friend? When she wanted someone to share the passing of time with, to share her dreams with, to laugh with? What about those times and that unconditional bond that allowed her to just exist with another person? Would she ever find that? Was she too eager in seeking that?

She'd never been overeager before, and she felt her face heat. He must think her a nut.

He had calmed, and his head rested on her shoulder, the shoulder that was about to go numb. Then he shifted and inhaled deeply.

"Scott was trying to save the children, but we'd been sent in to rescue twenty-one civilian women. They worked at the elementary school, only the school wasn't empty. It was supposed to be empty, but it was full of kids locked in the gym. A radio message told us to avoid the gymnasium and the children and for a split second we wondered why, and then the bomb went off . . . in the gym."

His eyes glazed over and his mind was no longer there with her. A few minutes passed while he said nothing. Then he shuddered.

"It was unimaginable. Indescribable. There are no words to sum up the magnitude of the evil I experienced."

She wanted to reach out to him and hold him and tell him what a wonderful soldier he was, but she was afraid he'd shut down and not finish what he needed to say.

"At that moment I became a liability. I just couldn't do the waste, the death, and the destruction any longer. Suddenly I couldn't recall what we were fighting for. Families had been destroyed in the blink of an eye."

He squinted his eyes, his pain palpable. "We got the teachers out, but all the children in that gym died. Insurgents had planted bombs around the gym." He gasped. "At an elementary school." His forearms tensed as he clenched his fists.

When she could no longer stand it, Mia laced her fingers around his neck, pulling Augie into her. She held him tightly for several minutes before she pulled back and searched his face and eyes. He was as lost as a ship at sea. Her hand under his chin lifted his eyes to meet hers.

"Break out of there and come with me. That place will always be part of who you are, but it doesn't have to consume you any longer. You need to let them rest in peace."

His eyes simmered with unshed tears and when he closed them, the tears fell heavily down his cheeks.

The train whistled and then rolled slower and slower until it stopped, but he still didn't stir. The man was an expert at sitting still. His forehead rested against Mia's chest, and she felt the moisture that had collected there.

When he finally looked up, his eyes were red and he offered her a shy smile. "I guess we should think about hittin' it, huh?"

She nodded and slid her right leg off his and dropped her foot to the floor, but steely arms held her in place. Soft, warm lips collided with hers. His kiss was urgent without being frantic.

And Mia felt it to her core.

"Thank you for being you," Augie said when he freed her mouth.

Her head lifted, and she smiled. That was the nicest thing anybody had ever said to her.

They exited the train, and he grabbed a map from a stand by the exit door. "Hungry?"

"Not really."

"You need to eat. We'll dash into that diner." He pointed across the street.

Maybe he was hungry. She'd just take a soda.

Outside the station, they walked toward the diner. They were seated at a corner booth next to a window. There was plenty of room, but Augie sat so close, their legs touched, and his hand remained laced with hers. The waitress, Corrine, was about Mia's age and when her gaze landed on Augie, she smiled and dialed up the charm.

"What can I get for ya?"

"We'll take two hamburger steak plates," Augie said.

"Great choice. Hamburger steak here is excellent."

"Glad to hear it."

"Fries, mashed potatoes, or baked potato?"

"Fries."

"Side salad or broccoli?"

"Er, how about corn?"

"Okay and what to drink?"

"Two Cokes."

"Pepsi okay?"

"Is it okay if I pay you in Mexican pesos?"

"What?"

"Pepsi is fine."

She took the menus and then winked at him. *Winked at him.* He seemed oblivious as he pulled out the map and routed their journey.

He pointed out the route and then doodled on the edges of the map while she drank her Pepsi.

Eventually he said, "It's roughly eight miles; I think we should walk. Think you can make it?"

"I'm good for it."

"Great, eat up." He nodded toward the waitress as she laid down plates laden with way too much food for her to eat.

She tried to release his hand because she needed her right hand to lift her fork, but he wouldn't let go. She twisted around to look at him.

"Use your other hand." Then he smirked. *Smirked.* Playful Augie was in the house.

After about ten minutes, the edge of the booth had her leg throbbing right on the spot where she'd been bitten. She reached down to rub it and winced.

He looked under the table. "What's wrong?"

"Leg fell asleep." She didn't want to fuss about the bite—they'd both already made a bigger deal of it than a simple bite warranted. But she wasn't a good liar and for a moment she thought she would be exposed. Then his focus moved to their plates, his empty, hers nearly full.

Corrine came to take their plates, but he held his hand over Mia's. "Is that all you're going to eat?"

"That's a lot for me."

"You didn't eat any fries."

"I got full."

"But we'll be walking for a while."

"I'll be fine."

He exhaled through clenched teeth and waved the plates away. Corrine complied as she grinned at Mia. In return, Mia rolled her eyes.

She pulled out her wallet and gathered some bills together and placed them on the table. Augie stuffed them back in her hand.

"I don't think so."

"You've been paying for everything. I've got this."

"No, you don't." He threw money down and pushed her out of the booth. "I've got to use a pay phone or a landline."

"I'm sure Corrine wouldn't mind you using the diner phone."

"Hey, that's actually not a bad idea."

"You might have to sweet-talk her."

"I got it covered." He pulled her behind him to the counter.

Corrine immediately sidled up to him. To be fair, he looked every inch the rough and tumble cowboy as he rested his elbows on the countertop, his long legs culminating in dusty boots. That ass in those faded and tight jeans made Mia's upper lip sweat.

"Howdy. I was hopin' you could give me a hand."

"Be happy to."

His cheeky grin could make panties combust, and Mia wished he would stop using it.

"Well, all right."

Her mouth fell open when Augie spoke in a silvery slow tongue that dripped with sex and a deep Southern lilt. He chuckled deep in his throat and said, "I need to use a land-line phone."

Corrine bit her lip and crinkled her brow, looking worried. "Well, my boss will be here in fifteen. Can you make it snappy?"

"Don't you worry, sugar, I'll take only two minutes."

"Come on back."

They followed her around a few dark corners, and then through an open door that revealed an office. On the desk sat an ugly black phone. Augie lifted the receiver and held up two fingers.

"Two minutes."

Corrine nodded and left.

He dialed a long series of numbers, and Mia wondered how he kept them all straight.

"Gloria, change of plans. I'll be at Silverlake Estates in East Bay. . . . Yes. . . . No, we're on foot. . . . Eight miles out. I won't know until we get there. . . . I'll leave some sort of sign."

He placed the receiver back in the cradle. That was it?

"We're all set."

As they began their walk, he pointed toward a store. "Hey, you need a jacket."

"No, I don't."

"Don't argue with me."

His eyes narrowed. This was a demanding Augie. He wasn't as easygoing as he had been before, minus the times they'd argued.

He held the door open for her, and she stepped inside. It was a boutique, where the cheapest jacket she could find cost two hundred and fifty-nine dollars.

"Augie, I really don't need it. I'm fine."

He grabbed sunglasses too. Altogether the items totaled over three hundred dollars. He pulled his wallet out and laid the money down. She wasn't used to going through so much money, and his doing it for her made her uncomfortable.

"Ready?" His eyebrows rose as he awaited her answer. She nodded, and he frowned. "I prefer an audible answer, Mia."

"I'm ready."

Outside he pulled the jacket from the fancy gift bag and took it out of the tissue. He used his teeth to remove the tags and then he held it open for her. She slid into it, the silky sleeves luxurious against her skin. It was a cream color, and she hoped she could keep it from getting dirty. Augie placed the glasses over her eyes and said, "Now you're all set." He kissed her forehead.

They'd been walking for what seemed like an eternity on government-granted parkland. The paths had started out clear, but now were thick with underbrush. The leg that bothered Mia at the diner was starting to throb, but she didn't want to slow them and so pressed on. To get her mind off of the ache, she started singing the song her mother had sung when they were kids. The one Augie had memorized. She smiled when she got to *hippity dippity hoppity doppity.*

Ahead of her Augie stopped and waited, then he wrapped his arm around her shoulders. They resumed walking as he chuckled.

He was laughing at her. She wanted to laugh with him, but couldn't. Maybe she could have if things had been different, but singing that song marked the happiest she'd been in her twenty-five years, when she'd actually had a mother in the truest sense of the word.

She searched his face, but sunglasses blocked his eyes. Without her asking, he removed them, revealing eyes honest and clear. In her gut she knew he was trustworthy and she would be able to tell him anything. She wanted to tell him about her past.

"Things weren't always good, you know." Oh God, she didn't want to come off as pathetic; after what he'd been through, her stuff seemed petty. She looked down quickly, and he rubbed reassuring circles on her back.

She couldn't remember the events that led to her mother's addictions, but she did remember how she'd been before she'd succumbed. They'd been a real family that took vacations and looked forward to picking out the yearly Christmas tree. Mom played with her, read to her. Let her help out in the kitchen, especially when she was baking. Then it all changed. Mom had become angry and belligerent toward all of them, and Mia had wondered what she'd done.

They walked across a meadow. Hardy wildflowers grew in shades of orange, yellow, and blue.

Augie turned to her. "For the record, I've been told I'm a good listener." He put his glasses back on and ambled ahead.

They walked in slow steady silence for five hundred seventy-three paces.

Mia had never shared about her family with anyone.

Five hundred eighty.

"Before my mother was diagnosed, before she got the medication she needed, we all had to live with her highs and lows. She was diabolical. The things she said to me, I'll never forget—like she should have aborted me. I know she was ill, but I didn't understand then. And it still hurts today. Eventually Dad left and took Evie. That caused my mom to spiral out of control. Even more pills were prescribed, medications that lead to addictions. To make matters worse, she nursed an old injury with Darvocet." When she started drinking, things got worse than they had ever been. Mia rubbed her jaw where it had been shattered by a vodka bottle. Just a shadow of a scar ran from her ear down the jaw line.

Augie's hand cupped the area that had been hurt so long ago, his thumb caressing the exact spot. "She hurt you." His eyes radiated compassion and something else. Irritation? "Yet you still concern yourself with her."

"I need to go to her. She'd been clean, had been keeping up with her little job as a receptionist, but then Dad died and she had a setback. I usually visit her every day. I'm worried she'll check herself out."

"Element of surprise is the only way we'd go undetected. No phones, no notice, but I promise, as soon as we take care of the Nicolas situation, I'll personally escort you to visit your mother."

She squinted up into his brown eyes. She could live in those eyes. "You will?"

"Absolutely."

She hugged him, feeling once again the power of his body. "Thank you."

"Let's take a break."

It was slightly chilly, and they walked out to the center of the meadow, out from the canopy of trees. With the sun on her face, Mia pulled wildflowers one by one until she had a handful.

When she'd made her bouquet, she looked around for Augie. He sat in the center of the meadow, lounging with his arms stretched behind him, watching her and smiling. She joined him in the grass.

She tied the stems of the flowers together with a long piece of field grass. She held the bouquet out to him and he took it to his nose and grimaced. She giggled.

"They stink."

"They're wild."

He dropped the bouquet, and immediately his lips were at her palm, then her wrist, her elbow, her collarbone. Soft, warm nibbles landed on her jaw. Moist, hot breath rolled over her lips, and her heart beat accelerated. A hand went into her hair, tilting her head as his lips molded to hers. He smelled like citrus and tasted like rain. She was finding it difficult to breathe, and her lips parted on a sigh. Their tongues met and she drank from him, exploring his taste and texture. His essence. Her hands cupped his face and her fingers traced the sharp, edible line of his jaw.

With his hands guiding her, she moved until she was on top of him. She felt his hardness immediately as she pushed against it.

Suddenly her butt met the hard ground, and he was on his feet. It happened so fast, Mia was disoriented. She shook her head to regain her equilibrium. And her composure.

"Come. We better keep moving."

"No!"

He took one large step toward her, his body so close and imposing that he blocked out the sun. "No?"

She shook her head. "No. I won't move from this spot until you tell me why you won't have sex with me when your body clearly wants to." She meant to point her index finger at his erection, but she overshot and her knuckles ran smack dab into it.

With no warning, her world tumbled sideways, and she plummeted toward the earth. But she never hit; her hips and waist rested against something hard, stopping her descent. Once she got her bearings, she realized Augie had thrown her over his shoulder caveman style and had resumed walking.

"Hey, you overgrown ape, put me down right now."

No reaction from him, so she began to beat on his back with her fists. Still nothing. Frustrated, she couldn't budge herself forward or backward. Not only had he hurt her feelings by dismissing her advances yet again, but now she was utterly humiliated. To top it off, her shin was starting to throb.

She couldn't believe how easily he carried her up the hill. Finally she pleaded, "Augie, please put me down. I get it. I promise I won't subject you to my attempted sexual promiscuity anymore."

Her voice was so low she wasn't sure he would even be able to hear her. Then she got an idea.

"After all, I'm just assuming you're into women. But men may be your thing. You were in the military, after all."

Once again her world swirled on its axis. She wished he would stop doing that. He tracked back to the meadow, walking angrily fast. The kind of pace her father used to take when he was mad at something one of them had done—like writing on the wall with crayons.

Well . . . *good*. Now they could both be frustrated.

He plopped her down on a tree stump and placed his hands on either side of her so she was enclosed in a blanket of Augie. His nose came just short of hers and stopped. He tilted his head and inhaled so close to her neck his breath heated her skin. She'd always thought herself giraffe-like and was self-conscious about her neck. She heard him inhale as he made his way from her collarbone to her jaw, not touching, just incredibly close. She felt his warm breath, the rhythm of his life, as he breathed in and out. Her eyelids slowly lowered.

His low growl in her ear made her giddy.

"You think I'm gay because I denied you?" His voice was raw, masculine, and deep.

She'd forgotten the circumstances that had gotten her here. That she'd teased him. Note to self—don't mock Augie. She was breathless and wasn't sure she could speak. She cleared her throat, but still couldn't find her voice. She pushed against him, one hand on each shoulder, but he didn't move a centimeter. He might as well have been a mountain for all her success at moving him.

His intense eyes froze her in place. He wasn't just looking at her, he was peering into her. His intensity exposed her every layer; there wasn't anything she could hide.

"You're not going anywhere."

He was going to strip her down, she could feel it. "I'm uncomfortable. Let me go."

"No."

"Why not? You're hurting me."

He smiled. But it wasn't a smile to comfort. It was the kind of smile she imagined stalkers gave when they happened on their prey. "I'm not even touching you."

"I didn't mean that kind of hurt."

"Mia, you shouldn't tease a master manipulator. I want to fuck you. I'm going to be clear here because we've been over this before and yet you're still at it. You were right about what you said back at the motel."

He stood and that meant she could finally breathe.

"I'm not a very nice guy. I don't do well with women, so I don't intend to ever pretend I'm a monogamous kind of guy." He removed his sunglasses and laid them on the stump next to her hip. "It may not matter to you, but taking your virginity isn't a small matter." He unhooked his large belt buckle, the eagle with spread wings. "You're innocent and fresh and God, you're young—too young for me." He started unbuttoning his jeans.

It was her turn to stand. "Um, what are you doing?"

"I thought I'd let you get a look at the goods. You have seen a man before, haven't you? I've only ever been with experienced women. I assume you've done your research."

"I saw *the goods* at the hotel."

"Not in the daylight and in all of their glory."

His fly was open, and he was pushing the waist of his pants down.

She saw his flesh, and immediately her eyes flashed up to meet his. Yet his penis was that quickly imprinted in her memory. It rose from his crotch, long and veined, smooth and thick; the base cushioned by his sack. Her mouth went dry, as if she'd been eating cotton. Her eyes throbbed from being stretched so wide.

She swallowed. "There's no hair."

His head shot back, making his erection stand even taller. He laughed so hard his entire body shook. "It's referred to as manscaping."

She didn't like it when he laughed at her, which he did a lot. She'd just have to see if she could get his attention another way.

She stood, reached out, and took his warmth in her hand and squeezed. His head shot back to its normal position, his demeanor anything but a joke.

"Are you done laughing at me?" she asked. She started the motion she'd seen in those movies her father watched. Augie's moans seemed to express appreciation for her actions. His eyes were hooded as he looked down at her hands. He slid down against the tree stump and she followed, kneeling and pumping him.

"Where'd you learn how to do that?"

"Movies."

"What the hell? What movies?"

"My dad watched porn."

His hand went into her hair and fisted there.

Her fingers squeezed over his tip.

"Ahh . . . " His eyes widened. "Did you . . . did you ever practice these moves on guys?"

She shook her head and grinned. Moisture coated her hand.

He leaned in and seized her lips, tugging, sucking, licking, and massaging. He felt moist and warm against her. They separated, and he pulled her down to the soft grass of the meadow. With her jacket, he created a pad, and then he rolled her to her back and he lay on his side next to her. His hands roamed her torso lightly as she watched. He was a man, not as young as she was. He knew what a woman had under her clothes, and he knew how to use that knowledge to bring them both pleasure. Mia wondered what it would be like to experience his masterful seduction in all of its glory, but she could tell he was holding back.

"God, Michaela."

"No one calls me that."

"Why not, it's a beautiful name. It's sophisticated. Like you."

His hand at her stomach burned through her shirt.

"Besides, Evie told me it's your full name."

"Yeah, well, I don't like it. It gives me bad memories. And she's wrong."

"What? Why?" He reared up and kissed her jaw as his hands held her immobile.

She felt vulnerable—she'd already shared so much. Truth told, she wanted to tell him. It would ease the burden, a release she needed, but would he think her a total disaster?

"I'm named for the boy the doctor told my parents they were having." She shrugged. "Dad was so upset when they presented me to him as a beautiful baby girl that he didn't even bother to have my name changed. Or my room at home. It was hockey themed until I was ten. On my birth certificate my name is Michael, but my mom told everyone it was Michaela."

He traced from her shoulders to her waist. "I was thinking we would conduct a little experiment." His brow arched at her.

"I'm going to use Michaela because I like it. But I'll only use it at certain times, because it's the kind of name you cry out when you're about to come."

CHAPTER 7

Her mouth opened on a gasp as his hands moved under her shirt and cupped her just under her breasts.

He willed himself to go slow, but her soft skin and the way she molded under his hands, like fine clay, left him desperate to taste that flesh. He dipped his head as he pulled up her shirt, and his hot mouth landed on the dip of her stomach. He tongued her belly button, and then his lips traced across the area slicked by his saliva. She tasted salty and smooth. And he needed to taste more of her.

As he kept up his survey of her torso, he expertly unfastened her blue jeans. Kneeling, he lifted her shirt over her head and held her in his arms as he delicately kissed the small swells of her breasts. He unclasped her bra as his stubble rubbed the skin there, making it pink. Her breasts were small, but her nipples were a barometer for her arousal as they darkened and elongated beneath his touch.

She responded like a goddess. She was soft and sweet, warm and moist. Her sounds were relaxed and deep, hypnotic guttural moans that he delighted in. He was lost in her. God save him, he couldn't even remember the mission. All he could do was touch, taste, hear, *feel* the woman falling to pieces in his arms. He nuzzled her ear to whisper, "I want to taste your sweetness." His hand slithered down past the rim of her jeans and into her panties where he felt her delicate wet flesh. "Will you let me?" Her breath was uneven as her chest rose and fell erratically. "Do you like it when I touch you?"

"*Yessss.*" Her voice was low and breathy.

"Do you want my mouth on you here?" He rubbed her core and sucked her earlobe between his lips.

She gasped, then moaned.

"I didn't hear your answer." His lips moved to her neck. "I said, do you want my lips on you here?" He used his finger to run along her seam.

Her neck and back arched. "God, yes, I want you to kiss me there."

So sweet. She was exquisitely responsive to his touch and words, and he loved it. He slipped to his knees, straddling her as he shimmied her jeans down her leg. Then he slid her silk panties down.

"You're a beautiful woman," he said.

She rolled her eyes and snorted.

"Are you calling me a liar?" He leaned down to kiss her lips sweetly.

"No." Her chest rose and fell and her breaths were heavy between words. "I just know how I look—all limbs and no womanly curves. I have the body of the boy my father longed for. I could probably pass for a Michael." She smiled at him.

"I like your limbs. And you have just enough curves."

His hand traced the small outer swell of her breasts, her collarbone, and her hip bones, then he slid his hand down her lower back and filled both hands with her ass, kneading firmly. "You have curves where it matters. You're efficiently built, no excess. In a way it's even better; there's no waste."

The women he usually bedded had ample curves but looking at Mia, Augie couldn't recall what he'd thought was sexy about them. He'd never been with anyone like her, but he liked her natural freshness. It had him hard as titanium. He moved down her body and pushed her legs back to expose her pussy to him.

"Did you watch this on your dad's porn?"

She tried to close her legs, but he wouldn't let her.

He rested between her legs and used his shoulders to keep her spread.

"Did you?"

"No, but I read about it." She took a deep breath. "In a magazine."

He delicately massaged her until he felt her clit grow taut. Then he spread her wider and used his tongue to explore her essence. She was sweeter than he'd imagined, softer than velvet, and completely at his mercy. Her legs trembled, her body bowed tight, but again she couldn't seem to let go. He wanted to be inside her, bring her that sweet release from the inside out, but he honestly didn't have a clue about virgins. Would he hurt her?

He let his fingers replace his tongue as he shifted so his weight rested on his shoulder.

"Please, Augie."

"Mia, remember you have to let go. Free fall."

Her body writhed and her eyes closed tight. He lay alongside her and kept massaging.

"Mia, open your eyes. Look at me."

Her eyes were deep amethyst with pewter-gray rims. Their color was incredible.

"Please," she pleaded.

He rimmed her opening with his finger. He slowly pushed past her barrier. She gasped but never broke eye contact with him. He massaged her clit, and she fell apart next to him, squeezing her legs around his hand so hard it actually brought him pain. She shattered, and he pulled her into his arms, whispering in her ear.

"You're the most beautiful and honest woman I've ever had the honor of pleasuring."

Her face was flushed and her eyes were returning to that lighter shade of purple gray. She smiled and reached for his erection, but he grabbed her hand and placed kisses on her knuckles.

"I want to taste you now," she said.

He shook his head, and her eyes narrowed.

"It's all about you this time."

"But I want more. I want you. And I know you want me too." She pointed to his crotch.

Yeah, he wanted her, but preserving her virginity, at least from him, was more important.

"Are you saying you're not satisfied? Because from here it sure seems like you should be."

"Oh!" Her eyes went wide, and she jumped to her feet, dressing in record time. Then she took off in the wrong direction.

He couldn't help but laugh. Slowly he stood, gathered her jacket, and turned to go after her.

The imbecile! Yes, the things he did to her were nice; yes, she was satisfied; and yes, she'd definitely enjoyed herself. But she felt as if a part of her was destined to go unfulfilled. When she'd held his heat in her hand, she'd wondered what it would be like to be that close to someone you were actually connected intimately with.

A steely band enclosed her upper arm and she yelped, startled.

"We're going this way."

"What?"

"In your haste, you took off in the wrong direction."

She stopped and considered his words.

He laced his arm through hers. "Come on."

She reluctantly let herself be pulled around.

They walked through the brush, leaves crunching underfoot. When the sun went behind the clouds, it turned cold and Augie placed the jacket on her shoulders.

"Are you still mad at me?" he asked.

"No. It's surprisingly difficult to stay mad at you."

In silence they walked for roughly twenty minutes until he stopped and turned her to face him. "What's wrong?"

"It's nothing. I'm just tired." She felt weird, numb. Her leg throbbed, and she was worried about her mother.

His hand went to her forehead. "You're warm despite the drop in temperature." His gaze pierced her.

"We'll get to your mom. One way or another, we'll get to her, but right now we have a mission to accomplish. I estimate two days. We can make plans to see your mom after that."

He was beginning to know her quite well and his promises comforted her. She cupped his jaw. "Thank you." When that didn't seem like enough thanks, she kissed his chin.

They walked a while longer. After an hour, her leg started to feel tight and the stiff spot in her shin felt hot, but then it went almost numb. Thankful, she thought the one thing Augie didn't need right now was to be burdened by a girl with an injured leg.

He walked ahead of her, clearing and holding branches out of the path when needed. She knew that looking out for her slowed him down, but he seemed content. As he held a rather low-hanging branch aside, she asked, "Is Augie your nickname?"

"Yeah, my full name is Augustine."

She stopped walking. "You're named after a saint."

"Exactly."

"Wow, that's some high expectations your parents had. I mean, if anybody was going to be named after a saint, I think you're a great choice."

He smiled.

"So tell me about this Saint Augustine."

"He was a philosopher who wrote some mumbo jumbo about the theory of self. He actually did a lot to establish the doctrines of the Catholic Church."

"So you know a lot about the Catholic Church?"

"Baptism, confirmation, holy communion, Catholic school, altar boy—trust me, you'll find no one more Catholic than me."

"So you attend mass every week?"

"No, I uh haven't stepped foot inside a church in years."

His lips tightened, and his jaw twitched.

They made it to a small fishing village where vacation rentals were tucked into the woods. The rental office was closed, but that didn't stop Augie. Mia followed him up to the back door of a house that had a long fishing dock. He twisted the knob.

"It's locked."

He squatted and dug through a potted plant. A few seconds later he produced a key that he used to unlock the door.

"Have you been here before?" she asked.

"No."

The door creaked when he opened it. Mia followed him in and through the house. Back in the living room he said, "Sit on the couch. Don't touch anything. I've got to secure a few things."

Sighing, she plopped down on the couch. She needed a nap, but felt guilty since he was doing all that work to ensure their safety. She tried to keep her eyes open, but lost the battle.

Images of Evie braiding her hair flashed behind her eyelids. Evie's fingers raked through her hair, soothing her. Rolling fields spread far and wide and they ran, hand in hand, all the way to the mountains. Only, the mountains were farther than they appeared and they weren't reachable on foot.

Fingers were now rubbing Mia's stomach in a touch that was more intimate than a sibling's. A masculine sigh funneled into her ears and woke her from the dream. Her eyes opened slowly to find Augie staring down at her.

Her head was on his lap.

"Hey there, sleepyhead."

Embarrassed that he'd been watching her dream, she turned her head into his lap and smiled lazily. His hand snaked through her hair and massaged the base of her scalp.

Mia groaned her appreciation.

"I've secured the place; you need to be aware of a few booby traps. At the top of the stairs I've strung fishing wire and attached a set of chimes, so be careful not to trip it."

"Where'd you get chimes?"

"Back porch."

"You destroyed their stuff?"

"You'll need to step over the wire." He ignored her concern. "Additionally I've reinforced each point of entry." He regarded her with a raised brow. "I used scraps I found in the garage; nothing was destroyed."

She smiled, burrowing against him.

"Each door and window has been secured. If I'm not available and there's an emergency requiring you to leave, simply pry the added wood apart and away using this crowbar." He lifted the tool. "It will be at the foot of the stairs. Then run like hell across the field to the neighboring cabin."

Lifting his butt from the couch, he slid one hand into a pocket. "Here's the key—keep it on you at all times. There's no electricity but there is a flashlight at the front door mat. Lock yourself in the cabin and wait there until morning and then you can walk down to Larry's Live Bait and use the phone." He pinched her lightly. "Questions?"

She scratched her head and sat up. "And why am I fleeing without you?"

"It's plan B. I don't think it will come to that, but if I am incapacitated, that's the protocol."

"Where'd you get the key?"

"Don't worry about it. Just keep it on you at all times." His fingers raked her back, but the way he spoke so coldly about the plans gave her a shiver. Like hell that was plan B. She wouldn't leave him behind to be hurt.

"You seem so serious."

"I am fucking serious. None of this is a joke. Those men that came after you work for an organized crime ring. Nicolas is deeply involved. Deeper than I ever thought possible." He clicked his tongue and shook his head. "I didn't want to involve you in any of this, but I think it's important you know just what you're up against."

She laced her fingers in his. "We're up against."

The silence grew, and her thoughts wondered. Did he plan to kill Nicolas? She worried for Augie's safety. And his mental state. He already had nightmares. Bad ones.

What would happen to him if he killed Evie's husband?

CHAPTER 8

She stared at his lips and just that fast, Augie wanted her mouth. Reading his mind, she took his bottom lip between her teeth and explored. He let her lead. Her little pants and moans made him ache as she squirmed atop his cock. Tentative nips and tastes turned into a hypnotic rhythm as her ripe lips softly took his mouth, her tongue slipping in and exploring.

In an effort to slow them down, his hands roamed up her ribs. His touch focusing on each separate valley and peak. Like his own breathing, hers was erratic and shallow. The fingers in his hair tugged hard while strangled sighs flared from her throat. If they didn't stop now, they'd go too far.

"Augie."

Whispered feminine pleas hit his ears.

"Please, I need you."

Heat ground into his crotch from where she twitched above him.

"I want to taste you." When her hand landed on his lap, expletives spewed from his mouth.

He couldn't undo his fly fast enough, so she took over. Soft fingers slid into his shorts and wrapped around his dick.

"I want you to take off your jeans."

"So bossy, Miss Brown." In a flash he was standing, leaving her on the couch, searching for him.

When her gaze locked onto his she said, "Shorts too."

Stopping his striptease, he contemplated her last prompt.

"What?" she said. "I've already seen it—in all of its glory."

He smirked. "My issue is that you're fully clothed."

Smiling, she pulled her T-shirt over her head and unclasped her bra. She held the cups to her breasts. "It's kind of cold in here."

"I'm counting on it."

He winked at her, and then a small silky polka dot bra landed on his head. She unfastened her jeans, lifted her ass from the couch, and shimmied out of them.

Both in their underwear, they were at a standoff as they sized one another up.

"Count of three: one, two, three."

Completely naked, he stood and she sat. Given her angle, looking up at his erection, he would have appeared huge. Her gasp confirmed his thought. He pumped his cock a few times. "You still wanna take this in your mouth?"

Her tongue darted out, and she licked her full pink lips. "Absolutely."

He sat and placed a pillow between his feet, then motioned her into position. She knelt, and his hands gathered her hair at her nape. Timid, she took his weight into her hands.

"Each time it's heavier than I expect it to be."

He smiled and collected her stray curls. She pumped his length, and a low growl escaped from her throat. Moist velvet euphoria blanketed him as she molded her lips around his glans. Her moans vibrated along his length, and he ached, harder than he'd ever been in his life. Sweet sighs combined with her gentle exploration had him reeling as he watched her gradually swallow his cock, cradling him with the underside of her tongue. Her small hands massaged the length not taken by her mouth. Twisting and squeezing, she worked him until he gasped for breath.

"Hey, if you don't stop that, I'm going to come in your mouth."

Intense eyes met his as she doubled her efforts, her gaze never leaving his, hands and mouth steadily working his cock. Come erupted from deep within, low in his belly, and curled outward toward his penis. Like a savage he shot long and deep down her throat. It took a while for him to empty. On a gasp he said, "Michaela." She licked her lips and slowly, so very slowly, licked him clean.

When she was done, she crawled up to his lap and straddled him. The skin at her back was cold, so he pulled the Afghan from the back of the couch, enveloping the two of them. His forehead touching hers, he kissed her nose.

"You're so beautiful." His hand rested on her cheek. "And that was incredible."

She smiled. "Really?"

"Yeah, baby. Fucking *blow my mind* incredible."

She giggled, and her hands went into his hair. "I want more."

"God, so do I. So much more."

"What do you want?"

Bringing their foreheads together again, he pulled her hair into a ponytail at the nape of her neck. "Michaela, my composure around you is waning. I want to be inside you, to be connected and feel your warmth, no ending, no beginning, just one. To feel you gripping and clenching me tight, feel the contractions as you drain my cock while you fall apart around me. I want all of it."

"Augie." Her voice was a whisper. He held his hand out to stop her from saying more.

"I'm not nice to women. I mean, in the past I haven't treated them very well. You would regret it eventually."

She shrugged. "Maybe you've been with the wrong women."

He looked away. Was that it? He'd been with the wrong kind of women? The closest thing he'd come to having an actual monogamous relationship was with Gloria. With her he'd proved he could be monogamous, at least for a little while. But then they'd both grown equally antsy and indifferent, just bored, and they'd done a mutual parting of the ways. No harsh words, no tear-filled goodbyes, no desire. Therein lay the problem. After sex, he'd just grow completely bored and ready to move on to the next one in line. The sex club he'd joined in Baton Rouge had helped with that, and nobody expected a commitment. But still sometimes women from the club showed up around town at the bars and clubs he frequented, hoping to hook up with him outside the anonymity offered by the Hoodoo Pot. Clay said his trouble was that he engaged in too much flirtatious conversation with the women beforehand, but how could one have sex with a stranger? Didn't work for Augie, he needed at least a foundation.

Mia leaned in and nipped his lip. "Hey, you're overthinking this again."

"I am not," he said, sounding surlier than he intended. He used the hand raking her back to pull her in close to his chest. She inhaled deeply and sighed, sagging against him, her chin under his.

"Do you think there's any chance those men will find us here?" Her voice quivered as a shiver racked her body.

"There's always a chance, but if anyone tries to touch you, I'll kill them."

"I've been thinking about Evie a lot and what she must have endured."

He pulled her back so he could look into her eyes. She in turn searched his face.

"Hey, all of that's in the past now. Evie is doing well. She'll forever be safe; no one will ever hurt her again."

Her hitched brow said she doubted him. "I don't think he intends to stop looking for her. You said he's a very bad man." She rubbed the bruised skin on her neck.

He pulled her wrists to his mouth and kissed the inside of each one. "I don't know what his game is. I don't intend to walk away from him unless I'm sure of your and your sister's safety."

Large lilac eyes stared into his. He filed their color into his memory—lilac, the color of her eyes when she was sated.

"How can you be certain?"

"Certain?"

"Of our safety."

His eyes narrowed. He knew exactly how, already had a plan B. Sure, he'd feel the guy out, but he knew what he had to do. Dawning spread across her face and her mouth formed an *O*.

"Augie." Her voice was a whisper.

Gripping her upper arm, he inhaled sharply. "I wanted to keep you far removed from the details, but I can't because you're here with me. Don't ask any questions. Don't even let your mind wander down that path. If anything happens, if questions come up later, you must remain unknowing, uninvolved, or else all of this"—he circled his finger in the air—"will have been a fool's mission."

Her lips tightened and she lowered her chin. When he lifted it again, he saw the pain in her eyes. "Tell me you understand what I'm saying."

Her hand went to the fingers he had clasped around her upper arm.

"I understand."

Her eyes turned to liquid and, wincing, she grasped his fingers. He hadn't realized he'd been squeezing her so tightly. He released her instantly.

"I'm sorry."

She rubbed her face across his warm chest, sticky skin to sticky skin. He'd never been this close to a woman before, except when engaged in sex. But never after. He couldn't deny it felt luxurious, but more than that, he wouldn't let himself deny how good she felt rubbing against him. He was aroused, but feelings he didn't know the words for welled up in him and when she pulled away, taking the blanket with her, he felt as if someone had taken away his favorite toy.

They dressed. Mia needed to talk to him about killing another man, even one as evil as Nicolas, but he'd made her promise to leave it alone.

"See if there's anything that could be made into dinner," he said. "I'm gonna look around." He held up two fingers. "Two rules: no technology and don't go outside. There will be consequences this time for breaking the rules. "

She nodded, distracted by the domineering personality he was displaying. Maybe this was his true nature. She rather liked it because she hated surprises and his expectations were clearly defined.

In the basement she found a deep freezer that contained what looked to be homemade ice cream. Tags read: rocky road, chocolate, and cherry vanilla. There were dozens of bags with frozen vegetables. No protein.

In one corner she found fishing rods and a tackle box. She carried them upstairs. The bait was spinners and minnows. Luck had always come to her when she'd used simple minnows on a jig, but the minnows she used were real, not artificial. She shrugged and pulled the rubbery bait from the box, attaching it to the line.

She headed outside to the pier behind the cabin.

She cast the line. The water was slightly choppy, which was actually not a bad thing for walleye fishing. As she waited for a pull in the line, she thought about how Evie hated fishing, said it shouldn't be considered a sport, but Mia was glad it was because fishing with her father had been some of the few occasions her father had beamed with pride on her behalf. She had a knack for casting and reeling. With a smile on her face, she inhaled deeply and tried to relax. It had been an unrelenting twenty-four hours.

When the line clicked, Mia bore down on the rod and slowly reeled it in. The tension was tight, but she steadily reeled. Eventually gold scales shimmered just under the water near the pier's edge.

Walleye status confirmed, she reached for the net by her feet and struggled to lift the fish. Fighting, the fish thrashed and jumped, but she fought back and turned the net into his struggles. Damn thing was heavier than anything she'd ever caught before.

She leaned the rod and net against the back door and went into the house. Rounding the corner to the foyer, she found Augie locked in an embrace. Eyes closed, a woman she assumed was Gloria had her arms around Augie's neck and her hands snaked into his hair. She was petite, and her feet weren't actually reaching the ground. No, Augie supported all her weight. Mia's gut clenched. Gloria was bronzed all over, both hair and skin. Her lips were thick and her lashes and brows were dark as coal. She was an exotic beauty and even her curves had curves. Denim hugged the swell of her thighs and ass. Mia imagined that men thought she was pretty spectacular.

They separated.

"Thank you for coming," Augie said.

"Augustine, you know you don't have to thank me for that."

Her chocolate gaze landed on Mia.

"Hi there, I'm Gloria. You must be Michaela."

"M-Mia."

Gloria's palm rested on Augie's chest. "I hope Augie has been treating you well."

She was even more beautiful when she spoke directly to you. All Mia could do was nod.

"Good. You let me know if he gets out of hand."

Grinning, Gloria grabbed Augie's hand and pulled him into the living room. Mia followed since she was on her way to the kitchen. Squatting to sit on the couch, Gloria said, "So brief me."

"Just one second." Augie turned to Mia, his face contorted into a menacing frown. He pointed to the fish and asked, "What is that?"

"Dinner."

"Where'd you get it?"

"I caught it out back."

"It's mighty impressive."

"I think it'll be tasty. It's walleye." Her voice was soft—she felt uncomfortable speaking with Gloria watching them.

"I have no doubt it will be. My issue is in how you caught it."

Was he being deliberately obtuse?

"I found a rod and tackle in the basement." She pointed toward the lake. "Then I caught it in the lake."

He folded his arms across his chest. "You went outside."

She nodded. What was he getting at?

"So you broke one of the two rules and jeopardized the mission yet again."

Her jaw dropped, and she felt her eyes blinking rapidly. Had she broken one of the rules? Her head was foggy on the rules. "Did I?" She swallowed.

"Yeah, you did, a big one. Tell me the rules, Mia."

"I don't remember." Her body felt hot and she had a headache.

He looked to the floor and used his thumb to scratch his eyebrow. She didn't appreciate being reprimanded in front of a stranger, especially one who looked like Gloria, and the fish in her hand was getting heavy, so she walked to the kitchen.

She plopped the fish into the sink and pulled some newspaper from a recycle bin and spread it across the counter. She pulled a fillet knife from the butcher block.

"The rules, Mia, what are they?"

She turned with the knife in her hand. "I don't remember, okay? I'm really tired. I was just trying to do something to help. I didn't mean to break your stupid rules."

He leaned against the counter next to her. "The rules exist to protect you. You could have been kidnapped or killed. How would I even know? You were supposed to be inside."

"Are you going to stay mad at me all night?"

"I'm at about an eleven."

"An eleven."

"On a scale of one to ten, one being the least mad, I'm at an eleven."

"That's pretty bad."

"You frustrate me. Every time you deviate from the rules, you risk all our lives. Mine, yours, now Gloria's. Maybe it would do you some good to think of someone other than yourself before you make a move."

He walked away, leaving her remorseful. Tears fell from her eyes and splashed on the newspaper, absorbed on impact.

"Say *I love walleye*."

"What?"

She turned, and Augie snapped a picture with his phone.

He grimaced. "How 'bout a mulligan?"

"What?" His mood swings disoriented her.

"You're not smiling in that picture. Do you want to retake it?"

"No." She picked up the knife and sliced through the belly of the fish.

"Looks like you know what you're doing."

"I do."

"Like I said, impressive."

"I take it girls in the States don't fish?"

He snorted. "No way. They do spa days, salon days, marathon shopping." He shook his head. "Their outdoor activities consist of lying out with piña coladas and those movie star magazines."

"Well, that's why you like them, right?"

"What's that supposed to mean?"

"I don't know." If he couldn't figure it out, she wasn't going to tell him.

"I made you cry again."

"And I made you mad again."

Cooking relaxed her, and she wished he would just let her be with her thoughts. He clouded her ability to problem solve.

"I can't believe you caught and gutted this mammoth beast."

That made her laugh. He squeezed her shoulders and walked off. Probably going to talk to Gloria. Mia watched him go, then turned her attention back to dinner. Digging around in the basement, she found everything she'd need to make walnut-crusted walleye. She also found a bag of potatoes and a loaf of French bread in the freezer and grabbed a can of tomatoes from the shelf.

Augie was leaning against the counter in the kitchen when she returned. He was sipping a beer. "What's that?"

She placed the food on the center island. "How about mashed potatoes and tomato gravy?"

"Damn, woman. Nothing I love more than tomato gravy." He squatted and began pulling wine bottles from beneath the island. "A nice wine is in order. They've got some decent ones here too. This pinot looks good. How about I pour us each a glass?"

"Where's Gloria?"

"Shower."

He slid her glass across the counter and sipped from his, tasting it like he was some wine connoisseur. "Mmm, it's oak-ey."

She laughed. After his playful drama, that was his grand conclusion? "Oak-ey."

"Yeah, I'm shit at wine tasting. Expensive, inexpensive all taste the same to me." He took another sip. "Don't get me wrong, I really do like wine, I'm just not good at being pretentious."

She held the bottle up and looked at the vintage. "Hmm, 2009. Hope this wasn't an expensive bottle."

"Trust me, no one leaves the good shit at their vacation home." He sipped the wine. "So what do you make of it?"

"Of the wine?"

"Yes, what's your expert analysis of this here vintage?"

His relaxed banter put her at ease. Playful Augie was once again in the house.

"Well, let me see..." Sipping and swirling the wine on her tongue, she analyzed the taste and then swallowed. "Oh!" She sputtered a little. "Wow." She held the glass in front of her face and eyed the contents. "With the way people put this stuff away you'd think it would at least taste good."

Augie smiled, looking like a much younger man. "Have you never had a drink then?"

"Na." She shook her head. "Strongest I've had is sparkling cider."

He took her glass to the sink. "Starting with wine was a mistake. You need to start with something like sex on the beach."

Spoon in hand, she turned away from her gravy making, her eyes wide. "Yes! I want that. How can I get it?"

Squatting to dig around beneath the counter, he said, "Relax, it's the name of a drink. Hmm, let me see. Basically any fruit juice will do." He set a can of pineapple juice on the counter. "And then you just need some fruity alcohol." When he stood, he had four bottles cradled in his arms.

"Oh my God. We're gonna drink all that?"

He looked down at his arms. "It's nothing. I'll make it very small."

"Do you drink it?"

"Well, see, I'm old so these sugary drinks give me a headache."

"How old are you?"

Looking up from his mixing, he offered a cocky grin. "Older by far than you, my dear."

He set about opening and measuring, pouring and tasting, before he nodded as if to say, *That'll do.* After plopping ice into the glass, he stirred the concoction with a spoon.

"Here you go, one sex on the beach."

As she took the glass, he winked. "Bottoms up."

She sipped, worried it'd be tart like the wine, but the taste was sweet. "Mmm." She rubbed her lips together, and then took a big gulp. "It's really good. Tastes like a Sweet Tart or fruit punch." She took another gulp. "I like it."

"I used a half ounce for each liquor, so there's two ounces of alcohol in there. That's a lot for a lightweight, so take it easy."

She sidled up next to him. "You want a sip?" She waggled her eyebrows.

He frowned. "Give me that." He took the drink from her hands and dumped what was left in the sink.

Gloria strolled in fresh from a shower, saying, "Hey, anything I can do to help in here?"

Mia coveted her thick shiny hair that was so long it almost touched her butt. "No thanks, I got it."

"I'm going to set up the laptop then."

"Sounds great," Augie said. "Thanks again for coming all this way." He smiled at her and she side-hugged him. "There's some of that beer you like in the fridge."

"Awesome."

She helped herself as Mia watched. Augie knew what she liked to drink and they had an ease around one another, far from what Mia had with him. He was always glaring at her for some breach in the rules she hadn't known she'd committed.

Augie held the plates so she could fill them. As she plated up the dinner, she was reminded of his hands catapulting her body into another dimension. Now that she'd had a taste of Augustine Roy, she wanted more. Hell, she wanted to devour him. It was all she could do to keep her mind off his erection. God, it had been heavy and hot in her hand. Whenever he was around, her eyes were drawn to his crotch. He was large, huge even, and she wondered how her body would accommodate him. But to spend all day trying would be bliss. He'd be sweet and worried about her comfort and safety like he always was. She'd be short of breath with an elevated pulse and desire strong enough to part the Amazon River.

Damn, what was in that drink?

"Michaela?"

She blinked. She'd gotten herself so worked up she hadn't known she'd stopped scooping the food.

"What—Are—You—Thinking—About?" He enunciated every word clearer than the last.

"Um, nothing." She cleared her throat. Steely hands grasped her arms and turned her to face him. His mouth whispered in her ear.

"You're flushed. Pulse is elevated, and I can guarantee you're wetter than an April day in Southwest Louisiana."

Her mouth opened on a gasp.

"Do you deny it?"

When she didn't answer, his hand snaked into her jeans, bypassed her underwear, and played along her seam. Coffee-bean eyes turned almost black at what he found.

"Fuck, you're the sweetest thing I've ever met." His hands trailed up her abdomen and his shimmering-wet fingers went straight into his mouth. Licking them like they were coated in melted chocolate, he never turned his eyes from hers.

Sparks ran through her core and belly, and she could no longer think of food; other hungers much too strong. "You have something I want," she said. Of its own will, her hand grabbed his crotch and fisted there.

He gasped and palmed her head, pulling her back by her hair to expose her neck. Laying a trail of kisses, his lips ran the length of her neck, to her jaw, and finally landed at her lips. Softly at first, he tasted her. Then his efforts turned frantic. His whiskers burned her sensitive skin as his lips and tongue explored her mouth. When his hand squeezed her breast and nipple, she broke away to cry out.

He backed away from her. "I'm sorry, Mia. When I saw you standing there all flushed and looking like a dominant's sex kitten, I lost it."

Her palm went to his cheek. "I like when you lose it."

And she did. But she'd clearly shocked him with her admission. He turned away and mumbled something about washing up.

Mia washed her own hands and then picked up the plates again. "Bon Appetite," she said, setting the plates on the table.

"It looks delicious." Gloria said.

"Well, don't eyeball it. Eat before it gets cold."

"Mmm, wow, Mia, this is truly amazing," Augie said.

Sounds of pleasure escaped from deep in his throat. "It's hands down the second best thing I've ever put in my mouth."

His eyes simmered at her, and she dropped her fork. It clattered to her plate with a crash. Christ, she'd lost her appetite for food. She needed him. Now.

Gloria cleared her throat. "So, Mia, you're a fisherman? Or should I say woman?"

She'd forgotten Gloria was in the room with them "Oh, I uh, I used to go out with my dad when I was young."

"What's this we're eating?"

"Walnut-crusted walleye."

"It's a really solid meal."

Mia smiled, not sure if she'd been complimented or not.

"Gloria hates fish." Augie smirked.

"Augustine, that's not true." She threw her napkin at him.

"Whatever. And stop calling me that, you know I hate it."

Augustine. Puke. Watching them banter made her want to hit something. Gloria perhaps. Yeah, she wanted to hit her in the face. She didn't know where these feelings of hatred came from she just knew she didn't like the connection Gloria had with Augie. She was jealous of their history.

"Delicious gravy too. You some kind of chef?" Augie beamed at her.

"Actually, my mom did work at Le Royal, this little French bistro, and it was great because she'd bring food home all the time and cook it up."

They talked in general throughout the meal, and after dinner Augie helped her clear the table while Gloria worked on locating a signal for the laptop.

"I'm going to go take a bath," Mia said.

His hand on her shoulder, Augie said, "That's a good idea. A long hot one. You need to relax."

She was glad to finally get away from the two of them. She certainly didn't need to hear Gloria pronounce the name *Augustine* again, in that sultry way she did.

CHAPTER 9

Mia climbed the stairs and thought about her dirty clothes. She'd kill for some clean ones. She'd left everything behind: her home, her clothes, her mom. She'd be leaving her country behind soon.

As the water level rose in the tub, she felt an overwhelming sorrow strike. She didn't even have a toothbrush. At least she had some dental floss in her purse. She supposed it could be worse—they could be dead and none of those things would matter. That thought made her even bluer.

She tried to channel her thoughts into something pleasant. As she stripped, she thought of her and Augie, cozy on the couch where she'd had him in her mouth. Now naked and cold and alone, she stared at herself in the mirror. No, no curves anywhere. Turning to the side, she leaned forward and stuck her butt out, trying to give herself the curves Gloria had.

"*Oh, Augustine.*"

"Mia?"

"Augie!" Straightening up, she felt her face flame. "Don't you knock?"

"What were you doing in the mirror?" He pointed at her reflection.

"Nothing. What do you want?" She covered herself with her hands, but he was there, patting them away.

"Don't do that. You've never done that with me before. Why start now?"

"I just . . . " She shook her head. "What do you want?"

A bag landed on the countertop. "I thought you might need some things, so I asked Gloria to grab some essentials on her way up."

"Oh my God, thank you." She sighed happily. "And thank Gloria."

His hand palmed her cheek. "Is everything okay?"

She nodded as warmth from his hand seeped into her cheek. She loved his touch. "Thank you."

He backed out, leaving her to tend to her bath.

In the bag she found jeans, a T-shirt, panties, socks, deodorant, toothbrush, paste, and a hairbrush. A smile broke across her face and she felt hopeful that things might just work out. Sinking into the warm bath water, she sighed.

"God bless Gloria for bringing me the necessities."

Mia could appreciate the other woman, but that didn't mean she had to like her. No, she definitely didn't like her. Augie and she seemed close. Had he dated her? And if he had, was that the kind of woman he liked, exotic looks and petite little curves? She was beautiful. Mia had never thought she was ugly, but standing next to Gloria, she would fade into the dust. She shook her head to rid it of negative thoughts and then plunged her body beneath the water, wetting her hair.

She washed and shampooed. As she toweled off, her body shook when pain radiated through it. It was her leg. It wasn't too red but it was slightly swollen. She placed her hand over the wound and felt warmth, too much warmth. Maybe she should ice it again like Augie had her do that first night.

She dressed in the new clothes provided by Gloria and brushed through her wet hair. Occasionally she heard feminine laughter, and she couldn't help feeling ostracized. She lay back on the bed in the room Augie assigned to her, but since she'd napped, she wasn't tired. Curious, she crept to the top of the stairs. After delicately climbing over Augie's booby trap, she took each step quietly. Halfway down, she could make out their words, so she sat on the stair and listened.

There was no denying it—she was eavesdropping.

"Not the first time I've saved your ass."

"Gloria, I owe you my life."

"How are the nightmares, Augie?"

"Not as frequent."

"Have you given anymore thought to reporting the botched extraction?"

"What good would it do?"

"It might help with those nightmares."

"Every day is one more day behind me. I don't need to report it. You saved my life that day, and we'll forever share that connection, but I can't relive those days during a court-ordered rehash. I have to move on."

"But you're not moving on. You may think you are, but your subconscious isn't. That's why you're having the dreams."

"Gloria, please. I don't want to go down that road. Besides, Mia helps with the nightmares. If she's near when I start to have anxiety or dreams, I don't get lost. It's like she anchors me to the present. Something about her . . . " He sighed. "No one has ever had that effect on me. Now my fear is that something bad will happen to *her*. I get anxious just thinking about losing her. I can't explain it."

Mia's jaw dropped. She'd no idea she'd helped him in any way.

They were quiet for a moment. Mia felt like a jerk for having listened to their intimate discussion, but she couldn't move while they were silent. They'd hear her for sure.

"So have you been intimate with her?"

"I'm not telling you that."

"You just did."

"What?"

"Your lack of information tells me all I need to know."

"Fuck, Gloria, why do you care anyway?"

"Did you tell her about us?"

"There's nothing to tell."

Mia heard Gloria snort.

"She seems innocent."

"She is, but she's not like other girls."

"What do you mean?"

"She's not into marriage and babies and doing her nails."

"Come on, Augie, she wants that."

"How do you know what she wants?"

"Because that's what every girl her age wants."

"You didn't want that."

"Oh, I wanted it. I just never had the opportunity to go after it."

"You wanted those things?"

"Desperately."

"But you never said anything."

"It's not like I would tell you and risk you running as fast as your feet would carry you away from me."

Mia didn't care if they heard her—she didn't want to hear any more. She stood and climbed the stairs swiftly, so fast that she got tangled in the damn fishing wire he'd strung. She went down amid the noise and knocked her shin against the top step. She hollered out in pain.

Flat on her back she saw Augie as he ran up the stairs, taking them three at a time.

He scooped her into his arms like she weighed ten pounds and carried her to bed.

"Are you hurt?"

She didn't want him to think she was more pitiful than he already did, so she said, "No, but I almost fell down the stairs."

"I told you to watch out for the wire."

"I forgot."

"You can't forget the things I tell you. Learn to focus. Do you remember what I said about getting away from here if it becomes necessary?"

"Yes."

"Tell me."

She huffed out a breath. "I run next door and lock myself in the cabin, and stay put until the coast is clear. Then I go to Larry's and use the phone."

Gloria had joined them in the room.

"And where is the key to the cabin?"

Feeling her empty pocket, she realized her error. "Uh, I left it in the other jeans."

"Gloria."

"I'm on it."

"Perhaps you should focus on the safety of this mission and less on eavesdropping. It doesn't become you."

Her face flamed at his criticism. Gloria handed her the key. She placed it in her pocket and turned away from them, feigning tiredness.

When she heard the door close, she sat up. To her shock, Augie was in the room, removing his belt. Then he started on his boots.

"What are you doing?"

"I'm getting ready for bed. Gloria's going to keep watch since I need to get some sleep."

She wasn't happy about his presence in her room. He'd made her feel like a child. An errant child. To be fair, she had been acting like a child. She scooted under the covers to put distance between them. "There are three bedrooms up here, you know."

"But those beds don't have angry warm females in them."

He slid under the covers and spooned her from behind. She fought him for a moment, but the strength differential was ridiculous.

"Stop struggling. You're not getting away from me."

More than aware he was in his boxer briefs, she was glad she'd kept her jeans on. Warm fingers slid around her waist and expertly unfastened her jeans. Hands slid inside and pushed the material down her thighs. "You can't be comfortable sleeping in these, and I want to feel your skin. Take them off."

She rolled over and sat up, removing her pants.

She leaned back in his arms and he slid his leg over hers and rested one arm on her hip, the other under her head. His breath heated her neck. Her frustration melted away and she went boneless in his arms, inhaling deeply. With the steady reassuring rhythm of his heartbeat against her back, she drifted to sleep.

Heat and moisture seeped through Mia's shirt, making it stick to her back. Something squeezed the breath from her and she tried to pull away, but she was trapped.

Gasps rang out in the otherwise quiet room, then she heard, "Go, go, go."

Augie. He was having a dream. A nightmare. Unable to free herself from his unyielding grip, she squirmed around in his hold until she faced him. The torment on his face had her gasping.

"No!" His expression contorted into one of pain and rage. His lips pulled into a snarl. "Don't touch her."

"Augie, wake up."

She wormed her hand free and stroked his jaw. His hold broke.

"I'll kill you!"

She pressed harder, and whispered, "Augie, it's Mia. You're safe."

More sighs and groans of despair escaped his throat.

"I'm here."

God, he was in so much pain, she just wanted to take it away. If she could have shouldered some of it, she would have. Since she couldn't, she kept whispering his name and stroking him, letting him know he was safe.

His eyes rolled underneath the thin skin of his eyelids, and his face smoothed.

"Yes, that's right, baby, I'm here and I need you." She kissed his lips.

His hand slid up her back to fist in her hair. Her lips parted, giving him access, and his tongue entered her mouth. He pushed at her aggressively, as if he wanted to consume her from the inside out. The intensity of his need stung her body and soul. No longer was it only about him being her savior. She needed him—that much had been clear—but he needed her too.

"Mia."

Raspy whispered notes hit her ears. She straddled him, palming his cheeks. She kissed him delicately to counteract his force. Yin and yang, they fit together as one.

"I'm here Augie."

Slipping his hands under the material of her panties, he kneaded her ass. He kissed her mouth, abrading her chin with his whiskers. In one deliberate move, he rotated her so her back rested on his front. His fingers slipped between her folds.

"Augie, I want you."

"I'm here, baby."

"I need more." He massaged her, but she wanted to be connected, she wanted him inside her. His thumbs hooked into her panties, and she lifted so he could slide them off. He did the same to his. When he resumed his assault on her body, she felt coiled tight. She needed him, but he thought himself undeserving and his perspective saddened her.

Her gasps came involuntarily, and she was unable to control her movements as his fingers brought her closer to that place she yearned to be.

"Take it, baby, take what you need. I want you to come on my fingers."

At his coaxing words, Mia's body began to tremble and writhe, and she felt moisture pool between her thighs. Surprisingly unembarrassed, she also heard the dampness as he worked between her legs.

She felt his stiff length when he rested it between her thighs, rubbing himself through her moisture. She tried to turn, but he held her in place with his other hand.

"Lubricate me with your wetness."

Frantic, she held him in place as his hand gripped her outer thighs and squeezed her legs together, cradling him in the gap at the top of her legs. Using the tight grip he had on her, he pumped her body up and down, creating friction as his cock rubbed between her legs.

She thought her sight blurred from the intensity of his touch, but her eyes could have been filling with tears. Tears for him and his self-condemnation.

"Augie, penetrate me."

"No, baby. I'm no good for you. You deserve someone fresh, like yourself. I'm used up."

Tears streamed in a river down her face. He was panting, breathing so hard her hair blew across the back of her neck. He seemed to grow even larger between her thighs. A strangled growl erupted from his throat, and she watched as the come spurted from him and dripped down her legs. She wiped her eyes.

"Wait here," he said, his voice low.

Where was she going to go? What just happened? She couldn't understand why he wouldn't just have sex with her.

He didn't want to use her in that way, but he was using her just the same. Every time they touched, their force solidified her feelings for him that much more. She already loved him for the man he was, saving her and her sister and her mother. She also loved him for the man he strived to be—a man worthy of her, an innocent, a virgin. It was a ridiculous notion that she now wished she'd never mentioned.

He returned with a washcloth that she used to clean herself. He turned out the light and this time they each moved to their respective sides of the bed—no spooning, no loving, no hugging. Alone. Two halves, but no whole.

Yet he needed her just as she needed him, and she would die trying to get him to understand that.

CHAPTER 10

Mia woke to an empty bed. Empty for a while, given its coolness. Sitting up, she glanced to the window. The sun was rising, so it must be around seven. She stretched and reached for her new hairbrush. No reason not to look halfway decent.

Downstairs she found Augie and Gloria at the dining room table. Augie sat in a chair staring into the screen of a laptop while Gloria stood next to him doing the same.

"My vote is for option B; it's a more direct route." Gloria said.

Augie's eyes greeted hers. "Morning. Will you make us some breakfast?"

Another command. "Okay."

"FYI, if Gloria eats eggs, she'll blow up like the Goodyear blimp."

"The what?"

"You know, the Hindenburg."

"Shut up, Augie. Where the hell's she going to find eggs anyway?"

"She's very resourceful, in case you haven't noticed. We had bread last night."

"Option B *is* the more direct route."

How strange to be spoken *about* but not *at* when you were in the same room. Mia needed caffeine. Surely there was coffee to be had in this place. And where could she get her hands on some eggs? She'd love to see that gorgeous, exotic face swell up. Remembering the basement filled with goodies, she headed that way. She found coffee, evaporated milk, and biscuit mix on the shelves. To her delight, there were frozen blueberries and pan sausage. They'd be enjoying a nice breakfast, sans eggs.

Determined to establish some sense of normalcy, Mia set about cooking and brewing coffee. Since they were at the far end of the dining room table, she set everything up on the opposite end. Never once did they acknowledge her. All they did was look at the laptop and talk about routes and plans. What the hell were they scheming?

With the table set, she took a seat at what would be considered the head. They still hadn't noticed her spread. She cleared her throat. "Excuse me. Take a break and come eat please."

Augie inventoried the smorgasbord she'd prepared and smiled. "Wow, looks great." He took the chair next to her and lifted her hand to his lips. "You certainly are inventive. I love that about you."

His words of praise left her staggered. The man was hot and cold, no middle ground. He'd ignored her all morning, not giving away anything of his feelings about last night, when it was all she could think about.

From her standing position, Gloria had a shot of their entire exchange. Her arched brow slowly lowered as her eyes narrowed and she set her intense gaze on Mia. She took her seat and poured orange juice all around while Mia served the coffee. They ate the muffins adding jam she'd found in the basement. The sausage tasted wild and earthy, and for a moment they all existed in a sea of harmony. It was the perfect way to begin the day.

"Mia, we have plans." Augie wiped at his mouth with a paper towel. "We're going to get loaded up and head back into town. You're going to stay with Gloria at a motel; she'll keep you safe. If I'm not back within four hours, she'll drive you to Louisiana to hook up with Eve and Clay."

He delivered the words as if he were giving a book report. Her eyes were too wide, but she couldn't help it. *If I'm not back . . .* Why wouldn't he be back?

"What are you going to be doing, where will you be, why would you not come back?"

His eyes bored into hers, and she realized there would be no compromise.

"It's just a backup plan, Mia. I'm sure nothing is going to happen, but we need to be prepared in case it does."

Maybe she was being selfish, but in that moment she resented Evie for putting Augie in this position. If he were to get hurt trying to obtain Evie's stupid divorce, she'd never survive it. It seemed silly for her to think that way, but she'd come to greatly care for him, this man who left everything behind to come so far to rescue her. She wished they could just leave now and head to Louisiana. She couldn't wait to see his hometown, for him to show her his favorite haunts and restaurants. Of course, she had no assurances he'd be doing any of those things, but she hoped like hell he would.

En route back the way they had come, Augie eyed Mia through the rearview mirror. She stared out the window and occasionally nervously chewed at her bottom lip. Things had gotten way out of hand with her. He couldn't believe he'd come so close to having sex with her. *Intercourse*, that is. Some would consider what they'd done to be sex. He'd wanted to pump into her, and she'd wanted him, but he had to be stronger than their desire. The only problem was, now that he'd had a taste of her, his brain wouldn't stop peppering him with visions of her at the height of her desire, no matter how hard he tried to keep those visions at bay. Mia's skin, slick with the sweat of their exertion; Mia's body bowed, the veins in her neck throbbing from the strain; Mia's sex swollen as he massaged her with his tongue. Fuck! He shook his head and swerved a little with that last image.

"Everything okay?" Gloria was in the front seat, navigating.

"Yeah. Some debris in the road." And now he was lying to Gloria.

Mia leaned forward and cleared her throat. "So how do you two know each other so well?"

He felt Gloria's eyes on him, but his never left Mia's in the mirror.

"We were in the field together. Afghanistan." Augie said.

"Oh." Her eyes widened. "Gloria, you did field work? That must have been tough."

She pivoted toward Mia. "Why? Because I'm a woman?"

Mia shrugged. "Well, yeah."

"I'll have you know I'm just as strong if not stronger in spirit than any man."

Mia's jaw dropped.

"Enough with the uber feminism. I don't think Mia's accusing you of being weak because you're a woman."

Mia shook her head. "Not at all. I think it's amazing. I was just imaging myself as best I could in your situation, concluding that I wouldn't be successful."

"You would have been," Augie said. "There's no doubt in my mind. You'd have surpassed them all."

She met his eyes in the mirror as they shared the moment.

"I saved Augie's ass more than once."

"And I in turn saved yours."

"*Once.*"

"Once."

"So after that you guys were together?"

Damn, but she didn't mince words. Ever. He could understand her curiosity, and it was within her rights to know the answers since he'd taken advantage of her body the way he had.

"We were. For about a year."

She turned to stare out her window again. Gloria kept eyes on them both.

"Since we're getting so personal," Gloria said, "I might ask what the hell is going on between the two of you. Don't think I didn't notice you two bunking together last night."

"I won't have her sleep where I can't keep an eye on her."

Gloria scratched her neck. "Please! You were walking around naked. I saw you make a trip to the bathroom in nothing but what the good Lord gave you."

"What are you getting at?"

"I'm just saying, there is more to the two of you"—she pointed accusingly at him and then at Mia—"more than you're letting on. More than you're admitting to one another."

Gloria was right. It would be hard to let Mia go once he reunited her with her sister. Did he want a relationship with her? His need for her was growing too strong. A thought that scared the shit out of him.

Mia leaned forward. "Will you pull over at that gas station?"

"Is everything okay?"

"I just need the restroom." She was tight-lipped and avoiding eye contact.

Augie sighed and ran his hand through his hair. He pulled into the station and Mia jumped out of the car before it came to a full stop.

"Mia!"

She ran into the store.

"Christ, Gloria, will you go after her, make sure she's okay?"

Shaking her head, Gloria took off.

He hadn't planned this very well. His ex-girlfriend in the car on an overland drive with his current . . . his current what? Fuck it all to hell. He strode inside and bought a pack of Camels and a lighter.

Leaning against the car, he inhaled the tobacco's soothing qualities long and deep. He'd be hearing from both Mia and Gloria about his nasty habit, but at this moment he didn't care. He wouldn't be getting back into the car until he'd smoked two.

He was just finishing number two when they approached. Mia broke off pieces of chocolate and put them into her mouth while Gloria sipped on a drink. Both women stared at him but said nothing of his smoking. He took one long last draw and stomped the butt out with his foot.

An hour and a half later they were at the motel. They'd purposely chosen it due to its proximity to Nicolas's condo. Through recon, Augie had learned that the guy stayed at a condo in town during the week. The setup was perfect for what he had in mind. He dressed in the clothes Gloria had brought at his request—black cargo pants, black shirt, combat boots. He grabbed the pack she'd also brought and removed the items he wanted affixed to his person. From a chair in the corner of the room, Mia watched him with shallow breaths.

Dressed, he secured the pack to his body. He pointed at Mia. "Don't leave for any reason. I plan to be back in a few hours. If I'm not back in four, you'll flee with Gloria. She'll get you to your sister and Clay."

"Shut up!" She stood abruptly and stomped over to him. "Just shut up, Augie. I don't like any part of this." She paced in front of him, wringing her hands. "Why do you have to do this? Can't you just mail him the damn papers to sign?"

"Mia, you know why I can't do that."

"But killing him isn't the answer. You'll be the one made to deal with the fallout for the rest of your life." A shaky hand rose to cup her mouth as she coughed around a sob. "And that's if you survive. What if he ambushes you? What if he's expecting you? What if—"

He tugged her over to sit in a chair and took the one across from her. "Mia, he's not expecting me. I'm going to do what has to be done. If I feel he's not a threat, he'll live. I have no problem letting him live out his days here in Canada, but he needs to assure me."

"What if he won't?"

"If he won't, then he won't live."

She shook her head and her lip quivered. Her eyes closed tight and tears streamed down her face, meandering like a river. He looked at Gloria, who just shrugged.

"I'm gonna go get a bag of chips," she said, leaving the room.

"Augie, please. Will you please promise to *try* to let him live?"

"He ordered you kidnapped. And with force. If you need a reminder, just look at the burns on your neck, burns that have screamed out at me every time I look at them. And what of Eve?"

She pressed her hand against her neck. "I know all that, but I don't believe in murder. I'm so glad you came into my life— the sacrifices you've made to help me are beyond anything anyone has ever done for me—but if something happens to me, then it's my time to go. I don't want to forge life from death. I don't want you to have to live with the emotional impact and the pain of the actions involved in killing a man. Knowing I contributed to your emotional pain would hurt me more than anything that could be done to me physically."

He was speechless. The woman was unconditionally selfless. He'd never in his thirty-five years known anyone like her. She would risk her life to save a man responsible for almost having her killed. He didn't know what to say.

Her concern for his wellbeing spoke volumes about how much she cared for him. He'd been in the business of helping people, but had never been cared for himself.

Mia stopped crying, bit her lip, and looked down at her feet.

Augie sat back in the chair. She was right. Hadn't he even questioned all the senseless killing? Killing in the name of freedom. Killing disguised as protection. Killing for oil, land, and religion. He'd had enough. In that moment he realized he didn't want to kill Nicolas. Probably couldn't even go through with it. Damn, she may have just saved his life. He hadn't had to kill in his line of work as a sheriff. The last time he'd taken a life was in that fucking desert.

Within a blink, soft, warm hands were around his neck, pulling him into her body with the fierceness of a protective mother bear.

"Augie, we can come up with a plan B together." Trembling hands palmed his cheeks. "Please."

He swallowed back the lump in his throat. Her emotion seeped from her and washed over him. He was too affected by her, but he was powerless to stop how she made him feel. "Yeah, okay," he whispered, feeling dazed. But he also felt as if a hundred-pound weight had been plucked from his chest.

She leaned in and kissed his lips, deepening the kiss on a sigh.

The door banged open. "So are you going or what?" Gloria rolled her eyes at him as she closed the door with her foot.

"We're going to make a new plan that doesn't involve Augie murdering a man."

"Are we seriously having second thoughts about killing that shitbag?"

"It's not good for Augie's recovery."

"Recovery?"

Augie stood. "I haven't killed since Afghanistan. I'm not sure it's such a well-thought-out plan after all.

"I'll present him with the papers and suggest he sign."

"That's a death mission." Gloria's eyes were intense and unwavering.

"I think we should ambush him at work."

Mia's suggestion, her *we*, was never gonna happen.

He cupped her shoulder and pulled her toward him. "I want to get something clear right now. There is no *we*. It's still just me, alone." He rubbed his upper lip with a finger "And right now I'm gonna go take a walk so I can clear my head."

Outside, he inhaled deeply, cherishing the sense of relief he hadn't known he wanted and needed. The thought of confronting Nicolas Renaud at work wasn't a bad one. He'd read enough about the guy to know that he had a commercial real estate business that served as a respectable cover for his covert illegal activities. For the most part the business was legit. It had even been investigated, and every little thing had been on the level. That was key because it meant he operated legally during working hours. If Augie did in fact confront him at work, Nicolas wouldn't be able to fight or kill. Further, enough had been compiled on the guy—enough of his suspected crimes south of the border—that were he to step foot on American soil, he'd be arrested and consequently jailed for a long time. Augie could use that information to threaten Renaud from ever coming to the States after the Brown sisters. Hell, the whole crazy thing just might work.

His mind filled with images of Mia's slim curves, wavy long hair, sincere lavender-gray eyes, and those hard, pointed nipples that made his mouth water. She even had a couple of crooked bottom teeth that he loved. He'd watch her lips when she spoke just hoping for a peek at those teeth. She had him hot and bothered by just standing in a room.

Shit, he had it bad.

He laughed at himself. And then he laughed at the memory of her carrying a fish and a rod. The way she captured and gutted that fish amazed him more than anything he'd ever seen a woman do.

He lit a cigarette and took a few drags to get the tobacco pumping through his system. His part of the plan was new, but the original rules would apply for the girls. If he wasn't back within the hour, they'd take off in the car. The more he considered the plan, the more he thought it was foolproof. The guy would sign or he wouldn't. Either way, Mia would make it safely to Louisiana and to her sister and Clay.

He stomped the cigarette out at the door. Tomorrow he'd be ready to confront Nicolas Renaud. Tonight he'd sleep— without the nightmares.

CHAPTER 11

"No way!"

"It's not open for discussion, Mia. You will let Gloria drive you to the States if I'm not back within the hour. Promise me."

"I will promise no such thing."

"Will you have my concentration divided then? I'll be so worried about you I might get hurt or worse. However, if I had your word, I'd be able to focus on the mission."

Gloria smirked, aware of his intention.

Mia frowned. "I hadn't thought of that."

"Promise me."

"I promise to go to the States with Gloria."

"And you're sure you don't want the nine?" Gloria held up a holster.

He shook his head. "Won't need it." He grabbed the folder that held the divorce documents and exited the car.

The glass building was shaped like an egg. From across the street, the designer mullioned windows shone metallic and black in the sun. It was quite the impressive and imposing structure, and Augie wondered if Renaud chose to rent office space in the building based on that fact alone. Inside he consulted the directory. Renaud Property Management was on the thirty-fourth through forty-second floors. The CEO occupied room 42 A-B.

Cameras were everywhere. One of two things was going to happen: Thug One and Thug Two would identify him in a matter of moments and chaos would ensue, or they wouldn't make an appearance and he'd be able to ease into a conversation with Nicolas.

The elevator whisked him with remarkable speed straight to the penthouse offices. A nicely subdued ping alerted him that the door would be opening. The elevator exited into a lobby, the soothing background music in stark contrast with his mood and the blood rushing through his veins.

A woman behind the counter stood at a computer.

"Good morning. May I have your name please?"

"Fletcher Smith."

"I don't have you on the schedule, Mr. Smith. Did you have a meeting with Mr. Renaud?"

"Er, no, I don't have a meeting."

"Is there something I can do for you?"

"Tell Nicolas I have information regarding Everleigh."

Her brow hitched. "Please have a seat." She gestured toward a set of black couches. "Mr. Renaud will be right with you."

She bounded across the marble floor in her well-fitted suit, heels snapping all the way to another office. The sound of shoes silenced immediately behind the frosted glass.

A moment later the efficient snapping advanced toward him.

"Mr. Reynaud will see you now."

He stood and offered his sexiest smirk to the overly blond woman. She held her eyes down, her hands clasped in front of her. How sweetly reserved.

Augie wondered what she knew of her boss's other businesses.

He entered an office with thick, plush, and expensive beige carpet, more black couches, a coffee table, and large windows overlooking the city. In the center of it all, at a mammoth desk crowded with files and papers and other office shit, sat Nicolas Claude Renaud. Expensive dark blue suit and tie. Dark hair, dark eyes, trendy facial stubble. Handsome, but a total dick. His fingers rummaged through papers and he seemed somewhat frantic and disorganized. Sweat beaded on his forehead and his jaw ticked. He scrubbed his face and started digging through a different stack of papers.

"Goddammit Francis I asked you for my fucking passport." He yelled without looking up from his papers.

Papers fell from the desk as he clumsily searched for something he could not find.

Augie started speaking. "The Brown sisters have been safely freed from your grasp, ensconced in a place of their choosing. Though *ensconced* may be the wrong word as they are not in hiding. That is, they are not hiding from you."

"Who the fuck are you?"

"I've been hired to serve you with divorce papers."

That did the trick. Renaud stopped searching, and his black eyes squinted at Augie, a stare so intense, blinking was out of the question. Augie gave back as good as he got. He held the folder on top of his hand, steady as a rock.

"I have the papers here for you to sign. Uncontested, of course. Your connection to the Browns ends now."

Renaud's neck went tight, and a thick vein funneled down the side and pulsed to life. He pushed his chair from his desk. "If we're not together it means one of two things: we're both dead or I alone am dead. Either way, somebody dies."

"That can be arranged."

Renaud wiped his face with his hand and stood. Tall and fit, he was a good match for Augie.

"The thing is"—Augie scratched his brow with his thumb—"they are in the States. Where there's a file an inch thick on you. You cross the border, you're going away for a long time. Your hands are tied, so sign for the divorce. It's time to move on."

"If I can't have her, I don't want anyone else to."

"Marriage to you hasn't stopped her from moving on. Clearly it's stopping *you* in your tracks, but she's moved on. Completely."

His intense dark pupils were unnerving. Augie's breath caught and even though he'd trained long and hard to remain cool, he felt a bead of sweat drip down the back of his neck. Would he survive this? It could go either way. Would Renaud blow? Would he concede? Augie stood steady, giving nothing away.

Please, God, if you're listening, I'd like to do this for the Browns and for Clay.

Nicolas exhaled through clenched teeth. "Damn bitch isn't worth it. She's always been a lousy fuck." He stretched his neck from side to side, popping the tendons. "You do understand, she'll get nothing."

"I understand."

"What claims has she made?"

"Claims?"

"A clean break for uncontested divorce is granted when one party admits to receiving mental or physical abuse. What has she accused me of?"

"Both mental and physical abuse."

Renaud leaned over the desk and scanned the document.

His sneer gave Augie chills.

"You seem quite nonthreatening. What's your role in all of this?" He stood to his full height and squared his shoulders.

"Obtain and file the documents and ensure the Brown family's protection. And it's more a partnership than a role. I'll protect them until I die."

Renaud's brow cocked. "You're the muscle? Do you really think I'm going to let you calmly remove her from my life?"

"She's already removed from your life. At this point it's all formality." Augie remained calm. When he was calm he was clear. He'd been told before that he appeared nonthreatening, but he'd always accomplished what he intended, so it worked for him. "The men you hired to go after her sister probably don't see me as a non-threat."

He smirked. "That was your work? You seem connected. Are you just resourceful or do you have actual power?"

Augie's eyes narrowed. Something was amiss. "Connected?"

"Connected, you know, as in making records appear or disappear in the legal system."

"I'm connected."

"You know I'm not going to fold without a fight." He stuffed his hands in his pockets and sat on the edge of his desk, legs stretched in front of him, tapping nervously.

Had Augie thought he'd give up his search for Eve just like that? He'd hoped, but it didn't look likely. Still, if Augie was reading the signs right, he seemed willing to bargain.

He had to have some ulterior motive for granting the divorce. And Augie intended to discover what it was.

"I work in law enforcement, and my father is a US senator. What do you want?"

"I want to disappear."

"I don't follow."

"I want out. Can you make me disappear?" Renaud's face contorted and his lip curled back as he inhaled shallowly. His composure waned and he seemed almost frantic.

Augie scrubbed his face and then crossed his arms over his chest. "The National Crime Syndicate runs deep and far. I could try, but I've heard it's damn near impossible to go undetected." Augie knew if anyone could make this guy disappear, it'd be his father. "I'll see what can be done."

Renaud signed the papers, placed them in the folder, and handed it to Augie. "If you don't follow through, I'll find one or both of those women and I will kill them."

Augie believed him. The man looked frayed. He ran a hand through his hair and his lip twitched. He was obviously more afraid of the syndicate than he was of Augie.

Augie took the folder. "I'll be in touch."

He'd taken the same efficient elevator back down and almost exited when something didn't feel quite right. He stood at the elevator threshold, peering into a dimly lit garage. Gloria and Mia waited across the street with the car, but he felt in his gut that something unwanted also waited for him.

He backed into the elevator and rode up. It stopped on the twelfth floor, but that floor was under construction. He depressed ten buttons rapidly. *Keep calm, Roy.* He took a deep breath and exhaled slowly. Deep lavender-gray eyes filled his thoughts. Her fresh untouched face and smooth dewy skin calmed his mind. The image of her ripping the guts from a fifteen-pound walleye made a smile break across his face. She'd been there to bring him out of the nightmares before they crescendoed, as they always did, leaving him floundering in fear and a cold sweat.

The elevator door opened and closed at each stop. He pressed the door-close button, but received no reaction from his action. He continually pressed. *Come on, dammit.*

He'd give his life in exchange for Mia's. She was fresh, she was pure, she was life. He'd lived his and it wasn't so pure or good. Mia's pleas haunted him. She didn't want him to kill the man even if it made her life better.

Renaud burst onto the elevator, sweaty and disheveled.

"What the fuck!" Augie fell into a defensive position.

"Close the goddamn door!"

They stood, one man on each side of the elevator, frantically tapping buttons.

"Fuck, they're coming; somehow they got through border patrol and passed through my checkpoints."

"Who got through your checkpoints?" The door finally closed.

"Lombardi's foot soldiers are here. All of my security team was on alert and trained to identify these men. Since they're in I can only assume my team is dead."

"Lombardi? Antonio Lombardi?" Augie recalled his research on Nicolas. His father was a Lombardi and Antonio was Nicolas's half brother. Sweat dripped down the sides of Nicolas's face. "So do you want to explain why your brother sicced his dogs on you?"

"They've been sent here to kill me."

The door opened and Renaud took off running while Augie watched his retreating back. Trying to regain his bearings, he shook his head. Using the elevator wouldn't be smart given the circumstances. Unless Renaud was putting on a performance for his sake. Still, the man seemed genuinely terrified.

Stairs.

Augie ran down the hall, looking for the fire exit. He turned and skidded to a halt. Four men whaled on Nicolas. Augie swiftly made his way toward the mass of men, but stopped when a wicked-looking knife gleamed under the fluorescent lights as it was unsheathed. Nicolas was repeatedly stabbed. Nothing could help him now. Augie backed away slowly, undetected. He gripped the folder tight to his chest. As he backed up, he bumped a decorative console table and his presence went undetected no longer.

The sick sounds of Nicolas's blood gurgled in his throat before he choked and was silent. Augie looked from man to man. He pivoted, knocked the console table into the space behind him, and took off in a sprint down the hall. *Fucking stairs! Where are the fucking stairs?* There! He saw the icon and halfway kicked and twisted the knob to open the door to the stairwell. He jogged and slid down fourteen flights of stairs, round and round like a rat in a maze.

Finally he pushed a door open and tumbled out into the grand marble entry, his lungs wheezing, but he didn't stop. He ran across the lobby and out the front door into the sunlight. He could just make out the white car Gloria drove. His focus was so intent on the car, he didn't notice the man barreling toward him.

Heavy footsteps thudded around him as more men scrambled, closing in around him. One, two, three . . . He counted four men as fists pelted his side and face. With no real chance to defend against them, he focused on accepting each blow. Repeated blows to his ribs made it more and more difficult to breathe. He could no longer see out of his left eye and felt as if his face had been lit on fire. He crouched to get his face out of the path of the destruction and spotted the folder. He snatched it up and held on as he curled into a ball and maneuvered out of their immediate circle using a combination roll and jump move he'd learned from some martial art.

Sirens wailed in the distance, and he ran on clumsy legs. A large man lunged toward Augie, arm extended. *Fuck.* Dizzy and faint, Augie felt the earth spin. Wetness ran down inside his shirt, and a burning seared him. He traced his hand over his stomach and side, stopping when he felt the coolness of steel. *Fuck!* He'd been stabbed in the gut.

He fell to his knees and then his world went dark.

CHAPTER 12

"Oh my God! Augie!" Mia pointed across the street to where Augie ran out of the building, and Gloria quickly put the car in motion.

Mia screamed, the sound deafening in the closed body of the car. Men ran up to Augie and beat on him. Her hands cupped her mouth. Horror gripped and held her close.

Gloria rolled over the curb, jostling the car and them. Mia was jolted from her shock when Gloria yelled, "Open that door!" Mia jumped out, opened the back door, and squatted next to Augie.

"Help me get him into the car," Gloria said. She lifted his shoulders and supported his head while Mia lifted his legs. He didn't respond.

"Oh my God! A knife. Oh my God! Augie!"

"Quiet, Mia. Focus." They slid him into the back seat. "Drive!" Gloria yelled.

Mia obeyed, speeding off. Tears blurred her vision and she wiped at her eyes. "Is he alive?"

"He's breathing. Pulse is shallow. I need a drugstore."

Mia watched in the mirror as Gloria ripped material away from the knife in his stomach. She pulled the car to a stop in a parking lot.

"You stay with him," Gloria said, already out of the car. "Don't let him pull that out. I'll be back soon."

The door slammed and she was gone, leaving Mia alone with Augie. His face had been badly beaten, but she knew that wasn't the worst of it. She prayed the knife wound wasn't fatal.

Her fingers traced his face, but she carefully avoided his wounds. Her lips touched his in a desperate attempt to wake him. She kissed him tenderly and tasted the tang of blood in her mouth.

"Augie, please wake up." Feathering her hand through his hair, she kissed his cheek. "Please, Augie." Tears poured from her eyes and landed on his face. Forehead to forehead, she rubbed him. "Please, I need you. And you promised. You promised me. Oh God, no. Please, Augie, I love you." Her head rested on his shoulder as she cried.

"Let's go," Gloria directed as she jumped into the car. "The hotel. Now."

"Hotel? He needs a hospital."

"No hospital. No records. Just drive to the hotel."

Mia watched Gloria efficiently tend Augie's wounds. Mia had gently scrubbed the dried blood away from his face and neck.

When Gloria removed the knife, Mia almost passed out and Gloria yelled at her. Her shrill voice sobered Mia up. He was patched up, but he still hadn't come around.

"He needs blood," Gloria said. "He's A, I'm B. Do you know what you are?

"I'm an O."

"Perfect. Come sit over here."

Gloria moved a chair next to Augie's arm. Mia hated needles, hated giving blood. Just the thought of a needle could incapacitate her. But for Augie, she'd give her life.

She sat in the chair.

Next to her, Gloria set up plastic lines that Mia guessed would carry the blood.

"This isn't the best setup, but it's all they had available. He needs blood now and that requires direct blood transfusion, which can be tricky, but I'm trained and have done this dozens of times in the field."

"I trust you."

Gloria frowned. "Thing is, it's uncomfortable; I'll have to expose an artery."

Mia looked away, her hand over her mouth. "Don't tell me any more—just do it."

She took Mia's wrist.

"Wait!" Mia said. She switched on the television, some reality shopping show. "Okay." She focused on the TV. Some girl was preparing for a wedding, but she was alienating her entire bridal party by being a caustic bitch. *Shit!* Her wrist burned. *Don't turn.* Her body wanted to turn, but her mind didn't want to know what Gloria was doing. She stared with renewed focus at the wedding cake. It was the cake as the bride had ordered it, but she pushed it off the table and onto the floor in a fit of rage. Honestly, who acted—

"Damn! That hurts!" Mia sucked in air.

"I know, I'm sorry, but we're almost there."

Gloria left Mia's arm resting on the bed and started in on Augie.

"Is he going to be okay?"

"Pulse is weak; I'll know more after the transfusion."

"And then he'll be fine?"

"Sometimes the blood clots or the body rejects the blood. It's rare."

Mia prayed to a deity she'd abandoned long ago.

"Given the flow rate, I'd say about twenty minutes should suffice."

Mia nodded. The show was ending, but Mia was so tired, her eyelids wouldn't stay up and she closed them.

A hand squeezed hers hard, sending pain shooting up her arm, and she cried out, jolting awake. Gloria was immediately there.

"He's contracted—give me a second. May have a cramp."

Augie's eyes opened and his dark gaze settled into hers. If his jaw were any tighter, he'd shatter teeth.

"Augie." Her voice was a whisper.

"Pulse is strong now. Hang on, let me unhook you."

His brow was covered in sweat, so Mia wiped his face with some gauze. She kissed the now-dry brow. Leaning down next to his ear so that only he could hear, she whispered, "Augie, I love you." She stroked his face, kissing his temple.

His brow furrowed. "You gotta stop sayin' that." His words were slurred.

"No." She shook her head. "I don't. And you can't make me."

Gloria ran through a list of his injuries. "You were stabbed in the gut, no arteries affected. You lost a significant amount of blood, but Mia gave you a direct transfusion. If you don't develop an infection from the nasty fucking knife, you'll be good as new in about a week. Oh, you've also got one cracked rib. We wrapped it."

Mia crawled up in bed with him and placed his head in her lap. His gaze was still focused on her in earnest. "Hey." She stroked the sides of his face. "That's a good report, huh?" She kissed the corner of his mouth. "Good as new, we like that. New is always good, unless it's your first day at a new school. Then nobody wants to be the new girl."

He smiled.

Gloria was busy cleaning the skin around the wound. She removed the rest of his pants and his boxer briefs without flinching, and Mia knew it was because she'd seen it all before.

"I bought you a pair of sweatpants, but I want the wound to get oxygen, so you get this clean sheet for now." She shook out one of the motel sheets and covered his nakedness. "You need sleep. I thought we'd take another room."

Mia squeezed his head to her breast. "I'm not leaving him."

Gloria gathered up the gauze soaked with his blood. "He needs rest."

"Then we'll sleep." She slid down next to him on his undamaged side and slung her leg around his thigh.

Gloria sighed. "Whatever." She walked to the phone on the bedside table. "What rooms do you have available closest to thirty-six?" She stared at Mia with tolerance. "I'll take it. I have cash, and I'm walking your way." She placed the receiver back in the cradle.

A knock at the door had all of their heads turning.

"That'd be dinner," Gloria said. She grabbed a takeout sack through the door and handed it to Mia. Then they both stared down at Augie in the bed.

"What happened?" Gloria said.

Augie swallowed thickly, "Mafia ring was hunting him. There was a hit on his head."

Gloria's worried face turned toward Mia. "No one can ever know we were here. Every move from here on out must be thought out. Whatever you do," she turned to face Augie, "use cash and don't use the telephone or computer." He nodded.

She checked Augie again, grabbed a syringe, and then pumped the contents into Augie's gut. "Penicillin. Call room-to-room if you need me. I'm in thirty-eight."

Mia sat Augie up as high as possible without hurting him and plumped the pillows behind his back. She opened Styrofoam containers of soup, salad, and sandwiches. She dressed the salad and cut it into bite-sized pieces easy for him to eat.

"I hope that salad is for you."

"It's for you." She placed the container in his lap and he just as quickly moved it to the empty side of the bed.

Hands on her hips, she glowered at him.

"I don't eat salad."

She leaned across his body and retrieved the container. "You'll eat it today."

"You have plans to make me?"

"Oh yes. You need to get your hemoglobin going. Leafy greens seem like a good way to do that."

She forked a bite and lifted it to his mouth. "Please eat it." He rolled his eyes, but took the fork in his hand and started on the salad.

About to cut his sandwich in half, she stopped when he said, "I'm not an invalid. I don't need you cutting up my sandwich like I'm a fucking child."

She set the plasticware down and placed the sandwich tray in his lap.

"And you can go stay with Gloria. I don't need you here."

Her eyes narrowed. She left him to it and went to sit at the table to eat the meal Gloria had included for her. Frosty orange juice came with her meal. She'd put his just out of his reach on the nightstand. Ignorant man was too macho to accept help, so she'd teach him a lesson.

She arranged her three-course meal in an inviting fashion on the table. She turned on the radio and started on her food. "Mmm, chicken noodle, my favorite."

Leaning back in the chair, she watched Augie struggle with his meal. When he lifted the sandwich to his mouth, a big fat blob of mayonnaise-covered tomato plopped onto his chest.

"Goddammit." He held his arms out, looking down at the tomato as if he expected it to jump up and waltz off.

Sighing, Mia set her soup down and walked back to him. She moved the containers from his lap along with the tomato. She wiped his chest with a wet rag, and then she cut his sandwich in two.

She held the sandwich out to him. "Will you take the lettuce off?"

She shook her head. "You need the vegetables."

He reluctantly took the sandwich.

"Would you like some juice?"

He grunted. She took that as a yes and poured some into a plastic cup.

"Here."

His eyes narrowed at her as he took the cup.

"Accepting help doesn't make you weak. *Not* accepting it, however, makes you foolish."

He grunted and growled some more, and Mia bit her lip to hide a smile.

"This is all I have to give you in exchange for what you've done for me and my sister. If you take this away from me I have nothing, so please accept my help without being an asshole."

She moved her food over to the bed, and they ate together in silence.

When they were done, she cleared the trash and adjusted his position for the night. She slid her jeans off and eased into the bed. He cleared his throat and she snuggled up next to him.

"What are you doing?" he asked.

"Sleeping."

"Why don't you sleep next door?"

"Shut up, Augie. And didn't I ask you to stop hurting my feelings? It won't do any good anyway, because I'm not going anywhere."

"Fine, but you should know I take up most of the bed."

His leg slid across the bed with purpose and his heel hit her shin just right, causing excruciating pain to radiate through her. She shuddered and winced and when she caught her breath, she sat up and grabbed at her leg. She lightly rubbed out the pain. The heat at the bite was stronger, and the skin around her shin felt tight. Exhaling noisily, she grabbed a pillow and walked over to the recliner. She set up for the night and found a position that should be comfortable for a few hours.

"You don't have to sleep in the chair. Come back to bed."

"I'll be fine here."

"I don't know why you left the bed. I was just playing."

"I said it's fine." But it wasn't. Her leg really throbbed. But Augie was the patient, not her.

"You're so stubborn. Just come back to bed."

She was stubborn? That was rich.

"I was playing around. If I'd known you couldn't take it, I wouldn't have."

"I can take it, Augie. It's just that your heel hit my sore leg."

"Oh, sorry. I wasn't trying to hurt you."

"I know."

"Will you please come back?"

"I wouldn't want to disturb you."

"You won't."

He wasn't able to move much, so she snuggled alongside him, her back against his side. His arm cradled her head.

"Augie, I love you."

"I don't know what you're talking about."

She smiled.

"No. Don't hurt her."

Augie's body tensed as he inhaled quickly through his teeth, then he cried out. Mia didn't know if it was from pain or his nightmare.

"Please, don't do this. You don't need to do this."

"Augie." She reached behind her and turned on the lamp at the bedside table. His face distorted with ghosted memories and his brow beaded with sweat. "Augie, it's okay."

He yelled something unintelligible, but she thought it was Mideastern. She grabbed the damp washcloth from the bedside table and wiped his face. His eyes popped open and went wide.

"Augie." She gently wiped down each side of his face as she cradled it with her free hand, careful to avoid his wounds. "You were having a nightmare." She dabbed at each brow. "I think you were speaking a foreign language."

"Farsi."

"I didn't know you were multilingual." She wanted to calm him so he didn't tense up and stretch his stitches. "Do you speak any other languages?"

"Persian."

"I took four years of French in high school. It was a disaster. The teacher said I was the only Canadian who spoke French with a Spanish accent."

He smiled at her. A big grin that included his eyes.

"Speak French to me."

"*Quand Dieu vous a créé les anges ont chanté.*" She rambled on, saying things to him she'd never be able to tell him in English.

He cleared his throat. She passed him some orange juice.

"Jesus Christ, Mia," he said after he swallowed.

"What?"

"I'm fluent in French as well."

Heat bloomed in her chest and blossomed out so far, she felt it to her ears. "You are not."

"I am."

"No."

"Do you recall saying when God created me, angels sang? Um . . . how about my ass is finer than the finest Eastern silk, and the sight of my naked body makes you so wet it's like the Congo is running between your thighs?"

She turned away from him, beyond embarrassed. Hot face in her hands, she mumbled, "I can't believe you didn't tell me you spoke French too."

"I'm glad I didn't."

"You're such an asshat."

"Hey." He leaned over toward her and placed his hand on her back, raking her skin, making it tingle. "I like it when you say things like that. You should say more things like that. Only thing is . . . I'm hard as concrete over here."

She turned to see the sheet tented over his groin.

Their eyes met, and he quirked a brow at her.

"I don't think so," she said. "You have to rest. All that's going to do is get you hot and bothered. Not so good for your prognosis."

"That's just not true. Hot and bothered is an excellent prognosis."

"Not when you've got stitches that close to your stiffy."

He laughed and coughed and laughed some more. "Oh God, it hurts. Don't make me laugh."

"Hey"—she poked him in the side—"think of your grandparents. You got an image of them?"

"Okay."

"Can you really see them?"

He closed his eyes. "Yeah."

"Now imagine they are French kissing with way too much tongue."

"Ugh. God, Mia, you're a dirty little thing. And mean."

"Didn't it help with your problem?"

"No, nothing can help when you're walking around in your underwear."

"What if you were to tell me about your dreams?"

His jaw tightened, and he turned away. "Nothing to tell."

"What are they about?"

"Afghanistan."

"What specifically?"

"Are you trying to psychoanalyze me again?"

"Just trying to help a friend."

He was quiet for a long moment, then he wiggled around in the bed.

"An extraction went bad. We were captured and eventually freed, but not before enduring a little torture at the hands of some insurgents."

"Is that where you are in your dreams?"

He didn't answer. Just stared through her.

"Augie?"

"Honestly, I thought that admission would shut you up. I didn't expect you to keep pressing me. Truth is, I don't really know where I'm at in the dream. It's a dark room, but the people being tortured aren't soldiers or Afghan civilians. They're my family and friends."

God, it was worse than she thought. She never would have imagined what he saw behind closed eyes. She smoothed his hair from his forehead and placed a kiss just above one eye.

He wouldn't talk anymore tonight; they'd sleep. She'd hold him and he'd let her.

CHAPTER 13

Two days passed. Augie wanted to get moving, but Gloria advised against it until his stitches set up and his knife wound started to close. By the end of day two, he was feeling much improved.

"We're leaving tomorrow."

"If I were in control of this op," Gloria said, "I wouldn't let you leave until the stitches came out."

"Don't be ridiculous; I can't waste away here for a week. We leave tomorrow."

She held her hands up surrender style. "No skin off my teeth—I'm catching the bus back to the East Coast tomorrow. You guys can keep the car, but nobody should do any commercial flying." Her head cocked to one side. "Or maybe I can leave tonight."

She flipped open the laptop. While she clicked away, Augie turned toward Mia. She'd fallen asleep in the corner chair, reading a paperback. He carried her to the bed, his ribs screaming as he lowered her. When he covered her with the comforter, she smiled sweetly and he kissed the corner of her mouth.

"You like her. A lot."

Gloria wasn't even watching him, but a smile teased at her lips.

He returned to the table. "What's not to like?"

"No, I mean you like her, like her."

"Again, what's not to like?"

"I think you may be in love with her."

"That's ridiculous."

She shrugged. "Never seen you like this before, is all. And don't forget, you and I were together for a year."

Scratching his head, he tried to make sense of her words. "She's different. You know, not like other women. But in a good way. She just does her thing, and she doesn't speak in code. She's a straight shooter, and she sure as hell knows how to handle me. I like being myself around her. I don't have to worry that she's going to hold a grudge against something I say or something I wasn't aware I was doing."

"So are you saying she's your soul mate?"

His lip curled into a smile. "Soul mate? I don't believe in that shit."

Gloria was multitasking, listening to him and clicking away at the computer. "Hey, I can get a bus out tonight. That'll put me there within twenty-four hours."

"You in a hurry to get back?"

"Yeah, I left my dogs at the kennel."

Her two pugs. "How are Dusty and Rose?"

"Just as fat as ever."

"Thanks for dropping everything and coming to my rescue yet again."

"Just don't forget, that makes three times I've saved your ass."

"There's no danger of forgetting because clearly you won't let me forget."

Bronzed fingers wrapped around his forearm. "Hey, I'd do anything for you, you know that."

He covered her hand with his. "Right back at you."

They never were big talkers or communicators; they were both action takers. That had been the major problem with their relationship. But it worked for friends.

He stood. "We'll take you to the station."

"You're going to wake her?" She nodded in Mia's direction.

Looking at her sleeping form, he said, "Yeah, I won't leave her here."

"Don't be silly, it's only six blocks. I'll walk."

"It's dark out."

"And?" She packed up her laptop. "You should be more concerned about me riding across the country on a bus."

"You have a point."

She stood and pointed at Mia. "Let her sleep." They both stared down at her asleep in the bed. "She's in love with you. And this next part you're not going to want to hear, but if your intentions aren't long term, you shouldn't be intimate with her."

"I know that. And I haven't had sex with her."

"There are many forms of intimacy. Anything that stirs strong desire counts. You should end it now or commit to her."

While Gloria went to the restroom, Augie was alone with his thoughts. Was Mia misinterpreting what was going on between them? For that matter, was he? Exactly how would he classify their relationship? They weren't having intercourse, but as Gloria had put it, they were intimate. He understood that and he loved that part, but why did it have to go any farther than that? He knew Mia liked their intimacy too, and she'd been the one to declare she didn't want babies or marriage or even expect a commitment from him.

"All right, I've got to get going."

On tiptoe, Gloria kissed his cheek. He hadn't even known she was back in the room.

"Let me know if you need anything, and I'll be here."

"Thanks, Gloria." They hugged for several seconds and then she was gone.

Shocked didn't begin to describe how Mia felt when she woke *in a car*. Evidently Augie had loaded her and their stuff—without waking her—into the car and, given the distance they'd covered, driven all night. He said he'd promised her a visit to her mother within two days and he always kept his promises. She *was* excited at the thought of visiting her mother. Now, hours later, she glanced at where his wound would be beneath his shirt. He didn't look any worse for wear, yet he'd been driving for over sixteen hours and sitting straight in a ninety degree position.

"Would it be possible to stop at a supermarket?"

"Sure, do you need something?"

"I'd like to get some flowers and chocolate."

"Next one I see, we'll stop." He smiled at her. "Mia, I never really thanked you for . . ."

He stopped talking, and she was dying. "For what?"

"You redirected me. Kept me from taking a life. You saved me from self-destruction. And then you saved me again when you gave me your blood."

"You almost died, Augie. I would give my life for you." She rubbed her wrist where the bandage stuck. He'd taken her blood, so part of her was inside him. It was a heady thought.

"Your blood runs through my veins. You're part of me now, connected by blood."

They were certainly thinking the same thoughts.

"Don't you need to rest?" she asked.

"I'm not tired."

"I mean for your wound. We should clean it and apply a new dressing."

His lips tightened. "It's fine."

"We could take a break. Stop for the night, get some dinner and a shower and a bed."

"I said it's fine."

She sighed. He needed to be whipped with a vine. She imagined her hand slapping his stubborn face. Hmm, he might benefit from a little antagonism. Tendrils of excitement rippled in her sex—*must stop thinking about slapping Augie.*

"You're doing it again."

Looking up, she realized they'd exited the highway and were stopped at a light on the access road.

She swallowed to clear the knot in her throat. "Doing what?" Her voice was a whisper.

"Your color is high and your eyes are hooded. It's like an instant aphrodisiac." He rubbed her leg. "Just what the hell are you thinking about when you do that?"

Shit, was she giving off some kind of signal? "I'm just going kind of buggy over here."

"We'll stop at the store, grab a coffee."

In front of a supermarket, he pulled into a parking slot. She reached down to grab her canvas shoes and he was at her door, holding it open. He always did that: front doors, car doors, gas station doors, restaurant doors. And not just that, but he always kept her next to him but slightly ahead, like he was protecting her. She delighted in that and enjoyed not having to take care of herself. Around him she was completely relaxed and worry free. Except when he'd been hurt. But despite his carelessness with his own injuries, he was faring well. His face was badly bruised, but he acted more like himself.

Inside the store, floral was just to the right of the entrance, and Mia gravitated to it. Augie followed, standing next to her patiently as she looked over the offerings. She ultimately settled on an arrangement of bright yellow gerbera daisies and petite roses. She held it out and lifted a questioning brow. He grinned and said, "It's guaranteed to put a smile on her face."

The coffee nook in the store was swinging. The line was long, so he left her to order their coffee and went to the restroom. She put in their order and wandered off to the produce section. Wheatgrass shooters were available and an advertisement read *Increases red blood cell count.* That would be good for Augie. However, getting him to take it would be a huge hurdle. He didn't like any vegetables, even on a sandwich or coated with dressing in a salad. She ordered two anyway and returned to the coffee corner.

"What's that green shit?" The raspy, low words came at her over her shoulder.

She turned and smiled wide, then kissed his cheek. "Green-apple shooter." She shot hers. It was awful—tasted like dirt and grass. Too green, but she was determined to have him swallow his. "Mmm, it's delicious. Here." She shoved the other cup at his chest. "Shoot it."

He took the little cup in his thumb and index finger and analyzed it. Shrugging, he held it to his lips and tossed it back. His face contorted, and she laughed until she cried. He shuddered.

"You're so going to pay for that."

He reached for her, but she squealed and took off running down the cereal aisle. He was gaining on her, so she darted left at the end of the aisle. Running through the store was rude and she got several unsavory looks from shoppers, despite her apologies. She hit the back corner and there was nowhere to go, so she whirled around. Steel arms trapped her face first against the frozen vegetables.

His nose tickled behind her ear as he lightly touched it to her skin. His breath a whisper when he said, "Where are you off to, Miss Brown?" His voice was raspy and low, and the sound delved deep into her core.

A chill started low in her spine, running like a flint line up her back, and she shivered. She turned in his embrace and faced him. Her nipples poked stiffly through her white T-shirt. His eyes widened and then narrowed as he watched her anatomy change.

He growled and placed one hand on the glass door near her head while the other squeezed her breast. His thumb and index finger pinched around her cloth-covered nipple, making her moan.

"Augie, there are cameras."

"Does that turn you on?"

"What? No!"

Warm, slick lips crashed down on hers. Teeth tugged at the soft tissue of her bottom lip before releasing it. His tongue slipped into her mouth and tangled with hers, and she tasted the wheatgrass on his moist breath. The moan from his throat vibrated through her. Behind them someone cleared a throat.

"If you don't mind, I need to get a bag of stewing vegetables. And might I remind you this is a family place."

Augie turned, leaving Mia pressed against the glass as he regarded the irritated customer. Mia was so drunk with passion, she didn't care that the gray-haired woman glowered at them.

"My apologies. She's just so damn beautiful, I can't help it." He put his hand in hers and pulled her along. "Come on, baby, let's go pick up our coffee."

Mia smiled blissfully at the old woman.

When they passed the dairy section, Augie pulled a can of sweetened whipped cream from the shelf.

"What are we going to do with that?"

He quirked a brow at her. "We're staying in town for the night."

"I thought we were pressing straight through."

"Plans have changed. Roll with it."

CHAPTER 14

They'd enjoyed a steak dinner at the restaurant attached to the hotel—swanky compared to where they'd been staying. As always, Augie had been solicitous. She'd ordered her steak medium rare, but it was delivered too rare to eat. Without her saying a word, Augie noticed right away and had it sent back.

Now, seated on the edge of the king-sized bed, he flipped through the channels, landing on sports news. "Fucking Stros can't get their shit together."

It was funny watching him shout at the television set.

She pulled his shirt off and pushed against his chest until he leaned back on his elbows. A huge smile erupted across his face.

"I like where this is headed."

"Where it's headed is right here." She circled her finger around his wound.

He frowned.

She pulled the breathable gauze away and found the wound appeared much improved. It had been three and a half days and the skin around the small incision had shrunk back to its normal size. She pulled the red antiseptic soap from a bag and walked to the basin. Lathering up a washcloth, she washed her hands as well. She'd been cleaning the wound twice per day, just as Gloria had instructed.

The task had become more and more unbearable and today was proving hardest of all as Augie relaxed on his elbows and let her have his way with him. Since he was practically healed, she noticed other things as she wiped at the stitches. Like the ripple of muscle across his side. She thought they were referred to as obliques, but she'd never seen any before. Not defined like Augie's were. And then there was the six-pack of abdominal muscle that she couldn't stop looking at no matter how hard she willed not to.

And speaking of wills, her palm landed on his lower abdominals and brushed across the dips and peaks there.

His fingers on her wrist startled her.

"No stitches there."

"No, I guess not." Her voice was breathy, her breathing shallow.

Taking the wet rag from her other hand, Augie tossed it in the direction of the bathroom. She was trapped beneath him in seconds; it took her breath away, how fast he could move. With his hands on her jaw, he held her head firmly in place and ever so gently licked her lips, moistening them, then he covered them with his own slick lips.

At her moan, his tongue slipped inside her warmth and he sucked on her tongue. She mimicked his every move, sucking on him hard and deep. One hand moved to the curve just below her breast, sending tingles to her nipples. He broke their connection in time to watch the peaks harden.

"I love how your body responds instantly to my touch."

She loved it too. The fingers on her jaw moved to her lips, and his index finger slipped into her mouth. She sucked on it just as she'd done with his tongue. Fingers squeezed her taut nipple, and she growled in the back of her throat. Bending her leg at the knee, she slid her foot along his side until it rested near his hip. With him lying between her legs, she was humming with need, and longing to take him inside her. But she was done asking.

He leaned over the edge of the bed, rustled through the grocery sack, and removed the whipping cream. Shaking it, he watched her intensely. "Take off your clothes," he said.

Demanding man. Yeah, she liked it, but she couldn't make it too easy for him. "Excuse me?" she said, one brow lifted.

"You heard me."

He cocked a brow back at her. Time stood frozen as he shook the can. They glared at each other, neither backing down. Who had the most to lose? She wanted him and knew he wanted her too, but maybe he was testing her to see if she really wanted what she said she wanted. She caved first. Her shirt and bra fluttered to the floor, her pants and underwear not far behind. Naked beneath him, her body trembled at the promises his held.

"God, you have the most beautiful tits I've ever seen."

Sounds of fluffy cream being funneled through the applicator hit Mia's ears just before the cold cream hit her breasts. Augie teased her nipple, pulling gently with his teeth before he licked the cream away. More cream hit her stomach as he licked a sticky trail down her side to her navel. She laughed when he touched the sensitive curve of her hip.

"Hmm, ticklish, huh?"

She shook her head.

"No?"

His teeth bit delicately, erotically, into her, and she squirmed and giggled beneath him.

Outside it was dark, and there were no lights on in the room, but Mia's senses were heightened. Every touch on her body elicited a purr from her. When he inserted the tip of the can into her core and pressed the applicator, she sucked in a harsh breath at the shock of the cold, wet cream.

"Augie!"

"Don't worry, your heat will melt the cream and it'll leak from you and into my mouth as I feast on your sweet little cunt."

Warm hands at the back of her thighs pushed until she was spread for him.

Oh God. She couldn't breathe. Her heart pounded away in her chest. This was it. Death. Her tombstone would read: *Here lies Mia Brown. Never penetrated, but died in an act of tremendous cunnilingus.*

Fingers parted her flesh and he blew over her exposed skin, causing a pulsing knot to form at her sex. She knew if he were to touch her, she'd explode.

"You're perfect, Mia. You deserve perfection right back."

She couldn't answer because his lips were licking and nibbling on her parted flesh and she was lost.

He was everywhere he wanted to be and nowhere she needed him to be. The knot at her core was growing larger, and she thought she might explode. She'd never been so aware of it before, but her clit now throbbed with its own pulse.

"Please." She needed him to move just a little to the right. "*Please . . .*"

"Not yet, baby. I want to feast on you for hours."

Oh God, not hours. He was teasing her to death. His velvet tongue barely made contact with the lips of her sex as he traced their shape. Parting her again, he entered her with his tongue and rubbed his face against her, trying to go as deep as he could. Plunging in and out, swirling around and around, his tongue kept a rhythm that had her almost where she longed to be. Her fingers fisted in his hair and pulled on him as her body bowed, but she couldn't reach the pinnacle.

"Augie!"

His dark laughter against her flesh sent shivers through her sex, further adding to her torment.

"What's that, baby, did you need something?"

"Augie." His name was a breathless whisper.

He opened her again, and then fingers massaged the knot where all sensation was coiled tight. She cried out.

"God, feel how excited you are. I never knew a woman's body could respond like this."

What was he saying? Oh God, she didn't care. She just needed release. "Please."

"Please what?"

Her eyes flew open and she tried to pull her legs together, but his hands held her thighs in place. She wasn't going to beg.

"Just tell me what you want."

"You know what I want!" she cried, her voice sounding different than she'd ever heard it before, laced with frustration and passion.

"But I like it when you tell me. Say the words."

Fine! "I want you to suck my . . . m-my . . . *me*." She wasn't used to saying those things.

"Your clit, baby. It's called a clit."

"Yeah, I want you to suck my clit. Suck it hard."

She practically screamed, and he chuckled against her again, sending vibrations straight to her core.

When his teeth grazed the tender nub, stars, comets, and asteroids—all of the heavens—collided around them. She screamed his name and pulled his hair as her back arched up from the mattress. With him sucking her into his mouth, wave after wave rolled through her body as she shuddered around him. Yet he was relentless. More rolling orgasms waved through her body, shaking her, as she bowed her neck on a moan.

He kissed up and down her inner thigh, rubbing the moisture from his lips across her skin. He kissed her belly and laid his head on her as her heartbeat started to slow.

Unspoken words electrified the room.

A loud commotion outside the door coupled with a crash had him on his feet in a flash.

"What is it?"

"Quiet—put your clothes on."

Gun in hand, he stalked toward the door like he was tailing a wanted man, looking more like a soldier than she'd ever seen him. As she dressed, she watched him linger near the door before he cracked it and peeked out. She heard laughter, then female voices swearing and carrying on. Placing the gun at the small of his back, he opened the door wide and stepped out.

"Hey, big daddy, you wanna play?"

Mia heard one of the girls coo. She actually cooed.

"Don't touch me. And no, I don't want to play. You're both drunk. Do you mind carrying on your conversation somewhere else?"

"Mmm. You're sexy when you're demanding, but then again, I bet you're always sexy."

His hands went to the gun at his back, but Mia was there. A simple touch of her hand to his forearm and a shake of her head brought him back from the bad thoughts. He smiled a smile that didn't reach his eyes, but he nodded at her.

"I said get the fuck out of here!" At his yell, the girls scurried down the hall.

He slammed the door. "Stupid bachelorette-party girls."

Stupid is right. Who knows where their escapades would have led had they not been interrupted.

She bet women propositioned him wherever he went. Funny, though, that he didn't seem to care for it.

"Never change, Mia. You're the exception." He pulled her to his chest and kissed the top of her head. "Stay the exception."

He was so cryptic, she had no idea what he was talking about. "Were you going to shoot them?" She smiled against his skin.

"What? No, just teach them a lesson."

"Wanna watch a movie?"

"Okay."

As they watched a newly released comedy, he held her tightly spooned. She had no idea what time she fell asleep wrapped in a cocoon made of Augustine Roy.

CHAPTER 15

The next day they set their course for Tricolor Bay, outside of Ontario. They'd driven half the distance and now were three hours out. Augie insisted on driving, which didn't really bother Mia since she wasn't all that fond of driving, but it was another element of their relationship that he controlled. He'd even order for her in restaurants. Sure, he'd ask her how she liked something cooked or if she even enjoyed steak or pork, but with that information, he'd make the final decision.

He didn't listen to music when he drove, or talk very much, which she found odd.

"Hey, do you wanna play I Spy?"

His brow furrowed. "Uh, I don't follow."

"I Spy."

"I spy?"

"Yeah, do you want to play?"

He gestured at the windshield. "Mia, I'm driving."

"It's a driving game."

"A driving game."

"Yeah, you play while you drive. Did you seriously not do this as a child?" She smiled at her memories. "Whole family loads up in the car and drives across the country singing bad karaoke and playing driving games. Occasionally you elbow a sibling or give them a rope burn."

He gripped the steering wheel so tight his knuckles turned white. "We never did anything like that." His tone was almost regretful, and she imagined Augie as a small reserved child. Had he always been this way?

"Now's your chance. We're gonna play."

"I don't think so."

"Come on, it'll be fun." She fished a pen and a sheet of paper from his backpack.

"You have an uncanny ability to make me do things I don't want to do."

She laughed. "Spare me. You don't do anything you don't want to do."

"Oh, really? Drinking that green shit, stopping at the hotel last night, not killing a man, eating a salad, helping crazy Russell with the mixer, and now this. I'm sure there are more, but I think that's enough to make my case."

"I think you'll agree those activities will only make your life better."

She made two cards with six squares each. "You have to find a McDonald's, a Montana license plate, a speed-limit-sixty-five sign, a green car, a school bus, and a blue semi-trailer truck. As you find the items, I'll mark out the squares. First person to find all six items wins."

His brow knit in confusion. "What do we win?"

"Um . . ." She dug through a convenience store bag. "How about a package of trail mix?"

He scratched his neck. "Seems like a lot of work for trail mix."

"What do you want to win?"

"How about winner gets a hand job?"

"What's a hand job?"

Smirking, he said, "See, if I win, you would take your hand and . . ." He placed his hand between his legs. "Wait, I've got it all wrong. If I win, I get to massage your beautiful cunt until you explode on my hand." He turned his head, probably to make sure she was still conscious. "You in?"

She swallowed back the lump in her throat. "I'm in."

"Speed-limit-sixty-five sign right there." He pointed out the front windshield to a sign she couldn't decipher since it was too far away.

"How can you see that?"

He shrugged. As it came into view, it was clear he'd just cleared one square.

"And a green car"—he pointed across the highway—"there."

What the hell? She went easy on him when she'd designed his game board. Her mistake. Dammit. Wait. Why did she care? She wanted him to win. Wanted what he'd described as his prize.

"Okay, so you've knocked out two squares."

"Three. There's a McDonald's."

"So three." She scratched out McDonald's.

"You're not trying very hard to finish yours. Maybe I can help you." He leaned over to try to glance at her board.

"Eyes on the road, Roy."

Straightening, he asked, "What's on your list?"

Holding up her list she answered, "A church, police car, dog, deer-crossing sign, and a blue Impala."

"Blue Impala? Don't think I've ever seen one of those in my entire life."

"I was attempting to make it easier for you since you're a rookie."

"Oh, is that it."

"Never mind." Looking out the window, she pointed. "Right there, a church."

"Look behind us."

She turned. "Police car." She fist pumped the air and marked her paper accordingly.

A dog that met his untimely demise was decaying on the side of the highway. "Um, dog . . . there." Again she pointed out the window.

"Yeah, but that's some bad karma, huh? Using the poor dog like that to get ahead."

She nodded. "It counts."

He threw his head back, and laughter filled the car. It was deep and infectious as it rumbled through Mia.

He found his last three before lunch and even though Mia was competitive when it came to I spy, she couldn't make one bone in her body feel remorseful at her loss.

After exiting the highway, they came to a stop at a red light. "Hungry?" he asked.

"Yes." She sat forward and searched through the windshield. "How about Chinese?"

He shook his head. "I don't like Chinese. How about a hamburger?"

Her lips tightened, but she nodded.

"Why are you pouting?"

"I'm not."

"You so are."

A strong hand clamped onto her side, and she squealed in laughter. "Stop it."

"First tell me why you're pouting."

"Okay."

He stopped torturing her, but refused to turn away.

"You never let me pick out any meals."

His forehead creased. "You don't like hamburgers?"

"I do, but why can't I pick the place?"

"Fine. Pick it." His eyes narrowed.

"Look who's pouting now."

The light turned green. "Where to?" Augie asked, moving slowly.

"Um . . ." She didn't know the area, so how was she going to pick? They passed a sign featuring a variety of food icons. One was a picture of a burger and beneath it read *drive-in.* An arrow on the sign led to the right. "Turn right at the corner."

He turned, and she kept her eyes focused on locating the burger joint.

"Where am I headed?"

"We're looking for a drive-in burger joint."

The next light turned yellow, and he stepped on the gas. "I think what you're looking for is just up ahead."

"How can you see these things?"

"What things?"

"The speed-limit sign, the green car, the burger joint. I can't see them, and I don't have vision problems. How can you see them?"

His hand scrubbed at his chin. "I have above average vision." Patting the space next to him on the seat, he said, "Get your jacket and come sit next to me."

She scooted across the seat. "Are you getting lonely over here all by yourself?"

"Yes." He picked up her coat. "Cover yourself with the jacket and slide your pants and underwear down."

Her head whipped in his direction. Eyes wide, she stared at the side of his poker face.

He didn't attempt to explain or comfort. He kept his head forward and drove. Her stomach stewed with nervous excitement. She would never be able to eat now, so she covered her lap with the jacket. She undid her jeans and then hooked her thumbs in both her underwear and the denim and lifted her butt off the seat to slide them down. When they rested at her knees, his hand landed on her thigh.

"That's good."

Under the jacket, his arm snaked around her thigh and his hand slid between her legs. His finger rubbed up and down her seam before breaking through. "You're wet."

It was exhilarating to listen to him state private erotic matters so casually. And she wasn't surprised when she felt herself grow wetter. Both his words and his fingers turned her on. Her lips parted, and she could barely breathe when he rubbed her clit.

"I can feel you getting hard beneath my fingers. Do you like it when I touch you?"

Her legs closed around his hand. "Yes," she whispered. Couldn't he tell?

He pulled into the drive-in and she started to pull her pants up. His hand pushed them back down.

"I don't think so."

She surveyed the parking lot. The place was jumping. It was lunchtime and there were people everywhere. He pulled up behind a car that was backing out and took the slot next to the oversized burger logo. Even the picnic tables were all full and the diners sitting there could see directly into the car. Since they were just outside the kitchen, carhops skated by on every side. Augie rolled the windows down, and a welcome breeze blew through Mia's hair.

"But, Augie," she whispered, "there are people *every*where."

"Mmm, I know. So you'll just have to be quiet and act natural." He fisted his hand between her legs, and she let out a strangled gasp.

A carhop rolled right up to the car and Augie started his order. His middle finger lightly circled her clit, not quite giving her enough. Her vision went spotty, and she laid her head back against the seat.

"Make it a double cheeseburger and a strawberry milkshake and she'll have a . . . Well, actually, let me get her to tell you. I wouldn't want to order for her." He turned to face Mia, still massaging. "Babe, tell the lady what you'd like."

Her eyes flew open and narrowed at him.

"I know you don't like it when I order for you, so tell her what you want." His finger entered her—slowly, so slowly— and her jaw dropped. Incoherent words emerged from her throat.

"I'm sorry, babe, Melissa here didn't get that. Will you say it again?"

The finger inside her danced as one on top circled round and round.

"Ah, the, the, ahhh . . . what . . . he's . . . having."

It was all because she'd confessed her dislike of him ordering for her. Melissa skated off to put in their order.

"Bastard," she whispered.

"That's a bit harsh." He frowned.

She closed her eyes and rested her head on the seat. A loud car pulled into the slot next to them. Augie whistled through his teeth.

"Look at that. A 1957 Corvette Stingray convertible."

Mia opened her eyes and tipped her head toward the window. The old man driving the car nodded at her.

"Nice wheels," Augie said, leaning slightly toward her but looking out the window.

Oh God, they were exchanging compliments about the car. Augie was playing with her clit, driving her crazy, and he was talking to some guy about his car. She was stuck in the middle and completely ravenous for his touch. She squirmed for more and he gave it to her, all the while conversing with their oblivious neighbor. Augie pumped his finger into her, and she ever so slightly rode him, but at this point she didn't care who knew. She just needed him to bring her to that sweet climax only he knew how to do.

"You guys from around here?"

Augie pointed with his free hand. "She is, born and bred. Right, babe?"

Her eyes opened again, but she didn't see anything. "Wh-what?"

"The man wants to know where you're from."

"E-Elora." His thumb massaged while his finger curled inside of her.

"Elora, that's near the gorge, isn't it?"

Her eyelids went down again.

"Babe." Augie whispered his hot breath into her ear as he worked his magic on her sex. "He asked you a question; don't be rude. He wants to know if Elora's near the gorge."

She blinked at the man in the convertible.

"You okay, miss?"

She felt the coil tighten like an elastic band, and then she exploded.

"Oh, oh yes, yes, I'm . . . oh, yes, I'm fine. Ah . . ."

Her back bowed against the seat as she exhaled and then inhaled long and deep, smiling at the stranger. "Elora is a small town outside Ontario, and you're correct, it's near a gorge."

His jaw hung open and his eyes were too wide. Next to her, Augie chuckled, and in that moment, Mia knew she loved him with everything she had. She couldn't imagine feeling this comfortable with anyone else. She trusted him, yes, even his shenanigans. She enjoyed sharing parts of herself with him *and* enjoyed the fact that he let her share herself. He'd indulged her silly game and even walked away liking it. Turning her smiling face toward him, she sighed. Augie kissed her nose.

"Miss Brown, I do believe you have just enjoyed your first public orgasm. I honestly didn't think you'd let me go all the way with it, but I can't tell you how glad I am that you did. You're very brave." He pulled his hand free of her and placed his finger in his mouth. She moaned at the sight that had her quivering all over again. She loved how contented and safe she felt next to him. He would die keeping her protected and satisfied. She knew he would.

CHAPTER 16

Leaving her hamburger half-eaten, Mia had fallen asleep against Augie's shoulder. Her sweet sighs in his ear as she slept—not to mention her show at the drive-in—had him aching. Smiling, he shook his head, but the girl was under his skin. Without being overly cloying, she'd managed to do what all the women in Baton Rouge combined could not—hold his attention. Okay, maybe that was a stretch, but hell, he wanted to wake her now because he was missing her chatter.

And she took his shit like a pro, something no woman has ever been able to do. When he and Gloria were together, his controlling tendencies had been at the crux of all their heated arguments. Gloria had liked to have control too, and they knew there was no way they would last as a couple. Yet it wasn't only that Mia let him have control; it was more that they controlled things together. They agreed on most major issues, so it was just easy. And when they didn't agree, she'd let him have a win, he'd let her have a win. Was that how a relationship was supposed to be? He wouldn't know since he'd never had a healthy one before.

What could he do with her? He tried to imagine himself with her, even married to her. But then what? He'd grow bored, she'd grow bored, they'd grow to hate one another like his parents had. It would be a disaster. He wasn't a family man. Hell, he hadn't even known what she was talking about in the car with her road-trip game. But he'd enjoyed that time with her. He couldn't make her eternally happy, he knew he couldn't. And if she grew to hate him, like his mother hated his father, he'd be devastated. And besides, what did he have to offer a woman? He had a nice home, he didn't want children, he was good in the sack, he wasn't romantic, and he had post-traumatic stress, although it had cleared up a lot. But he still suffered the nightmares. Basically, he would be the worst husband of all time.

He focused on the meandering road ahead, instead of the one in his head.

GPS led him to a tree-lined drive at the end of which sat a palatial red brick building sprawled across an acre or so. Parking in the designated area, he killed the engine. His hand went to her hair and petted there.

"Mia? We're here."

She rubbed her face in the crook of his neck. "I fell asleep."

"You were exhausted."

She smiled sleepily at him for several seconds. "I know it's out of the way, so I just want to thank you for bringing me here."

He kissed her cheek. "You're welcome."

He opened his door and walked around to assist her.

She held the daisies and chocolate in her hands and stood next to the car. "I'll be just a few minutes, if you want to wait in the car."

She didn't make eye contact, which wasn't like her.

"Why don't you tell me what's going on," he said.

She shifted back and forth and fidgeted with the flowers. Looking down, she sighed. "I've never really brought anyone around my mom. She's um . . . she's different."

His palm went to her cheek to comfort her and to get her to look him in the eye so he could read her emotions better. "Different how?"

"She may say something or act in a way that may upset you."

He wanted to tell her every parent would do that, but he didn't want to make light of her distress. His hand in hers, he pulled her along. "Come on, we'll tackle her together."

Inside, the place seemed more like a governor's mansion than a behavioral center. Silk curtains and antique furniture gave it an air of opulence. Before they cleared the entry, a woman in a navy business suit greeted them. She wasn't that old, but the way she pulled her hair back in a tight bun made her seem ancient. Her narrow glasses rode halfway down her nose.

"How may I assist you?"

"I'm here to see Mrs. Brown. I'm her daughter."

"She will receive you in the library." She held her still hand out to her side, indicating the direction they should walk, but she followed them. "Right in here. I'll just have someone go get her."

"Thank you."

Mia's voice was low energy, and Augie wanted, needed, to let her know everything was going to be okay.

A magazine on the coffee table caught his eye. *Car and Driver.* He lifted it. "Hey, look—blue Impala." Grinning, he showed the cover to Mia.

She pulled the magazine from his grip. "That's crazy! What a coincidence." Her smile beamed.

"You still would've lost. Face it, I rock."

"Hmm, I think a rematch is in order." She held her finger to her lips as she pondered.

"Same stakes?"

Her eyes grew dark, and she pulled up close so that only he could hear.

"Definitely not the same stakes; we need to up the ante." She kissed, slowly, up the side of his neck.

"Mia."

"Mom!"

Mia crossed the room and greeted her mother with a kiss on the cheek. She started to present the flowers.

"Where have you been? This place is awful."

"But you said it was better than the last place."

"I was wrong. This is much worse."

"But we can't afford to relocate you again."

They moved toward the sitting area. Mrs. Brown took a chair perpendicular to Mia on the couch. Mia still held the gifts in her arms, so to make her more comfortable, Augie took the items from her and placed them on a console table.

"Who the hell are you?"

"Mom!"

She waved one arm in his general direction. "Well, who is he?"

"This is my friend Augie. Augie, my mother, Pauline."

Standing in front of her, he extended his hand. "Nice to meet you, Pauline."

She shook his hand swiftly and eyed him coolly. "What is this?"

Her eyes shifted from him to her daughter. Augie took a seat next to Mia on the couch.

"Mom, I told you, this is my friend Augie."

"Friend?" She scoffed. "Men aren't friends with women."

"How do you feel, Mom? Still getting headaches?"

"Every day." She sighed. "Your hair is terrible; didn't I tell you to get it trimmed last time you were here?"

Mia wrapped her arms around herself and rubbed her arms. "Have you met anyone?"

"What is this, Club Med? No, I haven't met anyone." She crossed one long leg over the other and leaned back. "What I need is a cigarette."

Mia looked up at Augie expectantly, so he handed her the car keys. "Go get my smokes."

She geared up to say something, but he stared at her with intent. Receiving his unspoken message, she hurried from the library.

As soon as she cleared the door, he turned to her mother.

"Pauline, I realize we don't know each other, but we do both know Mia. Hear me when I say this—I'm here to protect her from those intending to do her harm. I will take her far away from you. Far—away—from—you."

She opened her mouth to talk, but he held up his hand to forestall her.

"She cares for you. Deeply. You should know that even when she is in dire straits that her mind is never far from you. You will act ecstatic at her lovely gesture of flowers and chocolate that you don't deserve. And I mean do it up big. I need to feel your excitement, your exhilaration. Are we clear?"

Rubbing her upper lip with her fingers, she inhaled deeply.

"Your daughter is the most amazing person I've ever met. She selflessly gives and gives and gives to people in need. I've never seen anything like it. You should spend the rest of your days getting to know her. You've created a gem."

Augie did a double take when he thought he heard her whisper, *Well, fuck me sideways.* Since she still sat primly, her nose high, he assumed he'd heard wrong.

Mia rushed in and dropped the pack of cigarettes in her mother's lap before reclaiming her seat on the couch. Silence filled the room. Augie raised a brow at Pauline Brown. She leaned forward in her chair. Pointing to the flowers she said, "Those are lovely."

Augie frowned.

"Just really beautiful. I love daisies."

Mia jumped up and grabbed the flowers and chocolate. "We thought you might like to put them in your room."

"That'd be great. I know the perfect place."

Mia beamed at Augie, and he wondered why this mother would be so hateful to a daughter with such an innocent spirit. This relationship wasn't good for Mia.

"So, Augie, what do you do?" Pauline asked.

"I'm a sheriff in Louisiana."

"Oh." Her eyes rounded. Her expressions and mannerisms matched many of Mia's. They even had the same body structure, and Pauline was extremely attractive when she wasn't being a bitch.

"Young, aren't you? For an elected office, I mean."

"My family is in politics." It was what had torn his parents apart, although it was also what had drawn them together at the beginning. They stayed together for the sake of his father's career, but their marriage was a business. Both of them had significant others. He'd never understood their reasoning and thought it a bizarre arrangement.

"How did you meet Mia?"

"Through a friend."

"Ah." She raked her hair through her fingers. She turned toward Mia. "I don't guess you've heard from your sister."

Mia wrung her hands. "Actually, I have. Through Augie. He's a friend of hers. We're headed to see her."

"I see. So you're leaving too. I'll be all alone."

Mia shook her head. "Not alone; I'll be back. I promise."

"Just like your sister. She promised the same thing."

"She had to go. She had no choice."

"There's always a choice, Mia."

Mia cleared her throat. "Anyway, I'm going to go to Louisiana to see her, set some things up, and then I'll come for you. I was going to apply for a visa; we could get one for you." She looked up into her mother's face. "It's warm there, Mom. You'd like it."

"Sounds wonderful. What do we do when the visas expire?"

"We could come home."

"You'd come back with me?" Pauline's eyes held pain. Maybe fear.

"Mom, I've been with you for twenty-five years. You have no reason to question my loyalty to you. I'll be back when you get done with treatment. Please don't worry; you won't be alone."

After they talked about insignificant things like the weather, Mia hugged her mother and they both said goodbye.

Once they reached the car, Mia asked, "What did you say to my mother?"

He lounged against the open passenger door and searched for the best possible way to tell her what he'd done. He hadn't expected Mia to ask about Pauline's change in attitude. "I told her she had a beautiful daughter she needed to appreciate more."

Her lips tightened as she whirled away from him. "You didn't need to do that."

Grabbing her elbow, he turned her to look at him. "But I did. She hurt you. I told you I would protect you, keep you safe. Just because she's your mother doesn't mean she's excluded. Besides, we trekked a long way to get to her, and she damn well was going to act pleasant. I'm sure she does it for her doctor and her other visitors. She could do it for her daughter."

Closing the gap between them, Mia lifted her eyes to his. Her purple irises shined with unshed tears. "Does everybody bend to your will?"

Since she kissed the corner of his mouth, he figured she wasn't too upset. At least not with him.

"It's not bending to my will, it's what's right, what's expected. But yeah, usually people do bend." He wrapped his arms around her. "Although *you* haven't."

And he rather liked that she pushed back against him.

Kept him on his game.

CHAPTER 17

Traffic was backed up going east so he'd headed west, and was now passing through Minneapolis. It would have been farther but Augie had driven until nine o'clock and then the idea of her warmth in the bed next to him had him yearning to fulfill that image, so he stopped for the night when usually he would have driven straight through.

After showering they had breakfast at a diner and hit the road again. Several hours later had them in St. Louis, and Mia was asleep again. She'd slept most of the way the last two days, which didn't seem like her, but he guessed that seeing her mother had taken its toll on her mentally and now she needed to regroup. It had been seven hours since they'd eaten anything, so he'd pulled into a barbeque joint.

"Mia?" He squeezed her thigh.

"Mia, wake up." But she wouldn't. Despite the air conditioned interior of the car, her head was sweating. He hadn't noticed that before. He pulled her toward him. Perspiration framed her delicate face.

"Shit. Mia?" Her eyes opened ever so slightly.

"Are we home?"

"No. We're in St. Louis."

"But I thought you lived in Louisiana." Her speech was slow and slurred. "Thiss line iss ssseparate."

Her words didn't make sense. Feeling her forehead again, he recognized that she was full of fever. He started the car and drove to the first drugstore he could find. He was in the downtown area now and pulled up next to the curb directly in front of a pharmacy.

He got her some fever reducer and juice, and headed back to the car. Maybe they could stay in town for the day, for however long it took her to overcome this bug. A hotel with room service would be perfect for that.

At the car he opened the passenger door and slid in, lifting her legs to slide beneath her. She winced and grabbed her left lower leg.

"Hey, take this." He handed her two pills and the juice. While she drank he lifted the material covering her leg. He gasped, drawing air through his teeth. The affected area wasn't larger than before, but what concerned him was the dark center. He knew staph infection from his days in the military— a nasty case could kill a man. Skin sores started out pink and red, then became dark as the head of the infection burrowed into the nervous system.

She smiled at him. "I think it's getting better; it's not as red as it was."

He took a deep breath and pulled her pant leg down. The wound needed lancing immediately to expel the infection. It was a painful process, and he winced at the thought of her enduring that agony. Given her fever, the sickness was already attacking her systems. It was serious, but he didn't want to upset her. "We need to get you to the hospital to get checked out."

She shook her head. "I hate hospitals and needles, so I'm going to pass." She shook her head, at the same time running her fingers through his hair. "You're a worrier, aren't you?"

He shrugged. "Not really. I just figured you wouldn't want a beetle-shaped scar on your shin."

Her nose crinkled. "Well, maybe it couldn't hurt to have someone look at it."

He scooted over to the driver's side, punched up *hospital* in the car's GPS, and drove. Her response to his nonsense told him that she wasn't thinking straight. After two blocks, Mia reached for the door handle.

"I'm gonna be sick."

He pulled over and before he could stop the car, she had the door open and hurled.

He put the car in park and ran around to her door. Bystanders gasped as they watched her lose her guts. He pulled her hair back and looped it in the clip she had on the seat. He reached for paper towels in the glove box and wiped her face.

"Mia." His words were barely a whisper. Her fevered eyes slowly closed.

When Mia woke, she was confused . They were seated on black chairs, and a lady at a desk tapped away on a keyboard. She felt a little better and was thankful for that. She could hear Augie's voice and it comforted her.

"She has a high fever and can't keep aspirin or juice down. She's nauseated."

"Sir, she's not a citizen of this country, so she will need to apply for the emergency assistance program."

"I already told you there isn't time for all of that nonsense."

"Well then we'll need payment in full for most of the procedure."

"Fine. Do it."

"I'll have to get a doctor out here to assess her needs. Wait just a moment."

Augie sat, exhaling long and loud and running his hands through his hair. It was the first time she'd ever sensed vulnerability in him while he was awake. He jumped to his feet when a young man in a white lab coat approached. His nametag read Dr. Williams. They shook hands.

"She's right here," Augie said. "Mia, the doctor's here to look at your leg."

She sat forward in the chair, and Augie lifted her pant leg. The woman from the computer, now holding a clipboard stood next to Dr. Williams.

"Incision and drainage of the abscess, necrosed tissue excision, staged debridement of the affected area, intravenous penicillin . . ."

Mia's mind wandered as the doctor spouted off his list. She watched Augie pace and saw despair overtake his features. What was he worried about? He stopped, looked at her, and then resumed his pacing. Dr. Williams stood and waited while the lady went to her computer.

"Excuse me, Dr. Williams."

He turned to her and squatted. His kind smile reassured her.

"Yes, Ms. Brown?"

"I just want to make sure you'll do everything possible to ensure I don't have a beetle-shaped scar on my leg. You see, it was this horrible beast of a beetle that bit me, and I sure wouldn't want to have a scar like that on my shin."

Augie took the chair next to her and reached for her hand. He squeezed it tight and carried it to his lips. The doctor smiled.

"We have lasers that can make you look as good as new, some say better. Don't worry, we'll hook you up."

"Sir." The woman called Augie to the computer and handed him a form. He nodded and brought it to Mia.

"Mia, you must sign this paper so I'm allowed to pay for the treatment."

"What?" Her head shook. "I don't want you to pay for it."

"Mia, please, it's the only way."

"No, Augie, I won't have you burdened with my medical debt." She tried to push the clipboard back into his hands, but he wouldn't take it.

He sat next to her. His face was drawn and his brow knotted. The desperation in his voice crackled the air when he said, "Don't argue. Debt and cost don't matter right now. The only thing that matters is getting you well." His breathing was ragged. "Please, Mia, you could die without treatment."

Of course he was exaggerating to get his way. That was a new one. And pretty low, saying she could die.

"Please," he said, "we help each other. That's what we do. You helped me, so let me tend to you. Just sign the damned thing. It'll all work out."

She would have granted him anything. She scrawled her signature across the page.

He passed the clipboard, along with his credit card, to the woman and reclaimed his seat beside Mia. He grabbed her hand and pressed his lips to her skin.

"Sir."

The woman waved his credit card in the air and he crossed to her. Mia heard them mumbling and then Augie's voice rose.

"Please, I can get the money. Just start the damn treatment."

"I'm sorry, sir, it must be paid in full."

"You can't be serious. She could die sitting in that chair."

"She's not considered a medical emergency."

"Are you fucking kidding me."

"Sir, would you like to call someone?"

Augie was loud and erratic. He threw his hands in the air. "No, I don't want to call anyone. I want you to start the fucking treatment." He pushed at her desk, and she stood.

"Sir, you need to settle down."

His erratic movements stopped. His hands in the air, he murmured, "You're right. I'm sorry, what can be done here?"

"The balance is fifty two thousand dollars."

Augie's hollow laugh filled the room. "On second thought, I would like to use that phone. Can you accept wire transfer, multiple credit cards? How shall we do this?"

"None of that. I can refer you to a bank."

"That's going to take too long. She's septic." The woman pushed a business card at him, but he brushed her hand out of the way. "Please, I'm begging you, start the goddam treatment, and I'll go to work on the money."

"We can't do that."

Mia was having trouble following and understanding what exactly was happening, but one thing was certain: Augie was more frantic than she'd ever seen him and it scared her. He begged and pleaded, but he couldn't accomplish his needs. His fists clenched at his sides and his shoulders slumped. He was hopeless.

He had the money. Hell, he had ten times that and with his family's money, they could buy half the hospital. But none of that mattered. He needed quickest access. Cashier's check. Bank.

When he tried to grab the business card off her desk, several items fell to the floor. "Come on, Mia." He helped her up and they hustled out of the ER.

What was he going to do? Augie wished she could just use his insurance.

She vomited on the sidewalk again before they got to the car, and he held her. God, she was getting worse. It would take at least an hour, maybe more, at the bank, and then they would have to get back to the ER. He guessed he would take his chances at the bank. What choice did he have? Her life hung in the balance, and he felt completely out of control. He couldn't even think straight, and hoped he was making lucid decisions. He fastened her into the car. The hair around her face was damp, and her temperature alarmed him. She was burning up. He couldn't believe the triage nurse wouldn't deem her a medical emergency.

"Mia?"

She smiled drunkenly and closed her eyes.

He started the car, punched up the bank's address on the GPS, and turned to drive away from the downtown area. At the corner he saw a happy couple dressed in wedding attire emerge from an ornate building. *Registrar of Marriage.* He whipped the car around and parallel parked in front of the building. He opened Mia's door and cradled her head in his hands, shaking her lightly to wake her.

"Mia, listen to me. Are you awake?"

"Mm hmm."

"We're going to get married."

Her eyes flew open. "Married!"

"Yes, married. My medical insurance will cover you instantly if you become my wife. Don't argue—we don't have much time."

She used his strength and the rest of hers to step from the car. "For the record, I was about to say yes."

"Shh, save your strength."

They walked in the building, and Augie spoke to the registrar. Evidently a marriage in Missouri amounted to filling out a piece of paper and providing any one form of identification. Mia presented her Canadian identification and Augie gave his driver's license. They were married in less than ten minutes.

The officiant's words rang in his ear: "By the power vested in me by the state of Missouri, I now pronounce you husband and wife. You may kiss the bride." Augie leaned over and touched his lips to Mia's. He heard a giggle well up from within her. In other circumstances that would have been comical, but her condition made it anything but.

"Congratulations Mr. and Mrs. Roy."

He signed his name to a form and passed Mia the pen.

She peered at the paper. "It says Michael Roy. I want it to say Michaela Roy."

"Baby, it has to be your legal name. We need everything to be on the level so when I call my insurance company, you can be added immediately. Please, no more questions. Just sign it."

With a groan and a pout, she signed *Michael Roy*.

Augie grabbed the license. "Thank you."

He led Mia out the door, loaded her in the car and drove the two blocks to the ER. Leaving the car double parked, he scooped her into his arms and ran into the building, arms and legs shaking all the way.

CHAPTER 18

Machines beeped, light seeped from under a door, and mechanical sounds hissed. Augie had watched her sleep for ten hours. When would she wake up? They'd admitted her when she passed out in the emergency room. Dr. Williams said the dehydration coupled with her infection had caused her body to shut down. *No fucking shit.* It was what he'd been trying to tell everyone. Since he didn't have a medical degree, no one listened.

Augie rubbed at the ache behind his eyes.

Why hadn't she told him about her leg? It must have been painful, yet she never let on. God, he'd been so scared. Were her vital organs shutting down? Dr. Williams assured him that was not the case. He hadn't been much of a prayer before, but he prayed to all the gods now. Her fingers fluttered and her eyes rolled beneath her lids. She moved to sit up and disturbed papers on the foot of the bed that then rolled to the floor.

"Easy." He jumped up from his chair in the corner of the room and went to her side. He picked up the stuff from the floor and dumped it back on the bed. "How do you feel?"

She opened her mouth and moved her lips, but her voice was gone. She held her hand to her throat. He pressed a button on the side of the bed and said, "We'll get someone in here to help in just a minute."

She looked groggy with her half-shut eyes and sluggish, imprecise movements. She examined the room, focusing on the machines and their strange noises, her forehead creased.

A short nurse with blond hair and large blue glasses breezed into the room. "Good evening, Mrs. Roy." The nurse's high-pitched voiced was loud.

At her salutation, Mia shifted her attention to Augie. She mouthed the word *Roy*, but her voice still wasn't working.

When he grinned at her, she gasped and her hands instinctively moved to cup her mouth. Next to her, Augie winked. "Careful," he said, gently pulling the hand with the IV down. It was her left hand and there was a new dainty ring on it, a ring he'd found at a pawnshop around the corner.

"How are we feeling today?" The nurse was next to Mia, shining a light in her eyes and forcing her to halt her excited inspection of the ring. Mia held her hand to her throat. "Thirsty?" the nurse asked. Mia nodded, and the nurse scooped up the pitcher from the bedside table and was gone.

Placing her ring-clad palm in her right hand, Mia brought it up close to her face for inspection. A myriad of emotions rolled across her face. Augie read shyness at first, then a pink blush that said embarrassment, and then a delighted smile that declared her joy. She bit into the soft flesh of her bottom lip and her eyes sought his. When they met, her blush deepened and her eyes turned dark amethyst.

Damn, what was going through her mind? Did she remember why they'd had to marry? God, she was like a schoolgirl with a new puppy. He'd only intended to provide her with the medical treatment that she needed to survive—that didn't include the provision that they'd be a legit married couple. But she kept eyeing him with those deep purple eyes and that shy smile that drove him wild, her blush creeping all the way down her chest. Christ, what was she thinking? Seeing her expression, he could guess. *Fuckety fuck.*

The ring he'd found was delicate and made of rose gold with a soft pink center stone that was square cut but was turned in the setting to resemble a diamond. Actual diamonds girdled the stone. Dainty scallops shaped the band, with diamonds following it around. He'd just happened into the shop, saw the ring, and immediately thought it was perfect and just big enough for her slim frame. He *hadn't* expected her to react in such a way. He just thought it would be fun for her to have.

The nurse was back with ice water, and Augie poured a cup while she took Mia's vitals.

"Ninety-eight point six." She moved around and slid a blood pressure cuff up Mia's arm and inflated it. "One twenty over eighty. Good as new. Doctor will be in to see you shortly."

The little nurse was efficient; no movements were accessory, all were deliberate.

"Here's your breakfast tray. I want to come back to an empty one." She winked at Mia.

He removed the lid from the tray and frowned; the food looked bland. No seasoning on the eggs and pasty gray oatmeal. He wouldn't eat it, but he hoped she would. She liked veggies, so how much worse could this be? He passed her the oatmeal and a spoon.

She smiled softly. "Thanks. I'm starving." The words were a whisper, but he understood. She scooped a spoonful of oats into her mouth and frowned, just as he had. "Eww. Not good." She set down the brown plastic bowl and pushed the food away.

"What do you want?"

Smiling, she said, "Nothing. I'm good."

He picked up her hand, squeezed it. "If you could have anything to eat, what would it be?"

"Hmm . . . Belgian waffle, over-easy eggs, bacon, crispy golden hash browns, tons of syrup." Her eyes closed, and she licked her lips.

"I'll be back soon."

"Where are you going?"

He waved to her from the door. "I'll be back soon."

There was a Waffle Hut across the street from the hospital but really, once he knew she was going to be okay, he needed a break from . . . everything. Even though he'd taken control of the situation with her medical needs, the mess was out of control yet again. The way she'd looked at him and smiled when she'd seen the ring . . . She practically glowed when she'd been called Mrs. Roy. Hadn't she understood why they'd gotten married? He'd made it clear, at the car. And she'd said yes.

No . . . Not exactly. She'd said *for the record, I was about to say yes.* As in, you asked me to marry you, and I said yes. But he hadn't asked her. He'd said, *We're going to get married . . . my medical insurance will cover you instantly if you become my wife.* Had she misunderstood? What could he say now? Whatever it was, it needed to be said now, before it got any more out of hand. He shook his head. Why'd he buy her that damn ring?

He sauntered into the restaurant and up to the cashier and ordered Mia's request to go, times two. Going over the possible things he could say to her, he recognized that they all sounded hurtful. His concern was that she'd take something the wrong way. He didn't want to hurt her. God, after observing the interaction between her and her mother, he knew to tread lightly. She'd endured enough crap. He scratched the back of his head. This whole mess was a giant cluster fuck.

Returning with the food, he was surprised at how nervous he was. Hell, he'd conducted raids in downtown Kabul that had him less agitated than he was now. With every step he took perspiration, beaded on his upper lip. Self-fulfilling prophecies could make or break a soldier in the field and so he'd apply the same rules here. He pictured himself successfully turning this situation around. Pumped, he was ready to face her. He barged into the room.

"Mia, we need to—"

Damn, she wasn't in the bed. And he'd been so prepared.

He rolled the table over to the bed and set up the breakfast.

"Augie!" In a flash she bounded from the bathroom to the bed. On her knees, her arms laced around his neck until she was weightless and hanging from him. She kissed his lips. "I missed you." She checked out the breakfast spread and giggled when her stomach growled. "Mmm, you're the absolute best most wonderful husband in the world. When we get out of here, I'm going to show just how wonderful you are." She grinned, winked, and then popped a piece of dry waffle in her mouth.

Oh shit, game on. But he couldn't break her spirit now. She was so confident, and he delighted in her newfound self-assuredness.

"The doctor is going to release me."

"He was here already?"

"Yep." She nodded. "Said I was good to go. Just got to wash, irrigate, and change the bandage until it's completely healed."

His eyes closed and he inhaled on a prayer thanking God that she was all right. In that moment it didn't matter that there was a misunderstanding. He didn't care if they stayed married forever as long as her light shone bright.

"Mia." He pulled her tight for a hug. "I've never been so scared in all my life. I thought you . . . you were out for so long I thought . . . "

"But I'm okay now. And if I was gone, who else would annoy you to death in the car?"

He kissed the top of her head. His eyes stung, but he blinked away the moisture.

"Hey, tell me one thing—and I'm hoping like hell the answer is no—but did we consummate this thing and I missed it?" She held her ring hand in the air next to their faces and wiggled her fingers.

Laughter exploded from his chest. Deep cleansing laughter that he couldn't keep inside. "No, baby, and what an insult. Trust me, if we'd consummated, you'd remember."

"That's a relief." She dipped a piece of bacon into the runny part of her egg and stuffed it into her mouth. Smiling at him she said, "I would have hated to miss it."

"You didn't miss it, baby."

The jury was in: Mia did not like hospitals. She'd been once before to visit a high school friend who'd had a baby, and she'd associated hospitals with joy and glee, but now she had another image forming. One of pain and apprehension. Every time a new person came into the room, they wanted to poke and prod at her like she was some breathing pin cushion. Finally, after she'd been checked over what seemed like a thousand times, they officially cleared her for discharge. It had been a long day, and she felt greasy and dirty and wanted a bath and a big soft bed.

"We'll be to Baton Rouge in about ten hours."

Downhearted at his seeming delight regarding the ten-hour drive, she sighed.

"You okay?"

"I'm tired and was hoping for a hot bath and nice big soft bed."

"Recline the seat."

"It's six thirty; are you seriously going to drive for ten hours straight?"

"Straight through, baby." He gestured at the highway. "Be there before sunrise."

She crossed her arms over her chest. "I don't want to be in this car all night. I want a bath, a hamburger, a big soft bed, some reality television, and I want to snuggle up next to you, and I want you there too if you're not going to be all *Augie's law* all night." She was frustrated, and her words were clipped.

He frowned. "What's Augie's law?"

"Augie's law is where you act crazy. You know, that thing you do where you act demanding and testy. What's that saying—*When I say jump, you ask how high*? I think it's because you're ex-military, but I'm not a cadet, so it's just not gonna fly."

Smiling, he grabbed her hand and kissed the knuckle. "No woman—hell, no man—has ever spoken to me the way you do."

"I'm just tired. I want to be in a bed with you."

"Okay, that's not an unreasonable request. We're going to have to stop to clean and treat your leg. So instead of stopping for a moment, we'll stay the night."

"Reasonable or unreasonable, I want to stop."

"Okay, baby."

They drove a while longer and swung around to drive back in the opposite direction. She'd learned he didn't like to be questioned, or at least she didn't think he did, so she tried not to ask him many questions. He'd proven to her time and again that he could be counted on to ensure her safety and see to her needs, and she trusted him completely. Leaning against his shoulder, she sighed contentedly as her eyes closed.

Electronic beeps filled the car and his biceps worked beneath her as he punched *Gateway Arch* into the GPS. He had something special up his sleeve, and she was giddy at the thought. The sun had set and as they turned a corner, her breath hitched at the sight before them. She'd seen pictures, but the pristine, sleek metal curved to perfection and magnified to its full glory took her breath away.

"The gateway to the west."

"It's breathtaking."

"It is quite spectacular." He pointed to a massive hotel across from the arch. "I say we get a room at the top of that thing."

"I don't know, it's like a four-hundred-dollar-a-night hotel."

"Should know how to make a good Belgian waffle then." He pulled the car under the porte cochère, and at once a valet opened her door.

Augie grabbed the little bit of stuff they had. He took her hand and pulled her inside. She slowed at the entry to admire the massive crystal chandelier with its many prism-like dangling teardrops. The ceiling had gold leaf detailing and a paint job reminiscent of the Sistine Chapel, and opulence simply dripped from every surface.

"It's gorgeous!" She gingerly padded to one of the many red velvet couches and rubbed her fingers over the material. Mini-chandeliers designed to be a likeness of the main structure hung over the couches and chairs.

A man in a tuxedo stopped at her side. "Would you like a drink menu?"

She sank down in the couch until only her eyes peered over the high back. An arm wrapped around her shoulders. She turned to see Augie standing behind her.

"Would you like a drink?" he asked.

"Um, I want a sex on the beach," she whispered back.

"You can't have alcohol with your medication."

She frowned. "Well, then, why did you ask me if I wanted a drink?"

He chuckled. "I thought you might be thirsty and you're sitting in the clubhouse area that serves as overflow for their nightclub and bar."

"I am?" Heat bloomed in her face as Augie pointed to the sign. It was a framed picture that hung on the wall and blended with the lavish furnishings. "Oh."

She started to stand.

"You sure you don't want anything? Nonalcoholic drinks are good. Do you like coconut?"

"Love it."

"We'll take two virgin piña coladas," he told the waiter. To Mia he said, "Do you want to sit out on the patio? The concierge said you can see the arch from there."

"Yes, I'd love to."

Passing by the tuxedoed waiter, Augie told him where they were going. When he said that the patio wasn't open, Augie whispered something she didn't hear and within a few minutes the man was back, carrying their drinks along with keys to unlock the door.

Outside, she took the green straw into her mouth and sucked up the cool treat. "Mmm, that's good. Pineappley and coconutty." She felt eyes on her and looked up to find Augie staring at her with a broad smile on his face.

"What?"

"Pinappley?"

"Yes." She sipped again. "Mmm. And coconutty."

They finally turned to sit and both gasped. The patio was set at an angle to the arch and the effect was mesmerizing. A sleek steel blade rose from the ground and jutted straight toward the sky until her eye couldn't follow it anymore. "Wow!"

"Gotta be the best seat in the house."

"Gotta be."

He sat on an outdoor pub chair. "Know what can make it better?"

"What's that?"

"Come sit here." He patted his lap.

She let herself be nestled against him.

"How do you feel?"

"Hmm." She shrugged. "I feel great. Why?"

He pulled her hair together and laid it over her shoulder before he pressed his cheek against hers. "You could have died, Mia." His breath whispered over her ear. "Why didn't you tell me you were hurting?"

"Well, you were so busy with everything, important things, and I didn't want to cause more trouble for you after my sister and I have caused you so much already."

He pressed her to him and kissed her temple. "It's not trouble, it's your life. You can come to me for anything. Have I ever made it seem any other way?"

God, now he was reprimanding her. "Of course you haven't."

"Think how I would have felt if something had happened to you after all I'd done to protect you. I would have been devastated."

To hear him talk so frankly made her long to be alone with him and show him how much he meant to her too. "I'm sorry. It was stupid. I won't do anything like that again."

He kissed her hair, and she leaned into his chest. "I love my ring."

"I thought you would."

"Thinking of being dead, you know what I thought?"

"What's that?"

"I could have died a virgin. It's the most depressing thought I've ever had."

He was still, quiet. In fact, if it weren't for the rise and fall of his chest, she never would have known he was still behind her.

"Augie, why don't you want me? The real reason."

He took her drink and his and set them on the table before he turned her in his lap.

"We've been over this. It's not that I don't want you. I don't want to take advantage of you or our situation."

"You can't control this too. You want me, and I want you. And tonight I want to have sex, you inside me. I don't want to be a virgin anymore. If you won't help me, then I'll find someone who will."

"You think blackmailing me is going to work?"

"I no longer care." She slid off his lap and squared her shoulders. "I'm going to go mix it up on the dance floor."

She headed inside, not looking back once.

She wasn't dressed for dancing, but she was going to prove a point. Wasn't she?

She stopped. What was she doing? Was she even thinking straight?

No, no, no, she wasn't going to think about her motives. She continued into the club. She took a spot on the dance floor and swayed to the music. The sound was syncopated, rhythmic, but slow. Several people were dancing, but she found a corner and pulsed with the beat. She followed Augie with her eyes when he emerged from the patio area and slowly sauntered across the club to a table. Crazy caveman wouldn't even come and dance. She knew she was being deliberately provocative, but his rules were ridiculous. They'd already been intimate many times and tonight she would lose her virginity one way or another.

Right. Who was she kidding? Deep down she knew she was all talk.

It would be Augie in bed with her tonight, or it would be no one.

CHAPTER 19

God, the woman was driving him crazy. And how many more times could he deny her? He didn't think he had it in him any more. Fuck it. He'd take her tonight and shut her up for good. She only *thought* she wanted him to be her first. Well, he'd be her first all right but he wouldn't, he couldn't, be counted on to hold back or coddle her because of her delicate condition. No, if she wanted it, she would have to take what he offered, and he wouldn't tolerate any whining, crying, or second thoughts. She wanted to see what he was like, and he was going to show her.

Her erotic moves on the dance floor were attracting the wrong kind of attention. A man had taken the space behind her and was moving in sync with her. When his hands went to her slim hips, Augie was on his feet, mindlessly pushing toward them, the only thing in his path, white-hot rage.

Get control of yourself, Roy.

He pulled her behind him. Eye to eye with the unwanted man, he said, "Get lost."

"Excuse me, asshole, we were dancing."

"If you want to retain the ability to dance, you'll run, not walk, in the opposite direction."

His voice was terse, his body rigid. The guy looked him up and down, turned, ducked tail, and ran.

Mia regarded him with that cocked brow of hers, the one that made him want to laugh on the one hand and pull her body under his and pleasure her for hours on the other. Her index finger was caught between her front teeth; that sultry look didn't induce the urge to laugh. He walked around behind her and slid his arm around her waist, pulling her back to him, her ass rubbing against his thighs and crotch. They danced, and he enjoyed her supple movements against his hard body. When the song ended, he pulled her away from the dance floor and to the elevator bank.

Once the door closed, he ran his palm over her jaw. He seized her lips and sucked, pushing her body slowly back until she was pressed against the cold metal shell of the elevator wall. He closed his fingers around her breast and squeezed her tit, hard. When she shuddered, he slipped his tongue into her mouth. She sucked sweetly on it. He grabbed the back of one of her thighs and lifted until she wrapped her leg around his waist. He ground against her core.

"You think I don't want you? What about what you feel between your legs?"

She replied with a moan.

"Baby, do you feel what you do to me?"

"Yes." Her voice was breathy and weak. "I need you."

"I know, baby. I'm gonna take care of you."

"Inside me."

He took her earlobe in his fingers. "You're ready for me, for all of me?"

"God, yes. Please, Augie."

The door pinged open and he carried her to their room. He set her on the bed and removed her shoes and jeans. "I need to change your bandage and clean the wound." He motioned to their bags at the side of the bed.

Shaking her head swiftly, she said, "No."

He grabbed the bag from the hospital and dumped out the contents. "I'm gonna go wash my hands. Psych yourself up while I'm gone."

He had to clean her leg. They could still play around, but doctoring her was more important. He was still hard from the elevator and needed a breather—before he ripped her clothes from her body and slaked his needs, taking what his body wanted.

Walking from the bathroom, he almost stumbled head first into the wall. In the center of the bed, standing on her knees, was a completely naked Mia. She had their marriage license on display in her hands.

"Augustine Charles Roy, I want you. Since I was passed out on my wedding night, this is it. Get over here and consummate this marriage now or so help me God, I will find someone who will. I would like it to be you, my husband. And besides, you've been sporting a canon in your pocket since I was seated on your lap at the patio so . . . What do you say?"

A growl escaped his chest as he ripped through his clothes, tearing them off as fast as gravity would allow. Naked, he stood before her and fisted his cock, stretching to his full length as she watched, her eyebrows slowly reaching her hairline and her eyes forming eggplant-colored spheres. Her tongue darted out, moistening her lip. He was ready to explode and he hadn't even touched her. Reaching down, he snagged his jeans and took out his wallet and a sleeve of condoms. She wanted it, she'd get it; he'd fuck her until they ran out of rubbers.

He knelt on the bed, lifted Mia's legs at the backs of her thighs, and she went down abruptly on her back, the wind knocked out of her. He pushed her thighs up, careful to avoid her bandaged shin.

"Keep your legs up and your hands on your knees."

He ran his engorged cock through folds soaked with her need, pushing just a bit at her opening. Her size would make the first coupling painful.

"You're small."

"I don't care."

"I won't hurt you." He wanted not to care about this little kitten of a woman, but damn it to hell, he did, and he would attempt to bring her as much pleasure as he could. They'd be taking it very slow. Even if his heart or his cock exploded with his efforts at holding back.

He stood, waiting for his blood to cool. Hands at his shoulders turned him.

"You can't leave me like this. Augie, I swear I'll hate you until I'm dead if you do. What's wrong with you?"

He saw the moisture collecting in her eyes. Her face was red hot and her lips were pursed into a tight line. His hand palmed her cheek. She was a sexually frustrated kitten, but he knew how to take care of her. He spoke the words he knew she needed to hear.

"Baby, we're not done. I'm gonna ride you all night long. I'm gonna be in you so long you're going to wish you never asked for it. You'll be begging for me to stop."

Her satisfied groan vibrated through his hand and down his arm. Leaning in, he kissed her, sucking her bottom lip into his mouth.

"Let me set the mood. After all, this is your first time. I want it to be good. And I'm under some pressure here since I'll be your first."

She smiled bashfully at him, and his cock jerked.

Walking around the room, he turned off the antiseptic white overhead lights and turned on two lamps. He opened the curtains and bathed the room in the glow from the arch. He searched the bedside radio for appropriate music and was in luck when he landed on an all-night dedication station.

Warm hands smoothed over the muscle of his backside. Placing her chin on his shoulder, she purred as she continued her caress.

"You have a most marvelous butt. How do you stay so muscular?"

"I run and box."

He turned until they were face to face, only inches apart. He kissed her nose, his hands slinking down to cup her slim curves. Pulling back, he slid his middle finger through her folds. "You're beautiful."

Her head went down. His finger under her chin lifted her face to his. "Hey, what's going through your mind?"

"I bet you've been with some really pretty girls."

"But you're more beautiful than all of them put together."

"With women's bodies."

She wasn't listening to him.

"Are you not a woman? I thought I'd checked on that a few times."

"I mean with cleavage and big round melon breasts and curvy hips and butts."

Yeah, usually that was what he liked, but she was more exotic than any woman he'd ever had. He couldn't understand it himself. She was pure, she was truth, she was his and his only, and he found those things to be more alluring than any physical feature.

He wanted her to never question her beauty again.

"Your graceful long neck"—he skimmed the line of her neck with his teeth—"your perky breasts and sensitive tits"— he drew them erect using his teeth—"the smooth column of your torso"—his fingers feathered down to the space at the top of her thighs—"and the delicate, dainty folds that hide all your treasures . . . Those are the things that make you the most beautiful woman I've ever had in my arms. You make me forget everyone else."

She preened at his words, arching her neck and back, showcasing her body and offering herself to him. Her skin glistened as she slowly rolled her hips, and she smiled seductively, revealing her pearly white teeth. His fingers manipulated the rigid knot of nerves between her legs, flesh already slick with her desire. Her legs gave out, and he pulled her into him, all the while keeping up his massage. It drove him wild, the way she responded to his touch, knowing too it had always been *only* his touch. He massaged until her panting and the leg climbing high around his waist told him she was ready to climax.

"Let yourself go, Mia."

"I don't . . . I don't want to until you're with me." Her breaths were shallow, her skin heated, her cheeks flushed.

"Baby, you're going to come again and again tonight, but we can't start until you're ready for me. I need you to come right now on my hand."

At his words, she bucked and uncoiled, releasing on his fingers. She was utterly perfect. Responding to his command as well as to his touch made her a goddess in his eyes.

Her eyes closed as the vestiges of her climax shuddered through her. Dropping her head back, she said, "Please tell me I'm ready to take you now."

His teeth grazed the pulsing vein in her neck. "No one's ever been more ready, baby." His hands cupped her ass, and she instinctively wrapped her legs around his hips. He set her on the edge of the bed, and her gaze followed his every move. Her body shuddered.

"Hey, you having second thoughts?"

"I have thoughts, but not that kind."

"What kind then?"

"You're big—I heard that was desirable."

He didn't know how desirable it would be for a virgin but yeah, he'd never had any complaints. But fuck, this was different. He'd never taken someone's virginity before. Would he hurt her? He thought it was inevitable. "It's going to hurt."

Her eyes held confidence. "I know. That's why I want it to be you. I trust you."

"Tell me if you want me to stop."

She nodded.

He fixed a pillow beneath her ass to lift her to him. Placing the head of his dick at her entrance, he rubbed through her wetness and slowly inserted the tip. The pressure he needed to breach her entrance was significant and if he was struggling, he knew she would be hurting. Shit, this was crazy.

Her chest rapidly pulsed up and down. He pulled back and positioned her better with her legs back and her hands on her knees, holding herself open to him. He inserted his middle finger and when she took it, he added his index finger. This was the fullest she'd ever been. Her breathing was heavy as her tension grew. Withdrawing his fingers, he licked her seam to apply lubrication and he rubbed her clit to keep her charged for him.

He pulled her to the end of the bed. "Mia, please look at me."

She opened her eyes. God, he could fall into those purple eyes and stay forever.

"Don't take your eyes off me." He had to get past this first part and then they could enjoy each other. A bead of sweat rolled down his temple. Mia held her knees up and he held the backs of her thighs as he pushed through the initial barrier in one strong thrust, inserting himself two inches.

A low groan escaped her lips, but her eyes stayed focused on his. As her body quivered, her tits grew harder and a shade darker. So beautiful. Her hips spread a little more as he pushed in another few inches. She closed her eyes.

"No, look at me."

Sleepy, lust-drugged eyes opened, half-hooded.

"Mia."

Her eyes opened wider.

"Can you take more?"

She moaned, her chest bowing off the bed. She stretched and whispered a breathy, "Augie, please."

Did that mean yes? Fuck it. His body was hurting from holding back, so he pushed in another two inches. God, it felt good to push into her soft, wet heat.

Her whimpers would have alarmed him had he not been watching her face.

"You okay, babe?"

"Need a minute."

She bit her lip and pushed against his thigh with her hand, her body feebly fighting his invasion. One more good push and they'd be home free. Her body writhed beneath him and her hips rolled sensuously.

"Are you ready?"

"Ah, yes."

He grabbed her waist and pushed in deep, eliciting a half cry, half sob from her, but God it felt good to stretch his full length into her, his balls resting on the curve of her buttocks. His hands slid up her back. Pressing her to him, he kissed her cheek, her nose, her lips. He pushed her hair from her face, the wet strands sticking to her neck. He took in her every contour and shadow, as though he hadn't seen her every day, nearly every hour, for the last seven days. Being inside her was as close to heaven as he'd ever get, and he wanted to memorize every sensation. What a gift she'd given him. He would always be her first; no other guy would be able to take that away from him. Shit, he didn't like thinking about her with other men.

"How do you feel?"

She lifted her face to his and delicately placed a kiss on his lips. "I love you, Augie."

"Mia, I . . ." God, she cut him to the quick with her innocent honesty. Did he love her? Had he ever loved anyone? He loved his brothers and his parents because they were his family. His feelings for Mia were already much deeper. But what did that mean? He pulled a few inches from her and pushed back in delicately, testing her ability to take what he gave. She moved her hips, meeting his thrusts, and he increased to a steady rhythm, not too rough for her delicate body. He'd never had sex like this before, never thought about his partner this way. He just took what he needed and hoped they got something out of it too.

Angling her body, he rubbed his cock against her G-spot, recognizing the moment she felt it when her eyes first widened and then the lids dropped. Staying steady, he tried to hold the position that was giving her immense pleasure because, God, he wanted this to be good for her. His mission was to brand himself so deeply on her, in her, that she'd never forget his name or this night. And wasn't that a radical fucking thought.

She started to buck against him and her mewls turned into sighs that turned into gasps.

"Are you there, babe? I want to be with you."

"Where?"

"Are you about to come?"

"I don't know." Her voice was raspy, low, and breathy.

"You are; I know your body." He increased his pace, not wanting to go wide open because he would kill himself if he hurt her. Could he even come this way? That didn't matter so much, since it was about her tonight. All about her lovely body melting around him.

When that body started to contract, her walls gripped him so tight it was almost painful. He stilled as much as the position and his body would allow, then without warning he exploded, the release deeper, stronger, than he'd ever felt before. It started low in his abdomen and radiated out. For one moment they existed perfectly together, both on the same fixed point, holding steady, a rapture of their bodies in both time and space.

He whispered, "Michaela."

He'd never remotely felt so close to another person. His lips took her mouth, coaxing her to open. When she did, he slid his tongue in and plunged deep, mimicking his body's movement. He laced his fingers through hers, linking as much of their bodies as possible as they rode out the waves crashing through them.

Then he simply floated in glorious, soul-healing peace.

Minutes later—maybe hours later—he kissed the shell of her ear. "That was the most precious gift anyone has ever given me."

She presented him with a tired, satisfied smile. "Did you . . . was it . . . I mean . . ."

He knew what she wanted to hear. "Your body molded around me so well, we fit together like a key into a lock, a connection deeper than I've ever felt with anyone. It's not always like this, Mia. I have to admit that it's not. You're amazing." He kissed her nose, loving the little button.

"But we are going to do it again?" She was very serious.

Laughing, he said. "Oh yes, but first we'll take a bath and get you re-bandaged."

She groaned and pulled a pillow over her face.

CHAPTER 20

Mia stretched long and deep, like a kitten just stirring from a nap, and it had her very aware of her body. There was a slight burn between her legs. Nothing painful, but it was like the burn of too many sit-ups. The thought had her giggling. What had happened when they came together was heavenly, nothing like sit-ups. She'd never known feelings like the ones that had coursed through her, that deep and utter longing to possess another human being. It was surreal. They'd connected, and while Augie hadn't told her he loved her, that didn't matter because he showed his love in every touch and action. His behavior, his attitude toward her, was precious, more precious than flowery words could ever be. To be fair, he wasn't bad at the words either. She'd never forget what he'd whispered in her ear. Those words were locked tight in her heart.

"Time for a soak."

He strode naked across the room, and Mia delighted in every inch of him. His cock was semi-rigid, and she eyed it without shame, feeling heat bloom in her cheeks.

"Like what you see, Mrs. Roy?"

"Very much." And she did. He had a beautiful body and he knew what to do with it.

He removed the bandage and inspected her wound. "Looks good. We're a matched set." Scooping her into his arms, he carried her to the tub.

She lightly fingered his stitches. "Tomorrow I get to remove your stitches."

"If I let you."

That didn't sound promising. She glared at him as he set her into the luxuriating, warm water of the large garden tub. "If you don't promise me right now that you'll let me take your stitches out, then I'm not going to let you clean and dress my wound."

"More blackmail, Mia, really? After all we've been through together?"

"Exactly. After all we've been through, you need to promise me this."

He sank his big body in the water opposite her. She yelped when he leaned forward and held her upper arms to pick her up and set her across his lap.

Looking down into her eyes, he said, "I've never made promises to a woman before I met you and your sister. You know that?"

"Nu uh."

"Well, I haven't. Don't know why I am now, but yes, Mia, I'll let you remove my stitches if it means that much to you."

Shifting her upper body, she stretched to reach his lips and kissed him, sucking his tongue into her mouth. After a few minutes of heated kissing, she felt something poke at her butt. When they broke apart, she bit her lip to stifle a giggle.

"That's what you do to me—make me insatiable. I can't get enough."

All thoughts of giggling left her mind as they were replaced with images of her body entangled with his and at his mercy. He began gently washing her with the fancy soap and super soft washcloth provided by the swanky hotel.

"Are you sore?"

"Hmm . . . When I move a certain way, I know you've been there."

He growled. "Can't say I'm not loving the way you're saying that." His fevered eyes met her gaze. "I like how it feels, being inside you. Like to know how close you are."

They sat until the water turned cold. She almost drifted to sleep atop him, but he stood with her in his arms and took them out of the tub. She loved his raw strength. Loved a lot about Augustine Roy, the warrior named for a saint.

He lowered her to the counter and pulled a towel from a cabinet. They dried off and then he had her foot on his thigh as he inspected her shin. When he made eye contact with her, his eyes were intense, his frown adding to the pained look on his face.

"I know," she said.

"What, baby?"

"I know you have to scrub it with that gauze."

"I do. Gotta scrape out that infection. Most of it is gone, but there's a little puss building around the edges."

"I know."

He looked away and nodded. "Sit tight."

Holding her leg straight out, she looked at the bite. It was nasty but looked a lot better since the black center had disappeared. Evidently that had been some kind of infection that got into her nervous system. She couldn't remember quite how the doctors put it, but she knew she'd heard enough about staphylococcus to last a lifetime.

Augie returned with the sack of items they'd taken from the hospital and a glass of water. "Here you go."

She held out her hand, and he plopped a pain pill into it.

"I don't want it."

"If you take it now, you should be good to go in about forty minutes. I'll be able to treat your leg."

"Treat it now."

"It's going to hurt like hell. I can't do anything until you've had the painkiller."

"It'll make me fall asleep and I don't want to do that. I want to stay up with you all night."

"Silly girl. Your leg needs to be treated."

She held out her free hand. "Give me the gauze and solution." She pursed her lips, steeling herself for the pain.

"I'll do it, but it's against my better judgment without the pain pill first." He kissed her wet head. "You're my stubborn little lady."

She basked in the little names he'd been calling her: baby, Mrs. Roy, lady, kitten. He left again and returned with his phone. "Here, play the bird game to keep your mind occupied."

He squirted a red solution onto the wound, and Mia sharply inhaled air through her teeth. Dammit. She didn't want to show any outward signs of distress, but she'd been unprepared for the cold shock. Her finger punched the home button on his phone and smiled. His wallpaper was her holding the walleye.

He clicked his tongue and tilted his head. "Stubborn woman," he whispered. He had the gauze ready, but first he adjusted the position of her foot on his thigh. "Scoot your butt against the wall." She pushed back, giving him a firmer hold on her leg.

When the gauze scraped the infected area, she gasped and bit into her lip. Turning her head away from what he was doing, she furiously punched through the phone.

"I'm so sorry, baby."

"Just do it, Augie. Fast." She aimed the bird at the target and shot. "But be thorough."

She wanted him to get all of it so she wouldn't have to endure this again.

Trying to think of anything but her leg, she wondered for the first time what the situation would be when they got to Louisiana. They were married now, so she assumed she'd be staying with him. "You have a home in Baton Rouge?"

"I do."

"And my sister is living with this Clay fellow."

"My buddy Clay, yeah. He's a fire chief. Can't wait for you to meet him. He's a great guy."

Pain burned through her shin, and she cried out, yanking her leg out of his hands.

"God, so sorry, baby, but you've got some here that doesn't want to let loose. Deep breath, okay?"

He squatted and worked at the stubborn spot. Her eyes filled with tears at the pain, but she didn't cry out again.

He stood and kissed her knee. "All done." He pulled her head into his chest. "I'm so sorry."

"It's okay."

"Let me get you bandaged."

He was still naked, so she sat back and watched her private show. When he was done, he carried her to the bed and pulled the covers up over her.

Back in the bathroom, he grabbed a robe from the back of the door and put it on. "Stay under those covers," he said, even though she hadn't moved. He was so peculiar, she giggled. He placed their soiled clothing into a bag and called housekeeping.

He pulled the room service menu from the table and plopped down in the bed next to her. "Mrs. Roy wants a hamburger, was that right?"

"And a milkshake."

"What flavor?"

"Chocolate, of course."

"Of course."

He flipped through the menu. "Sounds good." He started to punch up room service, but stopped. "How do you take it?"

"What?"

"How do you want the burger? What do you want on it? Don't want to be accused of declaring Augie law."

She threw a pillow at his head, and then said, "Cheeseburger, mustard, extra pickles, lettuce, tomato."

"This is thirty-two fifteen. I'd like to place an order for room service." He cleared his throat and tossed the pillows back on the bed. "Double cheeseburger, meat and cheese only, and a single cheeseburger all the way— mustard, extra pickles, but cut the onion—and two chocolate milkshakes."

A knock at the door had him tightening the belt on his robe. He collected the bag of laundry and disappeared around the corner to the entryway. The outer door closed and he came back around the corner, buck naked. He slid in under the bedclothes and pulled her against him. They were rounding third base when a knock at the door interrupted them.

"Shit. Stay under the covers."

He pulled on the robe before answering the door, depriving her of a visual treat, and Mia sighed, falling back into the pillows.

"Much obliged, thank you," she heard him say. "Everything looks delicious."

And she was suddenly ravenous for the burger she could smell.

He brought her the robe that matched his, and she pulled it on. It was soft and not too thick, but she felt like she was wearing fur. He arranged the plates on the bed and they ate right there.

"So you're a picky eater," she said. "Don't eat any veggies."

"I do so. I eat lots of potatoes. And corn. I love corn and corn products. Like Fritos."

"Those are not green or leafy, and corn-flavored products don't count." She pulled a pickle from her burger and bit into it. It was so tasty, she ate another. "Creole food is spicy, isn't it?"

"Yes, but I like spice."

"You just don't like veggies."

"I'll eat them if they're mixed in with something. Like in gumbo. There are veggies in that, and I eat it."

Mia reached for her milkshake and started eating it with a spoon. The cold metal container felt good in her warm hands. When she was halfway through, Augie plucked it from her hands and put the food tray in her lap.

"Eat your cheeseburger."

"I want the milkshake." Damn him and his authoritarian ways.

"If you drink all of that, you won't be able to eat your burger."

She lunged for the shake, landing across him, but he held it from her reach.

"Give it to me." She was on top of him now, straddling him, as he lounged back.

"Hey, I just want you to eat the burger because for what I have planned, you'll need your strength."

His dark eyes held the promise of something enticing, something taboo, and she definitely wanted to experience what he had to offer. His penetrating gaze hypnotized her into submission, and she reached for the burger and took a large bite from her position above him in the bed. She lifted her hips to move, but he held her in place. She shrugged and took a few more bites of burger. Once she'd finished half of it, she was allowed to reclaim her milkshake.

As she sipped the liquid through the straw, he tugged at the belt on her robe and then pushed the robe down her arms.

"Take it off."

She leaned over the side of the bed and set the container on the floor. Then she slid the soft robe from her body while he did the same with his. She straddled him, and he pushed her hips forward and back over his erection.

"Guide me in," he demanded, his voice low.

She fisted his cock in her hand. It was weighty and hard and she lined it up at her entrance. His hips lifted as he pulled her flesh over him and entered her slowly, on a groan. Once he was deep inside, she was so full, she couldn't move. It was different this time, skin on skin. He didn't use a condom but everything he did was so calculated, she knew he knew what he was doing.

"When you can, move a little; it'll help you take me."

She tested his theory and lifted herself an inch and then slammed back down. She winced.

"Easy. Warm up to it."

She tried again, this time slowly ascending and descending with his guided touch. He was deeper than she'd felt him the first time and their movements were slow and hypnotic. She was entranced, lost in sensation, using her core and hips in a steady rhythm as she rode his heat. She felt him as if he were part of her, as one, nothing between them.

"That's it, baby. Your little body is squeezing me so tight, I feel every quiver, every moan, as they vibrate through you and into me. It's crazy, like we're one person."

She'd realized they often thought the same things too.

"I feel it too."

His fingers parted her and massaged her clit while they continued their exotic dance. In a matter of minutes he had her on the cusp of climax and she panted heavily with the impending release.

He pushed harder beneath her, matching her thrust for thrust, massaging all the while until she exploded on a cry of his name and shuddered above him.

"That's it, Michaela, come all over my cock. I can feel you contracting around me, milking me. Fuck! No condom. Gotta pull out."

He held his cock in his hand, glistening from her juices. He fisted himself roughly, and Mia was mesmerized by the sight. He was a man in his element, raw and forceful.

"Lean back a little," he said.

She went back on her elbows and watched as his warm seed shot from his cock and landed on her belly. He groaned out with each shot, his hand tight upon the length and his fingers squeezing the tip.

"I can't believe I didn't put on a condom." He was panting. "That's a first. I'm sorry, babe. I blame you a little bit, though. You make me crazy impulsive with lust for you. I have a clean bill of health, if it's any comfort." He stroked her shoulder.

"I trust you." She smiled at him, unbelievably happy. She alone made this tightly controlled, dominant man lose control.

"Let me take care of you," he said.

He lifted her enough to scoot out from beneath her and walked to the bathroom. He brought back a warm, moist cloth and wiped her stomach. Sated, full, loved, and comforted, they crawled into bed, spooned with no space between them, and Augie held her as she drifted to sleep in his arms.

Half-asleep, Mia became gradually aware of warm hands and skin, hers and his, melding. Rubbing. Catching fire. His touch was everywhere—between her legs, on her hips, thighs, shoulders, arms, and breasts. He lifted her top leg, bent at the knee, and pushed it higher in the bed. From behind, his cock rubbed through the moisture he was responsible for creating. Ever so slowly he entered her tight passage, even tighter in this position, and she arched to accommodate him. Once he was entirely inside her, his hands went to her breasts. His fingers teased her nipples to tautness and her body bowed as she stretched and sighed from the extravagant attention. Lips tasted the skin at her collarbone and teeth grazed along the vein of her neck, pulsing wildly from the increased flow of blood. With each thrust, her ass hit his thighs, and she could feel how perfectly her body fit into his. His lips were close as he whispered words of adoration.

She'd loved all their lovemaking. But to her, this was the most provocative position they'd tried.

As she bit back a scream, she wondered what other provocative positions they could try.

She wondered what she could do to make Augie scream with pleasure.

CHAPTER 21

The morning after all their lovemaking, Mia was sore. Thinking about the reasons why made her giggle, but after satisfying Augie through the night, she definitely felt like a woman. She didn't mind the soreness because every subtle ache reminded her of the closeness they'd shared, and she never wanted to forget it.

They made love twice more after the sun came up, and she wished they could stay in their cocoon of carnal bliss forever.

A late checkout had them hitting the road at one o'clock. She sat close to Augie and leaned her head against his shoulder. When she'd done that before, he'd opened his arm, wrapping it around her so she could snuggle into him, but now he seemed deep in thought.

They drove for six straight hours before she asked him to stop so she could take a bathroom break. He gassed up the car, and she came back with a blue raspberry slushy and a cherry slushy for him.

As he placed the gas cap on, she kissed his cheek and handed him the drink. He frowned.

"Don't you like cherry? I'll trade you my blue raspberry." She held both drinks out.

"What the hell is that?"

"Slushy. You know—ice and flavored syrup."

"No thanks."

He sure was moody. And she thought sex was supposed to make people happy. She shivered; *she* was happy after the sex. And very relaxed.

They loaded into the car and ambled down the road. She drank both drinks and within the hour was looking to him for another bathroom break.

"You can't be serious."

"Well, I had both drinks."

"Why?"

"Seemed a shame to waste the second one."

He sighed and exited the highway.

"Is something wrong?"

He shook his head.

On her way out of the store, she thought she'd get him a Dr Pepper. She'd seen him drink them before, and he hadn't had anything since lunch over six hours earlier. She grabbed some sunflower seeds and a fountain Dr Pepper.

Walking out to the car, she saw him leaning against the passenger door, arms folded across his chest. For the second time she wondered what was bothering him. She smiled.

"You can't be serious." He snatched the drink from her hand and threw it in the trashcan next to the car.

"Hey, I got that for you. It *was* a Dr Pepper."

His eyes narrowed at her.

"What's your problem, Roy?" Her hand went to her waist.

Shaking his head, he scrubbed at his face. "Nothing. I'm just ready to get home." He opened her door, and she slid in, this time staying on the passenger side.

He backed out.

"Wanna play I spy?"

"No."

"How about the license plate game?"

"No games. I just want to drive quietly."

She sighed and leaned against the door. Each roll of the tires lulled her deeper into a numb state. She closed her eyes and focused on the sound.

She focused on becoming numb.

※~∞,※~∞,※~∞

"Mia." The hand at her shoulder shook her awake. "We're here."

Rubbing her eyes and stretching, she sat up. "What time is it?"

"Ten thirty."

She followed Augie up to the front door of a home where several newspapers and packages peppered the porch. A lantern hung overhead, casting them in a yellow glow. She could tell by the style of brick and the small trees and shrubs that the house was fairly new construction. He crossed the threshold, turning on lights as he went, and she followed him into the kitchen. He set the packages on the countertop and set about opening them.

The interior was open and inviting. Neutral earth tones made it comfortable and warm and even though she was in a strange place, it felt homey. The kitchen was decorated like a model unit, with canisters and greenery.

"Your place is nice," she said.

He dropped the mail and said, "Let me show you where you can sleep."

It sounded like he didn't intend for them to be in the same room together—what was that about? Maybe she misunderstood, but the possibility of having made a mistake didn't make her any less upset.

He turned a light on inside a room with beige-colored walls and soft and light plush carpet. The bed was large and full of fluffy pillows.

"Bathroom's right through there." He turned to walk out.

"Is this your room?"

"I'm down the hall."

"What?" She shook her head in disbelief. "I don't want to be in here without you. I want to be in your room."

He exhaled loudly and crossed his arms. His eyes were vacant as he glared down at her. She didn't want to hear what he was about to say.

Holding up her hand to stave him off, she said, "Forget it, Augie. Thank you for the room. Good night." She pivoted to go into the adjoining bathroom so he wouldn't see her tears. She turned on the faucet and splashed water on her face. A knock at the door interrupted her. She wiped away the water with a towel and opened the door.

Dark eyes greeted her. "I'll take you to see your sister tomorrow."

She nodded. "Thank you." She started moving the dress pillows to a spare blue chair.

"I just think we need to set some boundaries. It'll make it easier later when we separate."

She heard him, but she wouldn't let him see how much his words cut through her. It was as if someone had stabbed her with a samurai sword. "I get it. Makes sense."

"I've actually got a garage out back with a nice apartment above. It's empty right now. You can stay as long as you like. I'll take you to get whatever you'll need."

No, she didn't want him to see how affected she was, but she couldn't help it. She sat on the edge of the bed and looked down at the floor, stunned by his words. He didn't even want her in his home. How could she have misread all the signals? The gentle compassion he'd shown her, his solicitousness, his love making . . . It had all been a lie. And what was with the ring on her finger?

"Why'd you buy the ring?" Her voice was quiet, the words almost whispered.

He scrubbed his face. "Things had gotten completely out of control. I wanted to do something for you—your condition, the injury—but there was nothing I could do. There was a pawn shop near the hospital, so I walked in and saw the ring and thought, *She needs a ring, I can do that. I can give her a ring.* I want you to keep the ring."

Nodding, she removed her canvas shoes and climbed under the covers and turned away from him. She heard the door close and then she cried until she fell asleep.

CHAPTER 22

The first thing Mia noticed about Clay was how big he was. The guy was huge. The second thing she noticed was how gentle and loving he was with her sister.

"I want to know what's going on, Mia. Are you hurt?"

Evie's thick lips had pulled into a thin line.

"I'm fine."

She grilled Augie next. "What's your story? Who gave you those bruises?"

Her boldness didn't intimidate him; Augie was a stone wall. Mia knew Evie would get nothing from him. They squared off and stared each other down, neither blinking. Should she intervene? She'd never been able to placate Evie. She was about to speak up, but Clay stepped forward and spoke in Evie's ear. Mia's jaw dropped at how easily he handled her demanding sister.

Evie's tone softened, and she thanked Augie for going after her.

"I was happy to do it. She's a great girl."

Girl? She wasn't a *girl*, she was a woman. A woman he'd been intimate with. She was seriously depressed. She hated that Evie was happily in love, she hated that she couldn't despise Augie, she hated that she was in Louisiana and living above his garage, but most of all she hated that she'd never again feel him pressing into her, hot and frenzied with lust for her.

She sighed and watched as Clay and Evie laced their hands together. If she didn't leave soon she'd vomit at the sight.

The weeks passed and Mia saw Augie less and less. Occasionally she'd go out with Clay and Evie, but she didn't like being a third wheel. And there was one time they all went to Texas when Clay proposed to Evie, but after that, Augie had dropped her faster than if she'd been a nest of bees.

He'd been at work every day since he'd been back. She'd watch him jog every morning around five thirty. He'd return after about an hour, soaked in sweat. Then he'd leave for work around eight o'clock—dressed in a beige uniform, stiffly starched—in his fancy sports car. He'd return after dark, sometimes as late as nine, in the same outfit. She guessed he'd been catching up at work.

She'd gotten settled in the garage apartment. Evie and Clay had invited her to stay with them in Clay's cute bungalow, but it was just too intimate. The two of them were so close it reminded her of what she'd once had with Augie, if only for a moment. When she watched them, they were utterly tied up in one another and shame ate away at her for the jealousy she felt at their closeness. But she knew what it felt like. She'd had that closeness with Augie. Had known it and come to crave that intimacy with him so that *not* having it any more was worse than if she'd never experienced it at all.

Augie's garage apartment had been built with the home and was as new and as nice as his house, just lonely. She didn't know why she stayed there because it was torture to run into him, but the thought of moving away pained her, and she was glad to catch those glimpses of him in the morning and evening.

Today she thought she'd try out the public transportation. She had an interview at two at the local community crisis shelter, but first, lunch was on the schedule.

She'd been acquainting herself with what the locals called TexMex. A Mexican restaurant on the corner two blocks over was within walking distance and she'd been there several times for lunch.

She walked to the restaurant and ordered a Chupacabra—a monster-sized burrito—to go, with plans to take it to Augie at the station. It would be the first time she'd seen him up close in seven days. For herself she ordered bean chalupas. She hoped they could eat together and talk.

The bus had a stop right across from the station. Exiting, she carefully balanced the burrito so the sauce wouldn't leak out. She walked through the door and waved hello to the guys she'd met last week when she'd brought donuts, when Augie had been out on a call.

The door to his office was open and when he saw her, he stepped out.

"Mia, is everything okay?"

"Yes." She smiled. "Everything's fine."

"Then what are you doing here?" His hand at her elbow guided her to a chair across from his desk.

"I brought you a burrito. Don't worry, I told them no tomatoes, no lettuce."

His forehead creased and his lips pursed.

"Have you already eaten?"

"No, but you can't just drop in here whenever you feel like it. I'm busy."

She turned to see the guys in the station's main room playing cards. Augie sighed. She stood.

"I'll just be going then. I didn't mean to disturb you." She walked swiftly away, without looking back when he called her name. His message had been clear: he didn't want her around, even in a friendly capacity. She'd left both lunches on his desk.

The highlight of her week was accepting a position at the crisis center. She'd start next week.

After the fiasco of visiting Augie at work, she was glad that she was going out tonight. The Fireman's Ball would take her mind off Augie. Evie wanted her to go because Clay was going to receive some special award and be named permanent fire chief. She'd found a gown earlier that week at a thrift shop in town and had altered the bodice to fit her slim frame. Now she put the finishing touches on her hair and make-up.

The dress, a deep lavender, was beautiful. Strapless, it was classic with a sweetheart neckline and made of billowy silk chiffon. It rippled delicately as it flowed in waves down to the floor. When she moved, the material clung just enough that the effect was sexy, or so she felt. She borrowed silver heels from Eve, along with jewelry for the finishing touch.

Looking at the clock, she realized she had time to wait yet, so she put coffee on and sat at the table in the small kitchen. The apartment was an efficiency and painted mint green with white curtains. It was very beachy and peaceful, and she'd immediately loved it, but it did nothing to curb her desolate mood. Holding her left hand in front of her, she admired her ring just as she'd done a thousand times before. Tears filled her eyes. She stood and turned on the radio, refusing to give in to the emotion begging to be let out. She'd spent too many hours wondering what had happened, what she'd done, what could have been. A knock at the door took her attention from her musings and she was thankful.

She opened the door to Augie in a pinstriped slim-fit suit and tie. He was perfection. "Augie." Her voice was weak.

As she took in his entire body from head to toe, he was doing the same to her. He opened his mouth, but said nothing. He held his hand out.

Mumbling, he managed, "Your mail."

She opened the door wide to let him pass. "Would you like some coffee?"

"Yeah."

He sat at the small table and watched her every move as she poured him a cup and stirred in lots of cream, just as he liked it. "Here you go."

His hand landed on her arm. "You're beautiful, breathtaking even. Your eyes are the same color as that dress."

"Thank you. You look very handsome in your suit."

"The Fireman's Ball," they said in unison.

They were both going to the ball; she should have guessed as much. She didn't like the idea at all. He'd have to go with someone. A date. A woman. A large breasted blond haired Southern woman.

"I'll give you a ride."

"Thank you, but Keith is picking me up. He's one of the Fighting Nineteenth's candidates."

"I know who Keith is." His voice was harsh. His brow furrowed and his jaw clenched tight. "Here." He tossed the envelope on the table. "This came from the state. It's addressed to Michael Roy."

"Ah. That'd be my identification. Technically my name *is* Michael Roy."

"How'd you meet Keith?" Augie leaned back in the chair, hands in his pant pockets.

His suit pulled tight over his taut muscles and she missed running her hands over all of that hardness. "Evie and Clay invited me to dinner and he was there. Then he asked me to the ball."

"And you said yes."

He seemed annoyed.

"Yeah, I did." She played with the ring on her finger. "I never went to prom or any other school dances. I want to go; I think it'll be fun." She shrugged. Did he think she shouldn't have said yes? Her situation was so messed up. She was married to him, wore his ring, shared his name, he'd been her first lover, but then it had all dissolved into nothing. If he was bothered by her and Keith, it served him right. In fact, she hoped he was.

She got up when there was yet another knock at her door.

"Keith, you're early."

"And you're beautiful. Damn, girl, I'm one lucky son of a bitch."

"Thank you. You look very nice as well."

And he did, impeccably dressed in a three-piece suit. But where Augie was dark and brooding, Keith was too perfect.

"Oh, I got you this. Great minds, huh? Purple orchid."

"Thank you. Please come in."

She turned and almost ran into Augie. He was standing directly behind her, scowling at them both.

"Um, Keith, do you know Augie?"

"I do. Hey, Sheriff."

Keith stuck out his hand, but Augie only grunted and turned toward Mia. He seemed about to say something, but he stormed out, slamming the door behind him.

"What a dick. He's your landlord, right?"

"Um, yeah." She didn't like that Keith called Augie a dick, but he deserved the insult since he was in fact being a dick. Something hadn't been right with him since they'd been back.

"Nice apartment, though."

They rode to the ball in Keith's truck. He was a super nice guy, holding doors open and asking her what kind of music she liked to listen to, and at twenty-six he was closer to her own age than Augie was. There was only one problem: she couldn't stop thinking about Augie.

The event was being held at a nice hotel. The ballroom had been decorated in silver, black, and blue. Twinkly lights and silk draping had been slung over every available surface. She felt like a princess in a fairy tale. The festive atmosphere had her stomach feeling as if a school of fish swam around inside. The first thing they did was have their picture taken under a balloon arch. A local professional photographer snapped shots and charged twenty dollars for a five by seven.

"How many would you like?" Keith took her hand and pulled her over to the monitor. A picture of them emerged on the screen. "We're the best-looking couple here by far," he whispered in her ear. His outrageousness had her giggling.

She eyed their screen image for a long time. Having never been to prom or school dances, she wanted this picture for the memories. "I definitely want one."

Keith turned to the photographer. "Mr. Lewis, how have you been?"

The man was older, and Mia wondered how Keith knew him.

"Good, kid. How's the Nineteenth treating you?"

"Can't complain. Great work tonight; we'd like two please."

"You still over on Austin Street?"

"That's right."

"Got it." He noted something on a little pad he kept in his shirt pocket.

"Come, I want you to meet my buddies."

Keith put his arm in Mia's and they searched the room for his firemen friends. She spotted Augie at a table, alone, one finger rubbing his upper lip. His gaze followed them when they passed.

"There they are," Keith said.

She saw two guys about Keith's age leaning against the bar.

"Mia, I'd like you to meet Colin, and this is his date, Reese." The joke earned Keith a punch in the arm.

Reese put his arm around Mia while Colin nodded and said, "Beautiful."

They were nice guys and regaled her with firefighting stories while Keith ordered drinks—a piña colada for her. Keith had dark features, eyes and hair, and his skin had been bronzed from the sun, but Colin was quite blond and sported blue eyes and reminded her of the California surfers she'd seen in movies. Reese had quite the southern accent and wore cowboy boots and a cowboy hat with his suit. He had light brown eyes and a friendly demeanor.

His arm still around her, but now around her waist, Reese said, "I wonder if Keith has delighted you with stories of our first week as firemen."

"He hasn't, but I'd love to hear about it."

They walked to a table and sat. Augie was too close for her comfort. He still at alone, but it was early yet. She wondered who his date would be. He glared at them; she shifted her chair. And turned her attention to the young firemen.

The guys told her a story about Keith and how he had to wear a French maid's costume whenever he served fire department meals and when he cleaned the station. She laughed until tears streamed down her face.

"Why do you have to wear it?"

"I lost a bet to Clay."

"What bet?"

Colin said, "He bet Clay that he could beat him at a hose-binding drill."

Keith shrugged. "Turns out Clay is some kind of superhero." He sipped from his drink. "But I *was* top of my class."

She felt his embarrassment. "I'm sure you're a great fireman."

Reese added, "His nickname is Colette."

"Ah, the French maid thing. Funny."

Evie and Clay had arrived and now sat with Augie. Catching her eye, Evie waved her over. Mia leaned into Keith and excused herself. Nerves bunched in her stomach as she crossed to them. She caught Augie's eye, and he sucked her in, her forward momentum driven solely by him. At the table he pulled a chair out for her and she sat next to him, wishing harder than ever that she were his date for the night. .

"Mia, you look beautiful," Evie said. She shimmered next to Clay in an indigo-blue gown.

"Thank you. So do you." She smiled. Her sister looked happy. Perfectly content.

Clay cleared his throat. "You two are the most beautiful women in all of East Baton Rouge Parish." He kissed Evie's palm and she sighed, leaning her head on his shoulder.

Their obvious affection for one another made Mia nauseated. No, it was her jealousy that had her stomach roiling. Jealousy that shot through her like poison. She stood.

"Well, I just came over to congratulate Clay." She forced a smile at him. He was so nice that she started to feel like less of a fraud when the smile became sincere. Before turning to walk away, she looked down at Augie. She shouldn't have done it, should have just kept her mind focused on getting back to her table, but her body defied her. The room and everything and everyone in it fell away and in that moment it was just the two of them staring at one another. Stewing with words left unsaid. Deep brown pupils, almost black, searched her soul, stripping her bare. She was so overcome with emotion she was rendered immobile.

Immobile until someone pulled her hand and propelled her forward.

Colin. It was Colin.

"Come on, we gotta go bid before all the cool stuff is auctioned."

His excitement was contagious, and she practically skipped along with him. At the other end of the ballroom, behind a black curtain, a table was set with odds and ends of all kinds. There were restaurant gift certificates, vacation packages, cruises, concert passes, winery tours, spa passes, brewery tours, and even shotguns and pistols. The array was maddening.

They found Keith bidding on a fancy duck-call contraption. Leaning over his shoulder, Mia asked, "What is all of this?"

He wrapped his arm around her waist and pulled her into him. It felt strange, but she didn't dislike it. "This is the silent auction. Anything catch your eye?"

Her gaze landed on a life-sized plush Bengal tiger. "Wow, who would want that?"

"That tiger?"

"Yeah, it's so big. What would you do with it?"

He cocked his head at her. "Baby girl, are you not aware of the local college mascot?"

"A Bengal tiger?"

"Yeah, LSU tigers. That thing will go for hundreds."

"Really? Once you win it, what do you do with it?"

"Strap it to the top of your vehicle. Take it with you to every game. Some people actually buy a seat for their tigers."

"They don't."

"No shit Scout's honor." He held up three fingers.

"You were a Boy Scout!"

"Ten years."

She smiled at him and then the lights went down and dinner was announced. He escorted her back to their table, where a cup of crawfish bisque and a salad waited at each of their places.

He pulled her chair out for her and then took his seat. "Do you like crawfish?"

"Definitely, but we call them crayfish."

"Crazy Canadians." He smiled while shaking his head.

The next dish was sausage and shrimp jambalaya, and it was so spicy the first bite made her cough and her eyes water. Keith rubbed her back.

"You okay?"

Holding her hand flat against her chest, she said, "It's really spicy."

"That's Creole, baby."

Yeah, well, she couldn't really eat it, so she concentrated on the salad and garlic bread.

Ten minutes later the waiter removed her uneaten jambalaya and replaced it with a filet and scalloped potatoes. It looked delicious and her stomach growled at once, but this was a fundraising dinner and knowing how much Evie had paid for her plate of seafood, she said, "I'm sorry, I didn't order this."

"The gentleman at table sixteen sent it over."

Table sixteen? That was Evie's table. Not able to help herself, she looked over. Augie was watching her without even trying to hide his interest. What? He didn't want her but he didn't want her to enjoy herself either? Beyond frustrated, she turned her head and concentrated on the plate. It was too good to waste and she dove in. "Mmm." She savored the first bite.

"Steak a little better?" Keith smiled at her delight.

"Much better."

The steak was great and she wanted to enjoy it, but she was irritated. At whom, she didn't know.

Keith was a great guy, but Augie met her every need. And if he couldn't meet them, he found someone who could. She enjoyed having someone watch out for her. Since childhood she'd been the one holding everything and everyone together. She'd been a little adult from such a young age and she'd grown tired of having to always act serious and think about things like addiction and doctors and bills.

She ate every bit of food on the plate and when she was done, she crossed her knife and fork across the empty dish. She sat back in the chair and turned to find him. His smoldering gaze fired her up, and she smiled at him. His smile started at one corner of his mouth and slowly spread.

She didn't know why he was so intent on her. She'd given up trying to figure him out. The effort took too much of her energy without giving her anything in return. She'd never solve the puzzle, so she'd given up trying.

A local physician took the stage and announced the lineup for the night. Several society bigwigs presented awards, including the LSU football coach, who presented Clay with his new credentials as fire chief.

Once the awards had been given out, the first notes of music twanged from the stage. Immediately there was fast-tempoed excitement on the dance floor. She heard accordions and something she couldn't quite place. On the stage, one musician rubbed a washboard, and there were brass instruments as well, and the joyful sound had the dancers shuffling away in a two-step waltz.

Next to her Keith stood and stretched his hand to her. "Dance?"

She shook her head. "No way. I don't know how."

"This is perfect then. You just mirror me."

"I don't think so."

"It's really fun, and I promise no one will know it's your first time."

She stretched her neck to check out the dancers. Her feet wouldn't keep still and were jumping for a chance to move, so she placed her hand in his and let him lead her across the room.

"All right, just follow me. Couldn't be simpler. It's four basic steps. There's the water"—his foot went out to the side—"cayenne"—his foot went back in—"shrimp"—his foot went behind him —"and roux"—his foot went forward. His grin was huge. "Simple, right?"

She laughed with her entire body. She was having fun, something she hadn't experienced in a while. "It's officially the easiest dance I've ever attempted to learn."

He didn't need to know it was the *only* dancing she'd ever done.

"Only because I'm such a good teacher. *I* make it look easy."

"Of course!"

One hand clamped around her waist and one went to her palm.

"Ready?" Keith asked.

She nodded and they started to move. Once she had the steps down, they added momentum and she was whisked around the dance floor. He was a great dancer and the music carried such a celebratory beat that she was in love with all things Louisiana, including its men.

They danced for an hour before taking a drink break.

"So you like zydeco."

"Zydeco?"

Keith handed her a cup of fruit punch. Pointing to the dance floor, he said, "This music and type of dance is called zydeco."

"Yeah, I love it. I'm having a blast."

"Cool." He smiled and poured more punch into their empty cups.

When they finished, they joined his buddies. Each of them escorted a busty woman around the floor. Another hour passed and the music slowed, forcing them closer together. Other than with her father and Augie, Mia hadn't been physically close to any men. Keith's closeness was different. Not bad, just different. Augie was intense, but comforting at the same time. Keith was energetic and uncontrolled. His touch lingered for a moment and then moved on to some other place on her body: shoulder, waist, arm. His touch wasn't dominant or confident, it was just a touch. It felt friendly. When Augie touched her, she burned. And God help her, she wanted to burn.

Piano chords filled the room. The sound was different from anything they'd played all night and some of the crowd on the dance floor shouted out and booed. Mia looked around curiously.

"It's the last song of the night."

"How do you know?"

"Because in the South, Garth Brooks' "The Dance" closes out every event."

Mia was crushed because she'd hoped to dance at least once with Augie.

She stood on the dance floor in a daze. A hand at her back urged her to move.

"Dance with me."

That breath next to her ear, the voice that was so familiar, caused a Pavlovian reaction that was anything but friendly. His voice . . . His touch . . . She turned in his embrace.

"Augie." Her voice whispered his name, but it was more than his name. It was every emotion she had for him released into a single word.

He pulled her to him, her hand resting on his chest as his arm snaked around her waist. Her head cradled between his shoulder and his jaw. She could smell his cologne, its scent heated by his body temperature. In his embrace she was finally comfortable, comfortable because she was home. Heat radiated from his pores and into her body, traveling down to her core. God, she loved this man, this man who saw and met her needs without asking. This man who was conflicted about love. This man who was her first and who she wanted to be her last.

CHAPTER 23

Damn, he was barely holding it together. He'd wanted to tear Clay apart for helping Evie nail down a date for her sister—and Keith of all fucking people—only he couldn't think of anything wrong with Keith or of a reason to hate him. He'd touched her though, and that had damn near killed Augie. He had to bite the inside of his cheek until it bled to keep from getting up and beating the poor bastard into the floor. She was his, goddammit. She wore his ring, had his name, and he had her innocence. He held her waist tight, pulling her as close as possible to keep from feeling she was slipping away.

"Augie, you're hurting me."

He eased his hold. "Sorry." His voice was strained. He was in too deep, he was out of control. The song ended, and he reluctantly let her go. They were married; what was she doing at this dance with another man?

Walking back to his table, he heard her call his name, but he didn't turn. Wasn't this what he'd wanted? He should be glad she wasn't forcing his hand and making ultimatums.

He didn't want to be married. Knew he wouldn't be a good husband. What did that even entail? She'd be living in his home, in his bed. And then what? Kids? He couldn't be a father. He'd be a crappy father, just like his dad.

Passing his table, he kept walking out to his car. He got in and drove, no destination in mind. He just needed to clear his head. Racing through town he ran several lights, finally ending up at the station. He headed straight to his office and closed the door, ignoring the greetings from those on duty. He opened the folder on his desk and sat back and fingered through its contents. He'd been monitoring every move surrounding

Nicolas Reynaud. Cause of death: cardiac arrest. At first he thought it peculiar, but then it all made sense. The Lombardi family covered up the true cause of death. A news report had aired, but had been laundered through a publicist and was vague. It had been pretty quiet. This worked out well for him and the Browns. It meant they could put Nicolas Renaud behind them and start living their lives, free of fear.

Closing the folder, he leaned back and clasped his hands across his stomach. Shutting his eyes, he saw Mia, but he also saw something he didn't like—Mia with someone else, not him. A faceless man. She was happy and content, in love. He grew nauseated. Tremors racked his body until he replaced the distorted image with his own. Then it was the two of them, taking on life and all it had to offer, together. Another image emerged, one of her swollen belly, large with his child, his seed planted and nurtured inside her, two parts making a whole. And he knew for a fact Mia wouldn't let him be a bad father.

He got dizzy when something shifted inside of him. God, he wanted that image to be true with a fierceness that shook him. What a fool he'd been to deny her his bed, his home. To deny himself all that she was, all that she wanted to share with him. All that she wanted to give.

He'd been afraid of getting close to her, afraid their lives would be like his folks', but she was nothing like his mother, and he nothing like his father.

Jumping to his feet, he grabbed his keys and ran out the door. He ran more lights this time than he had on the way over. If he'd been in a squad car, he'd have turned on the lights. Thankfully he didn't have far to go. He was going to scoop her up and bring her into his bed where she belonged. She was his wife, Mrs. Michaela Roy. He was aware of a wide smile growing across his face. He loved her yet like the fool he was, he'd never told her. Even when she told him and the telling had eased the churning inside him. *Damned fool.* He'd tell her tonight. He'd show her too. She was his, and he'd love her until she felt the fierceness of his love running through her veins.

Turning on his street, he saw the silver Dodge Ram parked next to the curb in front of his house. Keith's truck. It was empty. At the back gate he saw the glow from the widow of the garage apartment, and his blood simmered. No, it boiled.

He started to walk toward the house, but he froze. If she could so easily give up on what they had, then he wanted her out of his life forever. He didn't care where she went, but she couldn't stay. Not when he cared so much and she cared so little.

He took the stairs three at a time and crashed through the door. Keith sat in a recliner and Mia in his grandmother's wooden rocker. They had the television on, and she cradled a bowl of popcorn in her lap, an Afghan around her shoulders. Large deep lavender eyes gazed into his soul.

"Augie?" She stood, passing the popcorn to Keith, and started toward him.

"Just fucking forget it." He stormed out, slamming the door.

"Augie!"

"Leave me alone, Mia." He heard her coming down the stairs.

"Mia?"

Augie turned at the sound of worry in Keith's voice.

"I'm sorry, Keith, but I'm going to have to ask you to leave." Mia said.

"Is everything okay?"

Keith was advancing on them in the yard.

"Everything's fine, just get lost," Augie said.

"Mia?"

"I apologize. Augie's got a problem, so if you wouldn't mind leaving, I'll give you a call tomorrow."

Augie's eyes narrowed. Keith approached Mia. Not wanting to watch a goodnight kiss, Augie went into his house.

What the hell had he been thinking? As he stomped to his bedroom, he pulled at the knot in his tie. He took off his shirt and threw it across the bed. He knew she was standing in the doorway behind him, because the molecules in the room had shifted. He always knew when she was near. Turning to sit on the bed confirmed what he already knew. He started removing his shoes.

She cleared her throat. "Augie, what was that?"

What was that? "I don't know, Mia. You tell me. I come home and you've let Keith into your apartment." He walked up to her, noting that her hands were clenched at her sides. "Did you have big plans, high hopes? Did you enjoy the goodnight kiss? Ready to put your loss of virginity to use?"

In slow motion, her hand came up to his face and made contact, leaving the skin stinging and hot.

She squared her shoulders, lifting herself to her full height. "You don't play fair. Be mad, angry even, but I never thought you would insult me. Have I ever given you reason to assume I'm going to be promiscuous?"

She hadn't. Far from it.

"No, but what am I supposed to think? I get here and he's up there." He waved his arm wildly. "You two all cozy and alone."

"Is that a crime?"

He knew he needed to answer her. "No."

"We'd just started a movie. And to me cozy implies touching, which we were not doing. And there was no goodnight kiss. But I don't need to tell you things you already know. Why don't you tell me what's really bothering you."

He leaned against the dresser, scrubbing at his face. "You bear my name, you're wearing my ring, for Christ sake, and we're married." He shrugged. "I thought that meant something to you, but I guess I was wrong."

She got in his face, her index finger pushing at his chest while her hand went to her hip. "Are you serious? We're not married. With a marriage comes companionship, intimacy, and love. You couldn't get me out of your house fast enough. No companionship there. Certainly no intimacy. You've completely ignored me and yet now you want to hold the vows we made against me? I cry foul. And what about you? You didn't keep any vows. Maybe you haven't slept around yet, but you sure as hell haven't cared for me the way a man cares for his wife. The way I thought you—" She dropped her hand. "The way I wanted . . ." She stepped back. "Forget it. I'll go back to Canada." The other hand went to her hip. "And did you ever stop to think that the only person I know here is my sister and that we've never been super close? She's been tied up with

Clay; where does that leave me? Do you think I should just sit home for weeks on end hoping that you'll invite me over?"

She was beautiful when she was pissed. Her hair whipped around her cheeks and waved with her efforts, mimicking the flow in the skirt of her dress. Her eyes simmered like dark purple lava, and her chest rose and fell swiftly, and Augie imagined sliding her dress down, exposing her breasts to his gaze. Delicate bare feet stole his attention.

"Where are your shoes?"

"What?"

"Your shoes; you're barefoot."

Hands still on her waist, her mouth opened, but she was speechless. Good. A perfect opportunity for him.

He lunged forward, capturing her lips with his, her taste as sweet as he remembered. Expertly his hands slid the zipper of the dress down and he let if fall to the floor until she stood in nothing but a white lace thong.

Gasping when she realized what he'd done, she bent to grab her dress and pull it up, but his hands intercepted her. "Do you honestly think I'm going to have sex with you?" she asked. "Have you even been listening to me?"

"I have and you will." His voice was raspy and low.

"You're such an arrogant bastard."

She turned from him, clutching her dress in one hand. He grabbed her free arm and pulled her to his chest, her back to his front. He swept her hair over her left shoulder, grazing his teeth down the exposed column of her neck. She trembled in his arms. He knew this woman, his wife, Mrs. Roy. It felt indulgent to touch her after what felt like an eternity. He wouldn't waste another moment denying what his body and his heart had known all along—he needed her healing touch to make him whole.

He nipped up to her ear, taking her lobe between his teeth. His free hand captured hers, causing her to release the dress. It fell to the floor, and he picked her up, moving to the bed. He released her, leaving a hand on her back so that she was bent over the bed. His hand snaked into her underwear, landing between her legs, and he fingered her soft folds. Using her moisture, he lathered her into a preclimactic state—that place where you would do anything to be freed. He stopped just short of giving her what she needed and wrenched her underwear in two with his hands. He pushed his pants and his boxers off.

He lifted her and threw her down on to the bed, turning her onto her back. His hands at the backs of her thighs, he pushed her legs to her chest, opening her to him. Opening her to his eyes and his hands and his intentions. Opening her to his determination to bring her pleasure.

She fought him, pushing against his shoulders and twisting her hips in an attempt to wiggle free.

He held her wrists and hovered over her face, his nose to hers. "You're not going anywhere, so you can quit struggling."

She squirmed some more, and her right leg straightened out. He felt the momentum and narrowly missed having her knee collide with his erect cock.

"That's not very nice, sweet Mia. After all this time, I thought you'd be happy to feel my stiff cock inside of you; hard from just the sight of you. After all, you told me enough times how much you wanted me to make love to you. Begged me to take you." Still holding her wrists tight, he bent over and kissed her brows, her nose, her lips. "Begged me to press deep inside you and rock you and fill you."

He bit her lower lip and tugged. Then he kissed her long and deep, her eager mouth telling him without words how much she wanted him.

"Are you saying no?" he asked against her mouth, teasing her.

"N-n-nooo," she sighed.

"No?"

"No, *not* no."

He chuckled. "So yes, yes or yes, no?"

"Yes, yes, damn you, yes!"

His knee pushed her legs open, and he slipped fully into her warmth, her welcoming, luscious warmth. She took him to the root and gasped out his name.

"What's that, babe? Miss me?" He laughed. Her expressive eyes were lost to his gaze when she closed them. "Forget the rules already, love?"

Her eyes opened, blazing at him. "Love? You never once told me you love me."

He smiled, trying to relax her. "Forgive me. I've been a total fuckbag." He didn't move inside her, just held her wrists. Her legs were kept bound by his thighs as he took her bottom lip between his teeth, then kissed her, slipping his tongue into her wet steamy heat. "Mmm, sweet Michaela, you taste like bananas."

She groaned, arching her neck to follow his mouth. "Lip gloss." Her voice was breathy.

Looking into her eyes, those beautiful lavender-gray eyes, he saw their future, their forever. "Mia, I love you. God, I love you so much I'm rendered useless by my obsession for you. I've gotten nothing done for weeks, just pushed papers around my desk. I've missed you so damn much. Missed your companionship. Missed your talk and your games. Missed you cooking for me and your nurturing spirit." He shivered. "I simply missed looking at you." He swallowed thickly. "And your touch, God, I can't live without your cleansing touch. You make my life worth something to me. I want to live longer just to experience more of you."

He leaned down again, kissing along her jaw. "Love is a short four-letter word; my feelings for you are much bigger than that. Grander. Wider. Deeper. I'm crazy with desire for you. I fucking adore you." He rained kisses over her face and chest and neck. "I'm out of control. This whole situation is out of control. I don't know anything except that to survive, *I need you*. Say you'll stay here with me forever."

"Yes." Her breathing was so rapid, she could barely speak.

"You and me. Together. Forever."

"Yes."

He placed a kiss at the corner of her mouth. "Tell me the words."

"I love you."

He wanted her to have no doubts where she belonged, where she was wanted. "And I love you, Michaela Roy. Forever and always."

They loved into the early morning, reclaiming one another.

CHAPTER 24

The first rays of sun entered through a crack in the curtains. Mia's body was too warm, and she realized Augie was wrapped around her. They were face to face, one of his legs resting between her thighs, the other on top of her leg. His arm held her close, wrapping around her waist, and one cradled her head. When she tried to escape, he tightened his hold. She craned her neck to whisper in his ear, "I need to go to the bathroom."

He groaned and then freed her. "Hurry back."

She immediately noticed she wasn't as sore as she'd been the first time they'd had sex. Studying herself in the mirror, she saw the smile on her face. It seemed to be her new permanent expression. She'd never been so happy, not even on her happiest days.

After she peed, she washed her face and brushed her teeth. She was naked and being so, knowing Augie would see her in just a minute, made her giggle.

He was fully awake and watched her as she returned to the bed. She added an extra sway to her hips simply to give him pleasure.

"I love to hear you laugh," he said. "I've missed it."

As soon as she landed on the mattress, he was on top of her, kissing all over her neck, shoulders, jaw, and the corner of her mouth. He pulled away in a quick jerk, catapulting from the bed like an Olympian.

"Hey, where are you going?"

"You've brushed your teeth, so I can't kiss you now. Gotta brush mine first. Be right back."

She watched his retreating form—actually, his very firm butt cheeks—as he walked into the bathroom. She smiled and stretched her arms over her head, rolling around in the mussed bedclothes and pillows. She inhaled fully, taking his scent deep inside her lungs. She truly hoped she wasn't dreaming. Pinching her arm, she said, "Ouch."

Watching him walk back to the bed from the bathroom had her stomach doing flips and her throat going dry. His cock sprang up like a Spartan warrior gearing up for battle—proud, erect, and ready for action.

Staring down at her tangled in the sheets, he asked, "What's ouch?"

"Oh, I may have pinched myself."

He grasped her wrist, inspecting her forearm. "On what?"

"No, I mean I pinched myself."

"You pinched yourself?"

She pulled her arm free and covered her face with her hands, feeling insecure and a lot silly. She knew he thought of her as a silly girl. Trying to see through his eyes, she understood why. "I pinched myself to make sure I wasn't dreaming and that this was all real. That last night actually happened."

Leaning against the headboard, he pulled her into his lap, cradling her with his legs. He wrapped his arms around her, his hands clasping just under her breasts, his head resting on her shoulder. "I'm sorry, Mia. I've never been in this deep. I got scared. I'm a coward. But you . . . you are so strong. No one has ever stood up to me like you. Would you believe me if I said you'll never have to wonder again if it's real?"

"I'm starting to believe." She leaned into his neck, but that wasn't good enough; she needed to see his expression. She needed for him to see *hers*, to see everything—the certainty, yes, but the doubts as well. She turned in his arms and her eyes met his gaze. "You hurt me. I loved you and you dismissed me and hurt me. Yet I forgive you and I want to trust you."

She lowered her gaze, but immediately looked up again. "Trust may take some time."

Please, God, don't let it take too long.

She needed their trust to build in order to be certain that his love was equal to the love she had for him. Without that trust, their love was powerless.

He could understand that it might take time for her to trust him again. But he'd never let her out of his sight again. He lifted her chin with his finger. "Marry me," he whispered and then he kissed her lips.

"I did marry you." She held up her hand, displaying the ring.

"And I'm happy that you wear my ring *and* my name. What I should have said was, *marry me again.* In front of our friends and family. I want the whole world to know you're mine."

When she smiled shyly, he added, "And I want them to know that out of all the men in that world, you picked me."

Her smile grew. "Are you saying a church wedding with a big dress and dancing?"

"Yes, and a limo and a honeymoon."

She was on her knees, her hands clasped tightly around his neck. "Oh my God, Augie, do you really want that? Because I'm about to get really excited."

He chuckled. She was so adorably sweet, it sometimes hurt. "I want all of it." His words were strained because her arms around his neck were cutting off his air.

He was released suddenly when she sat back on her heels. She held up her hand, flashing the ring.

"There's one more thing: I don't have any money. I think my sister does. I could ask her, but I don't really want to. Maybe we could just go take some nice pictures and post an announcement." She looked at him with bright smiling eyes. "I'd be completely happy with that."

She hadn't been paying attention, and he loved her for it. "Baby, haven't you ever noticed the car I drive?"

"The little sports car?"

"That's the one. Ever wonder why I'm not driving the standard issue Dodge Charger that the deputies drive?"

"I thought they gave you a special one since you're the boss."

His belly rumbled with laughter that started deep and radiated out. He'd never laughed so hard. "How much money do you think a sheriff in Louisiana makes?"

She shrugged. "I have no idea."

"It's a nice salary, but it's not enough to afford this house and that car. What I'm telling you is that the Roy family is, well, we're rich. Old money. Lots. That's how I got an elected office so young."

She nodded. Then her smile faded, and the sparkle drained from her eyes. "Why do you want to be with me? I have nothing to offer you."

How could she not know that she gave him everything? He obviously wasn't doing a very good job of convincing her how much she meant to him. He cradled her cheek with his palm.

"You're everything to me. You consume my thoughts. I was going crazy without you. I couldn't think, couldn't feel. Sometimes I couldn't even see because my head was filled with images of you. I was torturing myself because the truth of it is, I don't deserve you—your innocence, your sweetness, your beauty, your unconditional love. I can only hope in the years to come that I become man enough to merit all that you are and all you possess. No, your possessions aren't goods and money; they're so much more valuable. They're everything. They're life. And I love you."

He took her lips with his and when she parted them on a sigh of his name, he slipped in his tongue. They tangled and explored one another, and she melted softly around him in the way that told him just how much she loved him. He lifted her, setting her on top of him, straddling his thighs. Checking her wetness, he was happy to feel she was saturated. He brought his cock to her entrance, and she stretched around him, slowly taking him deep into her purity, cleansing him in the act. He sucked the nipples that were scraping his chin with each bounce of her body. When her hands pushed through his hair and she moaned, he felt the barbaric need to mark her with his seed. He wanted to shoot himself inside her, planting so deep and strong that she would always possess part of him.

He wanted every inch of her body to know him and carry his mark.

Between his thoughts and her baby-soft sighs and the squeezing walls of her cunt, he was ready to come within minutes. He brought his hand up to massage her clit.

"Baby, I'm going to come. Need to do it inside you."

Her mouth opened on a strangled cry as she quivered and fell apart around him. Moving both hands to her hips, he slid her aggressively back and forth on his cock, groaning out her name as he shot his seed deep inside her snug heat.

He tried to catch his breath. God, it felt good to mark her, brand her, connect her to him.

Her forehead came to rest on his. "I love you," she whispered.

"Love you. So much." His fingers traced lightly up and down her spine. "I just marked you with my seed and you wear my ring. You're mine. You've turned me into a Neanderthal. If I could figure out another way to mark you, I would."

"Why does Evie wear that rope?"

Hell, where had that come from? He smiled a knowing smile. "Do you really want to know about that, Mia? Once you know something it becomes impossible to un-know it."

He was still inside her. When she abruptly shrugged, his dick twitched.

"Tell me."

They stared into one another's eyes. When he could see she was ready, he nodded.

"She wears the ropes to remind her of Clay while he's away. The pressure the rope puts on her body is reminiscent of his touch. And he likes to bind her when they fuck."

Her eyes grew wide, and she gasped. He took her lips and kissed them until they plumped.

"Do you like to do that?" she asked.

He shook his head. "I'm not into that. But I would like you to submit to me. In all things, I'd like to lead us as a family. My every move would be about keeping you safe and happy and loved."

She leaned toward his lips and placed a sweet kiss on them. "I have no problem with that."

"Hey"—his brow rose as an idea hit him—"will you wear my collar?"

"Like a dog's collar?"

"No. Like a collar worn around your neck to indicate your submission to me."

"Does it *look* like a dog's collar?"

He chuckled. "No. Actually, the one I'm thinking about is owned by my mother."

"You don't ever speak about your parents."

He was quiet, wondering what to tell her about his family. How could he share his lifetime with them in just a few words?

"You'll meet my dad at Christmas and again at Easter. He's a U.S. senator, so he's never around. Basically lives in D.C." He inhaled and sighed. "Mom is here in town. She copes by consuming a daily cocktail of bourbon and Xanax and by fucking the yard boy."

Mia grimaced and dropped her head to his chest.

He stroked her hair. "You're so fresh, so innocent, so pure. I love that about you. I apologize. I should have been more sensitive in telling you, but speaking about my family is not one of my favorite activities. Still, I want to introduce my new bride to my mother. You up for that today?"

She nodded against his chest. "As long as you're at my side, I'll do anything."

"First we need to get breakfast; I worked up an appetite. I'll call Clay and see if they want to join us. We can share our news."

She bit the vein on his neck.

"If you don't stop that, we'll starve to death. Let's get dressed." He kissed her hair, inhaling her scent. *Their* scent.

"Don't take a bath," he whispered into her ear.

She peeked at him through her lashes and smiled.

CHAPTER 25

She hadn't been in his car before, but she'd seen him take a corner on two wheels. The car was sporty and the leather seats fit her like those rides she'd been strapped into as a child at an amusement park. His cellphone rested in the center cup holder.

"Can I use your phone to call my mom?"

"Of course. Find out when she'll be ready and we'll go get her, bring her down here. She can live in the apartment."

God, he was so wonderful. She hoped her mother wouldn't put up a fuss. Punching in the numbers, she started to tap her foot.

"Hello?"

"Hi, Mom, how are you?" She bit her nails as she awaited her mother's reply.

"I'm much better."

"I'm glad to hear that. Hey, when will you be ready do you think?" Mia sighed.

"A few weeks, maybe a month."

"Oh, yeah. Well, I'm here in Louisiana and I've got a real nice place for you." She rubbed the cold steel door handle. "It's my friend Augie's place; we'll come get you and move you down."

"A temporary move?"

Her lips pursed into a tight line. "It won't be temporary, it will be forever."

"It sounds nice. I'd like to move to Louisiana, to be close to you and Evie."

Her smile started small but soon spread across her face. "Really? That would be wonderful." She looked to Augie.

"Mia, I've got to let you go."

"Okay, Mom. I love you. Bye."

"Good?" Augie's brow rose.

"Yeah, she said she would like to move to Louisiana to be close to me and Evie." She shrugged. "I just don't get her change in demeanor. She's never been so accommodating and nice."

He squeezed her knee. "You deserve it. You're a great daughter to her."

She leaned her head against the seat and watched him drive. "I love you."

He smiled. "Love you too." They laced their fingers together.

He pulled into the diner and kissed her knuckle before releasing her hand to park. He killed the engine. "Ready to do this?"

"Ready."

"Let me get your door." As he walked around the car, she giggled. She'd never imagined she could be this happy.

At breakfast Mia met Clara, the youngest St. Martin and only female sibling of the bunch. A beautiful young woman, she was over the moon when Mia and Evie decided to do a double wedding. She appointed herself wedding coordinator. Both Mia and Evie were relieved. Evidently a wedding was an even bigger deal in the south than it was in Canada.

Augie drove fast and commanded the car with a dominant hand that had her wanting him again.

"I'm going to tell you what exactly you cannot say since that'll be easier than trying to come up with all the possible things my mother may or may not ask you."

"Okay." She had no idea what he was getting at, but his tone was serious.

"Don't ever allude to the fact that you're from Canada. Don't even say you're Canadian. Don't admit we married because you needed American medical services."

"Where should I say we met?"

He shrugged. "St. Louis."

"Why'd we get married?"

"Same reason everyone else gets married."

And what exactly did that mean? She frowned even as he stretched his arm across the span of the front windshield.

"This is the start of the estate."

Lining either side of a winding drive were large oaks that met overhead in an arch. The tree lined drive meandered spectacularly before them and was the epitome of what she considered a Southern plantation home.

"Ask me again."

"What?"

"Ask me why we got married."

"Why'd we get married?"

"Because I love you. I should have said because I love you." He clasped her hand in his and kissed it again. "I'm giving you these rules for a reason. I told you my father is in politics. I don't want him or my mother prying into our business. And they'll both try to breach our privacy and control our lives. Plus, the less people who know about you and Evie's connection to Nicolas the better. My father would shit if he ever found out about your sisters mafia connection. "

"I understand."

As they rounded the last bend, a huge two-story porch with pillars came into view. The house was large—mansion sized—with white brick and black iron balustrades and a black door. "It's a palace."

"Ostentatious."

"So you grew up here."

"Yeah, well, sort of. Me and my brothers were sent away for school. We came home for holidays." He shrugged. "It's what southern people with money do." His hand landed on her thigh. "When we have our children, I want them with us."

His eyes were dark, his look intent. Mia sensed that he needed her agreement on this.

"I wouldn't have it any other way."

"My mom is aggressive and will be in your business so fast you'll stop breathing. Share only what you want." His hand rubbed through his hair as he sighed.

"Augie?"

"Yeah, babe?"

"Are you okay?"

"Being here is strange. I check in about once per week, but what I meant is being here with you is strange."

"How?"

"I guess strange isn't the right word." His fingers curled around the steering wheel in a white-knuckled grip. "I almost don't want to expose you to my family. I'm afraid they'll rub off on you. You know my parents are still married, even though they don't see each other except during campaigns and holidays. They've made such a lie out of their lives, my life, everything they touch. Their lives are a mockery. I don't want to be like them. I want our marriage to be real."

She held her palm in the air and he clasped his hand over it, joining them. "We won't be like that. I love you. And just so you know, the thought of speaking in public makes me want to put hot needles in my eyes, so I can't see myself on the campaign trail." She winked at him and smiled.

"Thanks, Mia. Okay, you ready for this?"

She nodded and waited for him to walk around and help her out of the car, the way he liked to. Her hand in his, he pulled her along. As soon as they reached the porch, the front door opened and out popped a very attractive woman.

"Augie!" In a black cocktail dress and slim heels, the woman clicked across the tile and placed her arms around his neck. "I'm on my way out, dear, but I really want to catch up, so I'll come over after this library dedication thing, take my baby boy out for a steak dinner. Your brother's in there, so why don't you wait a— Oh, who's this?"

"This is Mia. She's my wife. Mia, this is my mother, Olivia."

Olivia gasped, then stared at Mia. "Augustine Charles Roy!" The pad of her foot tapped the tile hard. "Are you telling me my baby boy gets married and I don't even get an invitation? I could just die of heartbreak right now." Her palms went to Mia's jaw. "Jesus, you're beautiful."

"Mom, don't freak out my bride. And we're gonna have a big extravagant second ceremony, so you can die happy."

Mia started to laugh. She couldn't help it. Augie's mom was wonderful.

Olivia punched her phone. "This is Mrs. Olivia Diane Roy. An emergency has come up and I'm afraid I won't be able to make it. Yes, that's right. You may contact Mrs. Joyce Robichau." She slipped her phone into her purse.

"Welcome to the family, honey." Olivia linked her arm in Mia's and steered her into the house and to the living room. "You and I need to talk."

Mia looked over her shoulder at Augie, who winked at her as she was being led away.

Her vision was in overdrive processing the lavish surroundings at such a fast pace: chandeliers, Persian rugs, wall art, and rich ornate objects were tucked here and there. Plush velvet and leather furniture abounded and Mia would have liked more time to take it all in, but Olivia pulled her into the kitchen. "Coffee?"

"Yes, please. Can I help you?"

"Gracious, no." She swatted at Mia's upper arm. "Sylvia!"

God, her bellow was loud. Mia never imagined a sound that loud could come from a woman that small. "Sylvia!"

"Yes, Mrs. Roy?"

"Make a pot of coffee and do you have any more of those Neapolitan sandwich cookies?"

"Yes, ma'am."

Couches and high-back chairs made up a sunny nook in the corner of the kitchen and Olivia pulled Mia by the hand until they sat at a picturesque window in that nook. Augie's mother's posture formed a sophisticated line as she sat straight, crossing only her ankles, in a black sheath dress fancier than anything Mia had ever owned.

"Mia . . . Is that short for something?"

"Michaela."

"I love it. What a beautiful name." Her smile was like Augie's—a person could get lost in the intensity of it. "How'd you two meet?"

"We met in St. Louis, at the arch."

"Oh, how romantic." Olivia leaned forward. "Now you know, I've always wanted to have one of my boys marry here on the estate." She patted Mia's knee. "You could help me make that dream come true."

"I would love to get married here."

She winked. "Great."

A robust Latin man walked up to a set of French doors in the kitchen, and Olivia jumped up. "Excuse me a moment." He was a handsome man with olive skin and dark features. She spoke to him with the door ajar.

"Augie's here with his bride. Isn't it wonderful? Would you like to meet her?"

Mia couldn't make out what was said, but the man's body language said no, he wouldn't.

Augie and a man she assumed was his brother walked in When he saw what was going down on the porch, his eyes narrowed. Olivia turned and pulled the door closed.

"I'm just having coffee brewed; join us."

"What's he doing here?"

"He's my friend, you know that."

"I know what he is, Mom."

"Augie, please don't start." She indicated that the men should join them on the couches. "Mia, have you met Alex?"

She stood. "Hi." He shook her hand and she felt awkward searching for something to say, so she didn't say anything.

"Augie tells me congratulations are in order."

"Thank you." He was similar in height to Augie and shared the same coloring, but he wasn't as laid back in his suit and tie, and he held himself almost unnaturally erect.

She glanced to Augie and was immediately relaxed at the look of awe on his face. His smile grew until it reached his dark eyes. Walking toward her, he closed the gap between them and pulled her onto his lap on the couch, giving her a huge wet kiss on the lips. Heat bloomed across her neck and cheeks.

"Augie!"

Alex frowned. "On that note, I've got a call to make. Excuse me."

Olivia sat next to them on the couch, watching with a sincere smile and kind eyes. "I'm so glad you're here. I hope you two will come around all the time."

Mia turned in his lap so she could see his face. His lips were tight. She answered for them. "I would love to."

"I want to give Mia a family piece, maybe a necklace." Augie said.

Olivia squeezed Mia's knee. "Oh, that's a wonderful idea. Mia, when I married into this family, I was given buckets of jewelry from the elders. You need your own stash."

Mia didn't wear jewelry, not ever. But she had Augie's ring now and loved how it looked on her hand. Loved what it represented. "I haven't worn much jewelry, at least not until I got the ring from Augie." She held her hand to Olivia.

"I love the pink stone; it's just gorgeous with your skin tone."

"Thank you."

Augie slid her from his lap and stood. "I'm gonna go take a look at gran's jewels."

As he walked away, Olivia whispered, "I must show you his room. I haven't changed a thing since he left home. Come."

Mia followed behind her up the double winding staircase, down the hall, and through the door at the end. Inside, the first thing she noticed was the number of trophies lining the shelves and windowsills. Pulling one from the shelf, she recognized the figure on top to be an American football player. Others were for baseball, swimming, debate, track and field, and archery. There must have been over a hundred trophies.

"Wow, he's successful at everything."

Olivia was folding a blanket. "He pushes himself, too hard sometimes. But yes, he'll make a success of anything given to him." She patted the folded blanket with her hand. "He's just like his father, except Augie's fiercely loyal." She sighed.

Mia felt sad for Olivia, but she understood her a little bit better. "Augie's father doesn't live here." It wasn't a question; she knew the answer.

Olivia inhaled deeply. "No. I'm sure Augie told you we're estranged. Augie's upset with me, has been for years. For the record, I would have remained faithful had he . . ." Her fingers gently worried her top lip. "I just got so lonely here in this big house. Alone." Her voice was tinged with pain.

Mia took her hand in hers. "I don't know anybody here and I'm not very good at getting to know people, but I love Augie and I'd love to get to know you. I can get lonely also. I'll try to bring Augie around. He's a great guy and he loves you very much."

Olivia pulled her into an embrace.

Mia never knew touching like this; she instantly loved his mother. She would spend her days subtly trying to show Augie how wonderful this woman was, despite her flaws. She obviously loved her son.

"I'd like to be close with him again." Olivia pulled away and shook her head. "Enough of that. Now, the reason I brought you in here is so that you might consider taking some of these things home."

Home. To her new home. It hadn't even been her home for twenty-four hours. That thought had her giggling.

"I keep telling Augie to take these quilts, but he says no one will ever need more than two." She pulled blankets from a chest. "These were all hand quilted by his grandmother."

"They're beautiful."

"She was a beautiful quilter. If she were here, she'd already be picking out the pattern for your double-wedding-ring quilt. I'm not as good as she was, but I'll have to see what I can do."

"What's a double-wedding-ring quilt?"

"Let me show you the one she did for me." She dug through the chest and pulled out a beautiful quilt of greens, pinks, and purples. "See the interlocking ring pattern? That symbolizes unity. It's often given to commemorate a marriage."

"It's beautiful."

"I haven't been inside Augie's bedroom, so you'll have to get me a color scheme."

"Okay, I definitely will. Or better still, I'll have you over next week for dinner."

His mother smiled and sniffled. "I'd love that."

Looking again at the shelves, Mia traced over several bound books. Yearbooks. She pulled one from the shelf and started thumbing through it.

"Mom, you have a call." Alex came inside and handed a cellphone to Olivia. They left Mia alone in Augie's room. With five yearbooks surrounding her in the bed, she searched the index for pages featuring Augustine Roy.

After about an hour, she'd found all his pictures. He'd been in everything and loved by everyone. His roots were deep, and she was excited to become part of his world. She lay back on the bed and thought about the turn her life had taken.

Velvety lips on her cheeks woke her.

"Hey, sleepyhead."

Dark smiling eyes peered down at her, and Augie's fingers smoothed the hair from her face. He knelt and then pulled her into a sitting position and then to the edge of the bed.

"I like finding you asleep in my teenage bed," he said. He gathered her hair together at her nape and pulled it over one shoulder. He'd closed the door and had an expectant look in his eye, a little smirk on the corner of his mouth.

"What are you scheming?"

"Lots." He fiddled with something on the floor next to him. "Just thinking of all the things I'd like to do to you in this bed."

"Wouldn't that be weird? With your mom and brother downstairs?"

He laughed. "Yeah, I guess that would be pretty weird, although I think there might be something you could do to help me forget all thoughts regarding my family."

"No way."

He leaned in, taking her lips in his and sucking gently. The intensity increased when his tongue slid into her mouth. He tried to slide his hands under her shirt, but she was ready.

"Nah uh." She held his hands in hers. "Twenty-four seven at our home, but not here."

His playful mood became serious. "Our home. I love that. I've never thought of it as home, not really, until now." He released her hands and put his behind his back, contorting his body.

"What have you got and what are you doing?"

"Close your eyes."

She closed them, and he pulled at her shirt.

"Hey, I said not here."

"Do you trust me?"

"Yes, but I—"

Wait, that wasn't right. Mia lifted her hands to his cheeks and stared without blinking into his eyes. There were no *buts*—she trusted Augie with her life. She trusted him with her heart and her dreams and her future. She trusted him unconditionally.

"I trust you, Augustine Roy."

She closed her eyes once more and lowered her arms. At first Augie said nothing, did nothing, but then he pressed a kiss to her forehead, whispering, "Thank you." A moment later he removed her shirt and bra, but he didn't stop there. She let him remove the rest of her clothing until she stood naked before him.

"You're beautiful. Keep your eyes closed."

She felt a cold weight at her neck and heard the snick of a clasp. Then her hands were in his.

"Open your eyes."

He was on one knee before her as she stood, naked. "Will you wear my collar?"

Her hand went to her neck, and she felt the hardware there. "Have you ever given one to anybody else?"

"Never. I've never shared this, never wanted this, with another woman. It's yet another way I can mark and take possession of you and feel less out of control."

"I want to belong to you, want you to take care of me, so, yes, I'll wear a gift that says I'm yours. I never want you to doubt my love for you." She swallowed back the lump in her throat, hoping she wouldn't cry.

"I will take care of you. You'll never have to worry."

She fingered the choker. "I want to see it."

He stood and pulled her to the adjoining bathroom. "Look how beautiful you are."

She gasped, not recognizing her dark irises and the bloom of color across her chest and face. Her hair was wild from the bed, her lips swollen from their kiss. The jewelry at her neck was vintage and dainty. Small scalloped blush-colored flowers were woven into the gold wire of the necklace, and colored jewels made up the petals. Small vintage diamonds circled the edge.

"It's so pretty."

"It means everything to me that you accept it and trust me to take care of all your needs. I love you."

She couldn't talk because her throat was so tight, it burned. She eventually whispered, "I love you, Augie," and wrapped her hands around his neck.

Things would be different now. She would no longer be alone, responsible for holding everyone and everything together. Augie would help her, he would love her, and by proxy, her family. She loved him, and she needed him more than she needed air to breathe. And now he would always be there for her and she for him, sharing bits and pieces of one another until there was no distance left between them. *Oneness.* A joining. It was what she'd always longed for with her mom and dad, her sister, but never received. Augie'd given her the most precious gift, and she would cherish him and their love for the rest of her time on earth. He acted tough and macho and she loved his spirit, but he was gentle and reverent with her and she needed that part of him as much as the other. And he needed her too. He needed loyalty and friendship. He needed a woman who would put him ahead of all others, who would cherish him for the man he was.

The bonds of trust would grow and strengthen over time, uniting them together in a union that could never be undone. She once saw a little ritual performed at a small wedding in her hometown called a salt covenant. Each wedding party brought salt from their houses and combined the salts together into one container. Impossible to sort the salt after it had been combined, it symbolized the unbreakable vow of marriage and eternal love.

EPILOGUE

Two months after Mia met Augie's family, the big day was upon them. Clay and Evie were anxious to marry so Evie would have the St. Martin name and also so she could start the steps toward permanent residency. Since Augie and Mia were already married, they'd been happy to abide by the timeline.

The morning of the wedding, Mia awoke in a lonely bed. Lonely because her mother, Olivia, and Clara insisted she and Evie stay the night at the Roy estate. She'd had fun last night with the girls and her mother, but she missed Augie. They'd stayed on the phone until she'd fallen asleep. She reached for her phone now, intending to see if he was awake yet. Even as she lifted it from the nightstand, the display lit up with her favorite Augie picture.

She unplugged the charger and answered. "Hey."

"Baby, I miss you."

She giggled. They'd talked until two o'clock. "I miss you too."

"They won't let me in. I'm camped out at the pool house with Clay."

"Maybe I can sneak over."

"Doubt it; I already tried to sneak in. Whole place is on lockdown."

She smiled. "I know."

"There should be a breakfast tray in your room."

She looked around and found it on an ottoman in the corner. "Oh, good, I'm starved."

"Go get the tray and bring it over to the bed."

"Hold on." She started to climb down but heard his voice calling her back.

"Hey!"

She picked up the phone. "Yeah?"

"I love you."

She giggled into the phone. "And I love you."

"Glad to hear it. Go get the tray."

She carefully placed the tray on the bed and climbed back up. A thick envelope with her name on it was half-hidden by a plate. She wedged the phone between her ear and shoulder and picked up the package. "There's something here besides breakfast."

"Open it."

She found airline tickets to Bora Bora—Bora Bora!—and a note from Augie.

Michaela,

You, me, and the sea (too corny?). You're the love of my life. A life that didn't start until the day we met. You've taught me so much already, I can't wait to live and love side by side for the next half century. It will feel like but a moment, so I intend to savor every second. Our bags are packed. As soon as the ceremony ends, we're out of there. We can regale the family when we return. I need you.

Love you,

Augie

"Bora Bora! I can't wait."

"Did you see the huts?"

She picked up a pamphlet displaying bungalows perched above the water, complete with glass viewing floors.

"It's beautiful. I saw these huts on the Travel Channel. Oh, Augie, how wonderful."

"I ordered a meal package too, so we don't ever have to leave the hut."

"If you were here right now, I'd show you how much this means to me."

He chuckled "Damn, baby, I had no idea you were so cruel."

"I know. I'm sorry."

"Keep looking."

She dug through additional papers until she found one that read *Birth Certificate*. The paper was embossed and as she ran her fingers over it, she felt the roughness from the decorative etching. Confused at first, she read and then reread it. The name *Michaela Brown* finally jumped off the page. Mia gasped, and her eyes filled. She wasn't normally so emotional, but damned if he hadn't made her cry. And on her wedding day. She would look all puffy, but she didn't care. Tears fell onto the newly printed paper.

"Babe?"

She inhaled jaggedly and said, "Augustine Charles Roy, hasn't anyone ever told you that you shouldn't make a bride cry on her wedding day?"

"Oh, baby, don't cry." She heard some shuffling and then, "Fuck this shit; I'm coming to you."

A few minutes later she heard a commotion and then she was in his arms. His hand stroked her hair while he kissed the top of her head. The family—all of them, his and hers—stood in the hallway. Finally conceding, Olivia closed the door to afford them some privacy.

He squatted in front of her, so she had to look down to see his worried eyes.

"I just wanted to give you your identity—you are Michaela. I don't want anything standing in the way of you coming to know the woman I see. You're not a boy, you're a beautiful sexy woman. Your curves drive me mad, and I can hardly keep my hands off of you. You move with grace and elegance."

"Augie, it's so perfect. I could never have dreamed you would do this, that it could even be done. It's such a small little thing, one letter, but it means so much. You've always made me feel beautiful. Made me feel special. I can't wait to marry you again, this time as Michaela."

"Michaela. I'm glad you like your name now."

She wrapped her arms around his waist and laid her head on his chest. "I always liked it. I just didn't want to think about the missing letter."

"Now it's been found." He smiled. "Now there's nothing missing."

She returned his smile, "It *has* been found." *She* had been found.

And he was right. There was nothing missing any longer.

SURGE EXCERPT
(JACKSON AND CLARA'S STORY)
Excerpt has not been edited.
Content may change upon final publication.

Where are you?

Clara's man was extremely testy lately. She knew completing his hospital residency, along with his fulltime job as a paramedic, was taking a toll on Jackson, but she couldn't convince him to slow down. She'd have to see what she could do to appease him. It was Saturday. He had the day off. It was the big day, Clay was marrying Eve; Augie was marrying Mia. Again.

She typed a reply text using just her thumbs. *Be there in a bit. Had to get brides b-fast trays.*

She'd told him to sleep in. Figured she'd be busy as wedding coordinator extraordinaire—she added the flair to her title.

Hurry, I need you.

She whispered, "Oh Cracker Jack, I need you more." She smiled at the use of his namesake. He ate bags of the stuff while he completed endless mountains of paperwork and reports for med school.

She had known he wouldn't stay in bed since she'd had to leave. She grabbed two mimosas from the kitchen and made her way out to the pool house where the men were staying. She wore khaki shorts and a white tank top. She'd done her hair and makeup, but hadn't put on her bridesmaid dress yet so that she could move about freely. Surely there'd be a decoration to tape up, or some toile to adjust, and she wanted the freedom shorts could offer.

She opened the door to the pool house and found him slouched on the couch, a frown on his face. "Hey." She walked over to him and straddled him on the couch. "I brought mimosas." She teased him with the orange drink holding the glasses up but just out of reach. She kissed his lips and his pout started to turn. "But you can only have it if you promise not to be such an Oscar the Grouch." She offered an exaggerated pout of her own.

His frown was back. "Come on Cracker Jack, it's a most glorious day."

"I'm on call. I can't have it," *big bottom lip protruding pout.*

"I told you to sleep in. You look tired."

He traced a hair back behind her ear. "I missed my Bug."

She giggled. "I think we were apart for about an hour."

"I don't care. I don't like waking without you." His eyes tightened. "And I'm not happy about today either. It's been two years, we should be the ones getting married."

She took a large sip of the champagne and orange juice before setting the glasses on the couch side table. Smiling against his lips she said, "We will baby. Soon. But we can't move forward until we tell my brother, and we can't do that until you finish your residency."

"Why not?"

"Because that's what we decided."

"I want to revise the decision. Besides, I'm almost done."

"How about I kiss you here," she nipped at his lips, "and when we're done with that, I'll kiss you down here." She fisted between his legs. "See if we can't turn that frown upside down."

A moan from deep in his throat vibrated his tongue and hers. One of his hands slid up the back of her neck to grip her hair while the other cupped her jaw. His kiss was demanding and needy. He explored her deeply and alternated rough and soft strokes. She loved his kiss, his touch, his everything, even his brooding.

He was ten years older than her and she'd loved him since she was seven years old. They'd started getting intimate when she was sixteen, he was twenty-six. It was part of the reason they hadn't told her family.

Her hand fiddled with the hardware on his jeans, as she made a production of slowly undoing each button. She knew how it sounded; their admission wouldn't paint a nice likeness of Jackson. She knew Clay had suspicions and had even alluded to their relationship, but they'd thrown him off the hunt numerous times. A fact neither of them was happy about. Luckily, Eve had kept him exceedingly distracted.

She pulled his cock free and gasped at the readiness of it. He chuckled. His deep blue eyes shimmered like sunlight on the deep sea. She shimmied down his legs to kneel on the floor. He grabbed a pillow, "Here bug don't kneel on the hard floor." She rose up and he slid the cushion under her knees.

Fisting his weight in her hands she licked the head before taking him between her lips. She pumped the root while applying light pressure with the suction of her mouth. He palmed her head and aided her efforts. "God Bug, I love being in your mouth." She loved it too. Their connection had always been powerful. Their energy had been too potent to ignore. That's what had happened when she was sixteen. And they couldn't stop. It was as if one could not exist without the other. She took him deep, loving the feel of him and the groans he made for her.

"Shit! Your brother's coming." Her mind was disoriented but Jackson pulled her from the floor, the momentum throwing her forward onto him. His hands at her waist moved her onto the couch next to him. While he fastened his jeans, she lifted the pillow from the floor. The snick of the door opening occurred simultaneously.

Clay's wide ice blue eyes met her own before they narrowed to slits. His gaze migrated over to Jackson and back to her. "Clara Grace what are you doing in here?" His deep baritone reverberated around the room.

"I was looking for you." Jackson's hand had started to rub against his jeans. She knew he hated the lies they sometimes had to tell to hide their relationship.

"I saw you walking out here like fifteen minutes ago. What have you been doing?" His eyes darted from her to Jackson.

"Been talking with Jackson." His hand rubbed faster. "I brought mimosas, but he told me about being on call at the hospital." She jumped up and skipped to Clay throwing her arms around his neck and kissing him square on the lips. "Such a wonderful day. I love you. I'm so happy my big brother is getting married to his one and only love."

He squeezed her tight. "Love you too baby girl."

"Are you being a good boy?" She smiled up at his six foot five frame.

"Augie's the one you should be worried about. He's in Mia's room."

"Are you serious. That's not allowed."

"She was crying."

She gasped. "Why was she crying?"

Clay shrugged. "Augie made her cry."

"What?"

"Bug—err, better go check on her Clara." She turned to Jackson on the couch and couldn't help the slight smile that was forming at the corner of her mouth.

She kissed Clay's cheek. "Text me if you need anything."

"Will do."

She looked back at Jackson. He was always so serious. She'd seen him laugh just a few times and it was usually at something she'd done or said. She wished she could think of something now that would bring him relief. His eyes and his stiff body held so much pain it made her gut ache. Clay's head was turned away from her so she held up the universal hand sign for *I love you* and then she blew him a kiss. The right side of his mouth lifted ever so slightly.

Jackson loved Clay. He loved the entire clan of St. Martins. He didn't want to think about what would happen if they turned on him once they knew about his romance with Clara. And it was a romance, a huge whirlwind romance. God he loved her with everything he had. He was a man possessed. It wasn't just her beauty, but everything about her. Her laugh, and there was more than one. There was the cute half committed chuckle she made when she was tired. There was the short burst of laughter that bubbled out when she got tickled at something she'd read or heard on television. There was the sexy breathless half moan, half giggle she made when he nuzzled behind her ear, her ticklish spot. And she was so kind to everyone. He loved her spirit. The door closed behind her and it was like someone shut off the oxygen that was keeping him alive.

"You okay there brother?"

Clay took the chair across from him. "Yeah, just tired."

"You need to take better care of yourself. You've been working too many hours at the station. Along with your full days at the hospital, you're gonna run out of steam."

He wouldn't. Plus he had big plans for his future with Clara. Plans that required money. "I'll be okay."

They were basically living together and Clara had tried to buy things for his apartment, but Jackson Reid wasn't about to let that happen. He'd had to work overtime to provide for a few things she'd wanted to buy to make their apartment a home. Their home. He would provide for her. Wanted to provide for her. He knew she'd sensed his limited budget and lived much more frugally than she'd done in the past.

Sure things would have been easier if they'd waited until he'd graduated, but it was about survival. He couldn't exist without her and she'd said the same of him.

Clay cocked his head. "Still, if you need some vacation time, or if you need money, let me know."

He nodded. Clay had offered this before. Hell he'd tried to sneak money into Jackson's possession, but there was no way in hell he'd accept it. He wanted the world to know that he loved Clara for who she was, not for her name and money.

"So big day huh. I can't imagine how ecstatic I'd be on the day I marry uh . . . your soul mate."

"*You* marry *my* soul mate?"

"Or mine." He smiled.

"Have you met yours?" Clay's brow hitched.

Yeah, he'd met her and he wouldn't deny it. "I have secrets you've never heard." He smiled and Clay's loud rumbling laughter filled the small space. "Have you been exiled to the pool house for the entire day?"

"Supposedly me and Augie have been exiled but he's breaking all the rules."

"And you're following them. You've always been a rule follower."

Jackson's eyes grew heavy. It was true, he was behind on sleep. He'd worked last night. Got home around six in the morning, and it's not like he went to sleep then. He got in bed, but he and Clara couldn't be next to each other without touching. Touching led to kissing. Kissing led to sex. Totally worth it. He'd rather make love to her than get a wink of sleep. If it killed him he thought it'd be a sweet way to go.

"Jackson. You're so exhausted you're not even aware when I call your name. Stay here, get a nap in. I'll see that no one disturbs you."

"Thanks Clay. And hey, I'm happy for you."

"Thanks. And you know I couldn't imagine this day without you here. You're family, you're one of my brothers."

Jackson's throat burned with emotion. "Thanks. That means everything." His voice cracked before he could say all of the words.

He left Jackson in the pool house. The silence was maddening. His thoughts would always turn to his parents when the silence pervaded. If only his dad hadn't taken up flying. He'd logged the required number of hours and his parents had embarked on his inaugural flight. That day the air had been electric with the promise of excitement. The plane had crashed to the ground. Jackson had only been sixteen.

Tending to two brides at once was proving to be an act of monumental patience. Keeping Augie and Clay from their brides was damn near impossible and Augie had ruined Mia's updo twice. Clara was glad when the musical notes of Johann Sebastian Bach lilted in the air. She took her position in line, side by side, next to Jackson, she linked her arm in his. His free hand squeezed her upper arm and they were lost in one another's eyes. The couple behind them coughed to signal them to begin the processional. Slowly they traversed down the isle. She whispered, "Jackson, I love you." His hand squeezed tighter. She could feel his warmth even through his suit as it radiated into her body. As they reached the end of the walkway, his jaw twitched. His vice like grip was starting to squeeze off the flow of blood. Her arm was becoming numb.

"It should be us," his whispered reply.

They broke apart and each went to their appointed side of the stage. She stood and pivoted on the indicated mark just as practiced. Even from across the stage Jackson's eyes were intent on her. She agreed. It *should* be them, but they were both still in college and they really didn't have any money. Her family supported her and she had her own apartment near campus, but she'd moved in with Jackson and he didn't like it when she offered her father's credit card to pay for things. He paid for everything and she felt a little guilty. His joyful demeanor when he provided for them kept her from feeling too bad about their finances.

If she married against her family's blessing, and it would definitely be against their blessing, she had no doubt they'd cut off her funding anyway. They'd done it to Cash when, after four years of college, he hadn't acquired enough credits to graduate. Plus Jackson had said that he wouldn't accept, use, or even need money from them. He was adamant that he be the one to take care of them. She believed in him. He was disciplined and dedicated and unbelievably stubborn, but she'd watched him sacrifice himself for two years.

The other couples started to file in. It was a huge wedding party. Augie had two brothers and there was Clara and Clay and the rest of their five brothers and their wives. The colors were amethyst and gray, a combination chosen in part due to the color of the sisters eyes—both fiancés had been enamored by the color of his fiancées eyes. It was sweet and Clara knew the eyes were an expressive barometer into the soul. Jackson's eyes were a haunted deep ocean blue. He clung to her like a buoy in a storm and she loved him, wanted to help him, but sometimes she felt as if she weren't strong enough to keep them both afloat. She loved him more than anything but she wanted him to come to terms with whatever simmered beneath the surface.

The first chords for Canon in D rung out in the living room of the Roy estate and the sisters took their first steps. Since their father was deceased, they sauntered down the make do isle arm in arm, all smiles, a stark contrast to the men who awaited their arrival with intense eyes on their ladies. It was as if they were trying to ensure the women weren't a mirage and if they blinked would be gone.

She had her own version of intense. Jackson was still glaring at her, unblinking. She smiled at him. Nothing. She winked using the eye not facing out to the spectators. Nothing. Favoring that same side she put her hand on her waist and tilted her head, cocking a brow at him and then crossing her eyes. The corner of his mouth lifted ever so slightly and his gaze broke. He blinked and then his banked smile broke free. It hardly ever happened, but when it did she was rewarded with a sincere, honest and beautiful smile that only he could give.

As the vows were exchanged his eyes sparkled a little bit more as hers leaked like faucets. A few times she saw him look down and wipe away a tear.

The rings went on and finally there were kisses all around and each couple was announced. Still, he only had eyes for her. It was as if a magnet drew them together. The instant they reconnected she heard and felt him release the breath he was holding. His fingers gripped her in the vice of his fate, as if she alone were responsible for his wellbeing. Truth told his intensity scared her sometimes, but it was also a part of him that she cherished, unconditionally. As they walked down the isle he whispered in her ear.

"Gotta get you home. Need to be inside you, wrapped up in you."

"Cracker Jack." She squeezed him a little tighter. "I need you too." And she did. In a world where nothing slowed down and everything blurred, he'd always been focused on her. He'd always been around when she needed him. He was there for her when she'd had her accident. Her hero, her angel, her Jackson. He was the reason she was alive today.

ABOUT THE AUTHOR:

Gina Watson is author of St. Martin Family Saga. She lives in Texas where she leads a double life: university instructor by day, romance writer by night. She loves to be contacted by readers to discuss all things erotic romance.

Connect with Gina Watson online:
https://twitter.com/ginawatsongina
https://www.facebook.com/ginawatsonauthor
http://www.pinterest.com/gwatson/
https://www.goodreads.com/user/show/6713553-gina
http://ginawatson.net/

Reviews: Ratings and reviews are the lifeline of the book. Please leave book reviews, short or lengthy, all are appreciated.

Keep in touch: Join Gina Watson's email list at ginawatson@mac.com to receive alerts regarding sweepstakes, contests, giveaways, and upcoming book releases.

THE SAGA CONTINUES IN:

St. Martin Family Saga
Emergency Responders Trilogy

Sizzle
Seize
Surge

More books by Gina Watson:
Where it all began:

St. Martin Family Saga
Whiskey Cove Series

SCORE
SHAMELESS
SHATTER
SUITED
SMOLDER

Made in the USA
Charleston, SC
16 June 2014